"Look," I told her, "what we need to do is sit tight and hold them off. The cops will be here in a couple of minutes."

"*No!* You don't understand. I can get us to safety—I have the means. I just can't use it here, in public, where there are witnesses."

"All right. . . . *Run!*" As I shouted the last word, I rose up and started shooting. Then we were around the corner and into the alley.

I detached a fresh magazine from the holster belt and slammed it into the Colt's butt. Then I positioned myself between "Miss Smith" and the alley entrance, in firing stance.

That was when the world abruptly went blurry and gray and silent.

I didn't even know how to react. It was too unexpected, and too foreign to ordinary experience. She was holding an odd-looking device about the size and shape of a paperback book. She clasped it to her belt to free her hand. When she spoke, her voice was the only sound in the universe.

"It generates a field, large enough to encompass both of us, which—" she began. Then the first of our attackers was around the corner of the building, moving like a figure in a silent black-and-white movie in poor focus. I started to raise my gun, but she gripped me by the arm. "No! They can't see us or hear us. Just stand still, close to me."

My jaw dropped. Clearly, she was nuts. And yet . . . the ghostly figures were running past us, looking frantically around. One of them faced me, unseeing, from just a few feet away. Then their leader mouthed some inaudible command, and they regrouped and proceeded on down the alley, checking doorways as they went.

"Who *are* you?" I managed.

By Steve White

THE
PROMETHEUS
PROJECT

STEVE WHITE

THE PROMETHEUS PROJECT

Copyright © 2005 by Steve White

A Baen Book

Baen Publishing Enterprises
P.O. Box 1403
Riverdale, NY 10471
www.baen.com

ISBN 10: 1-4165-2097-X
ISBN 13: 978-1-4165-2097-9

Cover art by Bob Eggleton

First Baen paperback printing, December 2006

Distributed by Simon & Schuster
1230 Avenue of the Americas
New York, NY 10020

Library of Congress Cataloging-in-Publication Data:
2004027035

Printed in the United States of America

10 9 8 7 6 5 4 3 2 1

**To Sandy, for more reasons than
I can possibly number**

PROLOGUE

"Mr. President! Mr. President!" The White House press corps rose to its collective feet like an attention-seeking wave.

The President of the United States smiled into the tumult and the TV cameras, and raised his hands for silence. "That's enough questions for now, ladies and gentlemen. Let me just make a few concluding remarks." He waited until something resembling silence had descended on the Press Room, and his expression grew serious. "This has been a . . . vigorous campaign, and feelings have sometimes flared, as they will among people of strongly held beliefs. But that's over now. The electorate has spoken, and the Constitution admits of no doubt as to the outcome. Now it is a time for healing, and for unity. It is for that reason that President-Elect Langston and I called this joint press conference. And now, let me turn the podium over to the President-Elect."

Harvey Langston rose to his feet with a muttered "Thank you, Mr. President." He took his place behind the Presidential seal and smiled at the reporters who, he knew, had never really expected to see him there.

"Ladies and gentlemen, I want to add my voice to the President's. As we know, all sorts of things get said in a campaign . . . by both sides. But now the President and I share a common goal: a smooth transfer of power. My transition team has been in close communication with the President's staff to assure that my administration can hit the ground running. I intend to act without delay to deliver what the people have demanded by putting me in this house. The people want compassionate government. The people—"

"Forty-one percent of them, anyway," someone could be heard to remark, somewhere in the room.

"—want us to focus on our own domestic problems, and not on foreign adventurism," Langston continued without a break, forcing himself to ignore the dig. *Plenty of time later to stick it to that wiseass reporter*, he thought, knowing that Sal DiAngelo, his campaign manager, would have spotted the man and noted his name. "The people want us to abandon our weapons of destruction and seek peaceful solutions to the conflicts we ourselves have provoked! The people—"

From off to the side, DiAngelo caught his eye and frowned. *Stop campaigning, damn you!* Langston told himself. *You don't have to campaign any more. You've won!* He still had to periodically remind himself of that fact, as incredible to him as it was to most of the country.

"The people want continuity and the regular exercise of constitutional processes," he finished smoothly. He prided himself on these seamless recoveries. It was an ability that could be counted on to save his bacon as long as DiAngelo or one of his other handlers was around to shoot him warning looks when the shrillness started to creep back into his voice. "And now, I'll take a few questions."

He got through the questions from the floor, recognizing only those journalists he knew were friendly or, at least, predictable. Then it was over, and the President and his successor were out the doorway of the Press Room together, trailed by a gaggle of staffers and Secret Service men.

As they proceeded down the corridor into the West Wing, a tall, unfamiliar man on the outskirts of the President's entourage caught Langston's eye. He felt certain he would have remembered the man if he'd seen him before, despite his completely nondescript clothes. He looked old, with his thick mane of white hair, and yet his movements were not those of an old man. His features were bleak and harsh, and disfigured by a scar slanting across his left cheek. . . .

"Harvey . . . I mean, Mr. President-Elect," muttered DiAngelo, derailing his train of thought, "I still see no reason for this meeting. If there's anything that needs to be settled, the staffs—"

"Oh, it's all right, Sal. The President has asked for a private one-on-one conversation, and I see no reason to object. I'm curious to see what he wants. And besides, we can afford to be obliging."

"Yes, but—"

Before DiAngelo could finish, they passed by the Cabinet Room and the office of the President's private secretary, and reached the door that was their destination. Langston glanced around, but the mysterious old man was no longer in sight. The President led the way through the door. Langston followed, with Secret Service men politely but firmly shooing everyone else away. Then the door closed behind him, and he was in the Oval Office.

The President sat down behind the massive oak desk in front of the tall French windows of foot-thick armored glass that admitted the pale light of late fall afternoon. He motioned to a chair across the desk.

Langston was impressed despite himself as he crossed the carpet with the Presidential seal in gold and red against the deep blue. The momentary mood vanished as his eyes fell on the flags of the five armed services in their traditional position to the right of the desk, along the south wall. *Must get rid of those*, he made a mental note to himself.

Langston sat down and gazed across the desk at the man he would succeed in January. Silence and mutual loathing settled over the room.

"Mr. President," Langston finally began, "I trust that in the spirit we both articulated at the press conference just now—"

"Oh, cut the crap," the President interrupted in a voice as cold as his eyes. "I'm well aware that you have no higher opinion of me than I have of you. So spare me your trademark smarmy hypocrisy. We're alone now—*really* alone—and we can dispense with the pap we were feeding those hyenas in the Press Room."

"Do you seriously expect me to believe that? You're just trying to trick me into—"

"You can also spare me your paranoia. You know it's true, because otherwise I wouldn't be talking this way. Besides, what would be the point of trying to trap you into anything? It's too late for it to do any good. You've won." The President shook his head slowly, as though to clear it of a stunned disbelief that still hadn't worn off. "There's no getting around that fact . . . and I'd even go so far as to call it fifty percent just. You didn't deserve to win, but Ortega did deserve to lose."

Vice President Andrew Ortega had been the President's handpicked choice to succeed him, in line with their party's strategy of reaching out to Hispanics. He'd won the nomination with little opposition save that of isolationist commentator Frank Ferguson, a Holocaust-denial crank who had subsequently bolted the party and launched an independent candidacy with the announced aim of acting as a spoiler for "that spic." Still, Ortega's election had seemed a foregone conclusion. The opposition party, knowing it couldn't win anyway, had thrown a sop to the Old Left hardcases who were its shock troops by nominating one of their own: the patently unelectable Harvey Langston, congressman from a California district for which the term "La-La Land" might well have been coined.

Then the unthinkable had begun to unfold. Ortega's campaign had been a parade of blunders, bloopers, pratfalls and general ineptitude without modern precedent. The unfunny comedy show had climaxed the night of the final debate, when the Vice President—whose handlers had believed his drinking problem to be safely in the past—had managed to not quite fall on his face on prime-time TV. His apology to the nation the next day had made matters even worse than they would have been had he tried to brazen it out.

Voter turnout had been the lowest in the history of presidential elections, with most of Ortega's centrist base of support—not to mention the agonizingly embarrassed Hispanics—staying home in disgust. In spite of everything, he had somehow managed a forty-three percent plurality of the dismally small popular vote. Ferguson had gotten a once-unimaginable fifteen percent. Another one percent had gone to the usual assortment of minor-party joke candidates. But Langston's forty-one percent had been distributed with mathematical precision to give him exactly two hundred and seventy-one electoral votes.

Now he sat in the office he would soon occupy, filled with his triumph and his hatred of the man across the desk.

"Thank you for clearing the air, Mr. President. Yes, I know—or can imagine—what you think of me. And I make no secret of what I think of you." Oddly enough, Langston found himself believing the President's assurance that no one was listening . . . and it felt so *good* to be able to finally let it all out, without DiAngelo to rein him in. "You're a reactionary, warmongering dinosaur—a tool of the military-industrial complex and the multinational corporations! You've ignored the problems capitalism has inflicted on us—poverty, racism, sexism, suburban sprawl, cigarette smoking, meat eating, SUVs, and all the rest of our *real* problems. Instead, you've promoted economic growth to please the fat cats of Wall Street, and invented imaginary foreign threats to justify military spending."

The President raised one eyebrow. "As 'imaginary' as the terrorism we've faced ever since the 'imaginary' destruction of the World Trade Center back in 2001?"

"What you call 'terrorists' are heroic freedom fighters whom our own greed and imperialism have forced to defend themselves against us! We brought the 9/11 attacks on ourselves, by our support for Israeli oppression of the Palestinian people! Besides, the Israelis knew about it in advance and didn't warn us. They *let* it happen, to inflame public opinion against the peace-loving people of the Arab world. That's been clear all along, at least to those of us who aren't blinded by the propaganda of the international Zionist conspiracy!"

This time both presidential eyebrows rose in arcs of irony. "The Vice President-Elect might not see it quite that way."

Langston flushed. "Senator Goldman and I have had to agree to disagree about some things. But on matters other than Near Eastern policy, we share a broad philosophical common ground."

The President gave a short, scornful laugh. "Translation: you had him rammed down your throat as your running mate. The grown-ups in your party weren't about to accept a loony tune like you as nominee, even for what was supposed to be a kamikaze run, without a sane moderate to balance the ticket."

Langston rose to his feet, quivering with rage. "If you've asked me here simply to insult me, Mr. President, I believe I have better uses for my—"

"Insulting you is impossible. Now *sit down!*"

Without recalling having done it, Langston realized he was seated again. His conscious rejection of his country's past could not immunize him from the sheer power that pervaded this room, all of it focused and concentrated in the one man behind the desk.

For now, he added to himself grimly. *Until January.*

The President drew a breath and released it slowly. "Well, none of that matters now. Thanks to the vagaries of the electoral system and the buffoonery of Andy Ortega, you are—God help us!—going to be President of the United States. So it's time for me to pass the burden on to you. That's why we're here now."

Langston was puzzled. "But the inauguration isn't until—"

"Never mind that circus. And never mind everything the presidency is officially about. I'm talking about the *real* burden. Something every president for the last six decades has had to live with after learning of it in private from his predecessor."

"I have no idea what you mean."

"Of course you don't. The little ritual we're here to enact is not generally known. Nor will you find anything about it in the Constitution."

Langston felt a coldness slide along his spine.

"I am," the President continued, "about to impart to you certain information which has been handed down by each president to his successor ever since Eisenhower took over from Truman. I will not swear you to secrecy, because it would be a meaningless formality. After you've heard what I have to say, you will *know* that it must be kept in confidence. All your predecessors have understood this—even the ones who looked like they might present problems. I've heard a few stories . . ." The President gave a chuckle of amused reminiscence. "There was one president-elect who had to have it put to him as a religious imperative, on the Sunday school level; it seems he genuinely believed the infantile pietism he spouted. And then there was a later one who turned out to be perfectly happy to go along with anything that didn't interfere with his extraordinarily single-minded pursuit of every pair of panties in sight. In fact, I understand he was tickled pink to know—for once—something his wife didn't know!" The President sobered. "The only break in the chain was before either of those, at the time of the Kennedy assassination. Afterwards, Johnson had to be informed by other means. I gather there were complications. But he had no trouble grasping this information's . . . 'sensitivity' is hardly the word. Neither have any of the others."

The thinly veiled slights to a couple of former presidents whom Langston particularly admired helped break the spell. He leaned forward, glaring. "If you think I'm going to unquestioningly accept this vague, unsubstantiated mystification—"

"Of course not. I wouldn't expect you to. On your standards, you're actually being rational. No one should take something like this on blind faith. And we all know that photos and film can be faked. So in order to assure that you take me seriously . . ." The President reached into a desk drawer and withdrew a foot-square sheet of gray metal. He wordlessly passed it to Langston, who handled it gingerly. It was lighter than he'd expected, and unyieldingly rigid.

"Well, what do you think?" asked the President.

Langston handed it back, irritated. "What am I supposed to think? Steel, I suppose, although it's very thin for something that won't bend at all."

"So it is." As Langston watched in dawning amazement, the President took out a block of what looked like soft wood and placed the square of metal atop it. Then he produced what looked like a metal-punch, placed it in position above the metal, and held up a heavy mallet. "The Secret Service gets upset at people putting bullets through things in here," he explained, and, without warning, brought the mallet down. Langston jumped in his chair as the bit punched through the metal and into the wood.

The President held up the metal sheet, which now had a small round hole with a slight lip on the underside.

As Langston watched, the metal around the hole began to . . . *do* something. The lip grew even slighter, and then smoothed itself out altogether. And the hole closed, and vanished. The metal was as flawless as it had been before.

"It's an application of nanotechnology known as 'smart matter,' " the President explained matter-of-factly. "Actually, these particular molecule-sized robots aren't all that smart; they can only return it to its original shape."

The chill Langston had felt along his spine now rose to his neck, and the short hairs bristled. He found he could not speak.

"There are limits to what I can show you here," the President continued. "I'm pretty much restricted to things that don't make much noise and don't set off any alarms. So flashy or spectacular stuff is out. However . . ." He took out what appeared to be a thick headband, made of some flexible substance that seemed neither plastic nor metal. "Put this on."

Adrift in unreality, Langston could only obey. He slipped the device—it was heavier than it looked—over his head. The Oval Office grew dim and indistinct.

"Prepare yourself," he heard the President say.

He was no longer in the Oval Office. He was in what looked like a ski lodge, judging from the dramatic mountainscape beyond the wide windows. A fire roared and crackled in a massive stone fireplace, and the heat tingled on his face. He squeezed the armrests of his deep lounger, and felt the soft leather yield. The President— now dressed in khaki cords and a green turtleneck sweater—gazed at him from a similar lounger.

"Ask me something," urged the phantom President.

"But you're just an image," Langston heard himself say.

"But an interactive one." The unmistakable face formed its equally well-known smile.

For the first time in Langston's life, sheer panic took him. He tore off the headband and flung it away. With vertigo-inducing abruptness, he was back in the Oval Office, drawing deep, shuddering breaths and fearing he was going to be sick on the carpet with the presidential seal.

"So," he finally gasped, "this is all about some covert top-secret research project?"

The President shook his head. "I can't blame you for not being a scientist. I'm not one either. But if you were one, you'd know that this stuff is whole technological revolutions ahead of anything that could be seriously considered for R&D by anyone in this world." He paused significantly after those last three words.

Langston looked blank.

"You still don't get it, do you?" The President reached inside the desk again. This time he produced a plastic container the size of a large lunch box, but with tiny readouts on the side which Langston couldn't interpret. Its top clamshelled open at a touch of a button. The President took out . . . something.

"This animal is, of course, dead. But it has been preserved in molecular stasis by means whose details are immaterial at present. Here—take it. Feel it. Look at it."

Gingerly, Langston took the small, unmoving shape, flinching involuntarily from the lifeless flesh. That flesh was brownish-gray, smooth . . . and it didn't feel like flesh. He wasn't sure why it didn't, for this was inarguably a formerly living animal. The mysterious preservative to which the President had alluded had left it limp and flexible. Overcoming his queasiness, Langston found he could feel the outline of its skeleton. But it didn't feel like a skeleton. Instead of four limbs branching from a spine, there were six, radiating from some bony something in the center . . . but the animal was nothing like a starfish. One of those limbs, he realized, was no limb at all, for it terminated in a tiny face. At least Langston assumed it must be a face, for it had eyes. Three of them.

Belatedly, he recalled the emphasis the President had laid on the words *in this world.*

A cold draft seemed to blow through the Oval Office. It didn't stop sweat from popping out all over Langston's body.

"I think," said the President gravely, "you're now ready to look at these and not automatically dismiss them as fakes." He slid a sheaf of photos across the desk. "You'll note," he commented as he put the preserved animal away, "that not all evolutionary pathways are as divergent from ours as this guy's—especially the ones that culminate in tool-using races. The way it's been explained to me, a bilaterally symmetrical vertebrate—that's us—is a better arrangement for an active animal than a radially symmetrical one like his. It helps to have a definite front end."

Langston wasn't listening. Nor was his mind processing everything he was seeing. The various beings in the photos were too foreign to his accustomed world to fully register. But they had a certain indefinable quality of reality which he could now recognize, having seen the animal from the plastic case. And they had another quality: a sheer, skin-crawling *wrongness* far beyond the adolescent imaginings of Hollywood special effects. Oddly, this was most true of the ones that came closest to the human form.

"Do I now have your undivided attention?" the President asked.

Langston looked up from the photos and managed to nod.

"Shortly after the end of World War II," the President began, "the United States government was contacted by a man—yes, *man*, human but of unknown origin. He called himself 'Mr. Inconnu,' thus demonstrating that his originality had limits. He brought incontrovertible proofs that he was for real, stuff that made it impossible to dismiss him as a nut-case. He also brought news the human race wasn't—and still isn't—ready to handle."

Langston found his voice. "You mean the fact that there really is, uh, life in outer space?"

"Not just that. The galaxy isn't merely inhabited; it is *taken!* There are mighty civilizations out there. They have all the prime real estate already nailed down. They have no interest in technologically backward, politically fragmented worlds except as pawns in the power-games they play. And at the time Mr. Inconnu arrived they were just about to uncover one more such world: ours.

"It was necessary—urgently so—to do two things. First of all, we had to bluff the aliens into thinking Earth had a central political authority and was technologically advanced enough to rate at least a certain perfunctory diplomatic courtesy. Secondly, we had to begin living up to the second half of that bluff, and bring Earth up to speed as quickly as it could possibly be done. Mr. Inconnu provided the means to commence the crash course."

"You mean . . . the kind of things you've shown me?" Langston gave a headshake of bewilderment. "But if, as you say, we've known about this technology since the late 1940s, then why isn't it commonly known? You yourself just said it's still beyond our horizons."

"It couldn't be released all at once. It is a sociological truism, worked out by cultures older than ours, that a society simply can't survive the abrupt, wholesale intro- duction of technology more than one level above its own. God knows there've been plenty of examples in our own post-Columbus history! Mr. Inconnu's stuff has had to be doled out gradually, to avoid causing cultural and social collapse. Although," the President added with a grim smile, "I sometimes think it hasn't been avoided by a whole hell of a lot! Have you ever read much classic science fiction?"

Langston shook his head emphatically. The stuff was just *so* politically incorrect.

"Those writers foresaw the things that lay within the potential of their early-to-mid twentieth-century world: nuclear weapons, spaceflight with chemical rockets, and so forth . . . including 'electronic brains.' But not one of them ever foresaw the culture of ubiquitous information access that arose by the end of the century: practically every middle-class person with a computer on his or her desk at work, and another one at home." The President paused significantly. "The transistor, you see, was one of the first of Mr. Inconnu's revelations to be released, in 1948. Once society had had enough time—barely—to absorb that, the silicon chip followed. Society managed to adjust. The side effects and by-products, such as the rise of an objectionable computer-geek subculture, weren't quite fatal. But the point is that if the techno-logical progression had followed its normal course, we'd now be living in the future visualized by those Golden Age science-fiction writers: massive computers with lots of flashing lights and buzzers, and clunky Robbie-the-Robot type cybernetic devices, all using advanced vacuum tubes.

"At the same time, an analogous process was going on in molecular genetics. The same goes for any number of other fields. Materials technology, for example; none of those writers foresaw Kevlar. Nor did they foresee the laser. 'Death rays' were just a lucky guess."

Langston struggled to comprehend. "But . . . but *who* has been releasing these innovations? Who decides when they're to be revealed? And . . . what was that you said earlier about deceiving these aliens into thinking Earth had some kind of world government?"

"The answer to all your questions is the same. You see, this *had* to be kept secret. If it had gotten out, the result would have been global panic and hysteria that would have blown the whole deception. So a secret agency known as the Prometheus Project, answerable only to the President, was formed for the purposes of interfacing with the aliens and conducting a double security operation: keeping the truth about Earth from the aliens, and keeping the truth about the aliens' existence—and our relationship with them, including the agency's own existence—from the human race. It also controls the dissemination of extra-terrestrial technology.

"It's been a staggering job—all the more so because the overriding imperative of secrecy has made the personnel problem almost intractable. Nevertheless, recruiting for the Prometheus Project commenced immediately and proceeded on a continuing basis . . ."

PART ONE:
1963

CHAPTER ONE

I still remember my first glimpse of Mr. Inconnu. It's easy to remember, because it was also my last one.

It was while I was in training. I was hastening between Quonset huts, to the mess hall. It was raining. It's *always* raining in the Alaska panhandle, except in the winter when it's snowing. And this was spring, shortly after the Good Friday earthquake of 1964. We hadn't gotten the direct impact, for the epicenter was five hundred miles to the northwest, at the northern end of Prince William Sound. But the tsunamis had swept to the far reaches of the Pacific, with twenty-foot waves as far as California. We had been mostly shielded by Chichagoff and Admiralty Islands, but we'd gotten some messy aftereffects. And now the rain was worse than usual. So I wasn't able to get a

really good view of the group of men emerging from the
HQ Quonset, including the elderly guy—or at least he
seemed elderly, although for some reason it was hard to
be sure. His hair, which I could see before he pulled the
hood of his parka up over it, was gray, shading to white at
the temples. His left side was turned to me, and even in
these conditions I could see he had one hell of a facial
scar. Then he turned toward me, and for a very small fraction of a second our eyes met.

Then he was gone. That was all there was to it. I'm
certain I wouldn't have noticed him at all, except that
something about him seemed oddly familiar.

Afterwards, I described him to my roommate Dan
Buckley, who'd been at the facility longer than I had and
fancied himself the ultimate repository of insider knowledge. Even while condescending to enlighten my
ignorance, he couldn't entirely conceal his surprise at the
glimpse I'd gotten.

"Hardly anybody ever sees him," Dan explained. "The
only people he has direct contact with are the higher-
ups. I guess he's up here for consultation or something."
Evidently feeling he had somehow lost ground by
revealing that he was impressed, Dan leaned close and
spoke in his wisdom-imparting voice. "They say he's got
direct, automatic access to the President."

"I suppose he'd have to, considering . . ." As I replied
absently, most of my mind was contemplating the fact
that I'd seen the man who was the ultimate reason all of
us were there, up the Lynn Canal Inlet from Juneau, not
quite halfway to Skagway. And now that I knew who he
was, I remembered the one slide, made from a poor-
quality photo, that I'd seen of him. Of course, he looked

older now, as was only to be expected. But the scar was still a dead giveaway.

But I'm getting ahead of my story. All this was, of course, after I'd been recruited for the Prometheus Project. I remember the day that began, too. In fact, I'd remember that day even if I'd never been recruited. It was the day no one of my generation can ever forget.

Those of the younger generations (God, have I actually lived long enough to hear myself using a phrase like that?) find it very difficult to believe that not so very long ago Washington, DC, was like some sleepy, comfortably down-at-heels southern state capital.

It's true, though. At least as recently as the early 1960s you could just drive your car into the Capitol parking lot, and if you could find a space that was neither reserved nor already taken—which was often possible—you could simply park and walk into the Capitol building. No metal detectors. No Delta Force wannabes waiting to swoop down on you. And as for the White House, you just strolled along the street—it *was* a street then—to the East Wing and got in line. I swear it's true.

And it wasn't just the big-deal government buildings. Washington had at least its share of large hotels, of course, but even those had character. And the city was full of smaller places with dark wood-paneled bars that had aged well, their walls covered to practically the last square inch with framed, faded, autographed photos of politicians who'd gotten soused there. Those places had even more character. So did the sidewalk cafes that lent a delightful suggestion of Paris or Rome in the days before the freaks took over the sidewalks. The whole city oozed character.

It was a great town. Really. May I be sentenced to live in *today's* DC if I lie.

I was there in November of 1963. It was a little over a year after I'd parted company with the Army. (No, I don't want to talk about it.) My new career had taken me out of town, and I liked this particular job because it brought me back to Washington, where I was based. I loved Washington—especially in the autumn. Forget those famous cherry blossoms in the spring. Autumn was best.

Not that I had all that much time to appreciate it. I was there on business. Business took me to a certain bar in Georgetown—an area recently made fashionable by the Kennedy administration types, but still recognizable. The bar was a little place on one of the side streets off M Street, not far from the footbridge across the canal. I was to meet George Stafford there.

As I approached the place, I became aware that something was not quite right. People were hurrying into the bar in abnormal numbers for early afternoon—people who didn't look like regulars. I immediately realized I shouldn't go in. Even if the meeting hadn't been blown, any out-of-the-ordinary event at the venue meant it would be, or at least should be. Either way, it was time for me to take a leisurely stroll along the Potomac riverfront.

But a zillion generations of monkey ancestors told me to follow the crowd, out of sheer curiosity to see what all the fuss was about.

Inside, the sense of wrongness grew. People were clustered at the bar—but they weren't drinking, to speak of. And they were strangely quiet. They were all staring at the TV above the rows of bottles. The voices from the TV had the unmistakable tone of news announcers trying to fill a silence.

I shouldered my way through the oddly passive crowd. I got to the bar just in time to see the latest of the cruelly interminable reruns of the motorcade in Dallas, focusing on one open-topped car and on the famous chestnut-haired head which suddenly slammed forward with the impact of a bullet.

You have to understand. We didn't know any of the stuff that came out about him later. Like the fact that he was the kind of guy who, at the time his wife was undergoing a difficult and possibly life-threatening childbirth, was off cruising the Med with a boatload of bimbos. The kind of guy who cheerfully signed his name to a book Daddy had had ghost-written, and afterwards cheerfully accepted the Pulitzer prize Daddy bought for the book. In fact, he hardly ever did anything in his life for any reason except to please Daddy. And Daddy was, with the possible exception of Meyer Lansky, the most successful organized criminal in American history . . . besides being a Nazi sympathizer, unlike most crooks, who at least are refreshingly apolitical. A good match for Mommy, whose religious bigotry would have been considered a bit much in the sixteenth century.

No, we didn't know any of that at the time. All we knew was that he was young and vivid and stood out like a flame among the bald, boring old farts who in our experience— I was twenty-seven then—made up the political establishment. Call us naïve if you want. I can't stop you. I can't even disagree with you. All I can say is that he *meant* something to us, as though something new had come into our world with him. And now that something had been snuffed out.

That was why, for decades afterwards, in the teeth of all the evidence, people went on believing in various conspiracy theories, the more far-fetched the better. We couldn't accept the fact—and it is a fact—that the assassination had been the stupid, pointless act of one lone, pathetic little loser. That truth was unacceptable because it somehow diminished us. Surely the obliteration of what had meant so much to us—defined us, in a way—had to *mean* something, because *we* meant something. Didn't we?

In my case, it didn't help that I'd been in the Army's Special Forces before . . . never mind. He had always been kind of a special patron of ours. He'd reviewed us once, and passed within a few feet of me.

Anyway, I don't remember much of the rest of that day, or the next few.

At some point, though, I ended up at Matt Kane's, not far from the Fourteenth Street sleaze strip, late at night.

That place was another great thing about the old Washington. If you walked in through the storefront-like entrance, it was just a medium-seedy Irish neighborhood tavern. You had to know the side door, off to the right, that led through a slightly alarming-looking corridor to the "Bit of Ireland" bar in the back. The business about the whole thing having been brought over from the Auld Sod brick by brick was probably bullshit. But it was full of banners and Gaelic road signs and all the rest, and it hosted the best Irish bands to cross the Atlantic.

Tonight, though, the usual liveliness was gone. And I was ignoring the justly famous beer list. I had ordered another Irish on the rocks when I became aware that the barstool beside me had acquired an occupant.

"Better go easy on that stuff, Bob," said George Stafford.

"You missed the meeting in Georgetown," I stated. Even on that day, I'd retained enough presence of mind to check out the crowd. He hadn't been there.

"I know. I was unavoidably detained. There was a lot going on that day."

"Golly, George, thanks for telling me that. What would I do without you? I never would have known if you hadn't—"

"Cut the goddamned sarcasm!" Stafford kept his voice low with an effort. He looked like he hadn't slept in days. "It just happens that the present situation is especially difficult for the people I work for."

"About whose identity I've never been entirely clear." I was pleased with myself for being able to navigate through that sentence. In fact, the accomplishment seemed to call for a drink. I suited the action to the thought.

"You don't need to be 'clear' on it. All you need to know is that I represent people who sometimes need certain services on an *ad hoc* basis, with no questions asked. The very fact that you've never shown an interest in their identity is one of the main reasons you've gotten their business."

"Point taken. Okay, what do you—sorry, I mean the people you represent—need this time?"

Actually, I had a pretty good idea, if only in general terms. Stafford was something in the government, I knew that much. I didn't know what agency he worked for, but it clearly wasn't the FBI or the CIA or anything like that. Those wouldn't have had any need for the services of a freelancer like myself—they had their own people. No, his agency just had occasional, obviously somewhat irregular contacts with some superspooky outfit or other . . . and it didn't want to use its own people to make those contacts. Instead, it used intermediaries—independent contractors like yours truly, who had no idea who they were ultimately working for, and could be disavowed and forgotten like a bad smell if such became necessary or convenient. (The English language hadn't yet become debased enough for a term like "plausible deniability," but that was the idea.) Which was fine with me. The money was good, and since I was expendable, they had no reason to be concerned about my background. A marriage made in heaven, you might say.

"The matter concerning which we were supposed to meet in Georgetown has been canceled indefinitely. But now there's something else we need you for—something related to the situation that has arisen over the last few days." I patiently endured Stafford's circumlocution, knowing his inability to communicate without it. "There's somebody coming to Washington. Several people, actually. But you only need to worry about one of them. She'll be arriving at National Airport tomorrow." He passed me a typed itinerary. "You're to meet her and bring her to the address in here." He slid a sealed envelope along the bar. "Don't open it until you've actually picked her up."

My eyebrows rose. This exceeded even Stafford's usual capacity for cloak-and-dagger theatricality. But I was perfectly willing to play his games as long as I was paid to do so. "How will I know her?"

For answer, Stafford handed me a wallet-sized photo. It showed a handsome brunette, not too much older than me but too severe-looking for my taste.

"You will address her as 'Miss Smith,' " Stafford went on, "and identify yourself to her as 'Mr. Jones.' "

"While keeping a straight face?" I inquired, straight-faced. Stafford looked pained, and I raised a hand to forestall him. "I know, I know: 'no questions asked.' I will ask one question, though. Are you expecting trouble?"

"There shouldn't be any." Stafford's tone seemed oddly at variance with his words. It wasn't an assurance, but a kind of desperate, almost truculent assertion, as though things were happening that had no business happening. "However, it seems that the possibility can't be entirely discounted. Why do you think we're hiring you?"

"Skip the flattery. I expect a hazardous-duty bonus."

Stafford flushed. "Why? This is simply what we pay you for in the first place."

"Nope. You pay me—and, I imagine, others like me—because you want to keep your hands clean. Fine. But I get the impression that this isn't exactly routine. If I'm going to be risking my ass, I expect to be compensated accordingly."

"Don't push it," Stafford snarled. "Remember, if it wasn't for us, you wouldn't be in business at all."

There was an element of truth to this. I'd put out the word through various acquaintances that I could provide certain services discreetly. The result had been my first contact with Stafford. Shortly after that, my license to operate a private security service had come through, despite the less-than-fully-honorable discharge from the Army that I had on my record. I couldn't pretend that the two had been unconnected.

Still, I didn't appreciate him reminding me of it. So I

turned my attention back to my drink, ignoring him and
waiting patiently while he jittered.

"All right," he finally blurted. "I can't make a firm commitment. But we'll talk about it after she's safely
delivered."

"Fair enough," I allowed, deciding it wouldn't be a good
idea to push him too far in his present emotional state.
Shortly thereafter, I departed, seeking my car. Even the
hookers on Fourteenth Street seemed subdued. Everybody was subdued these days—except Stafford, who acted
like he was fending off a nervous breakdown.

My apartment-*cum*-office was east of Rock Creek Park,
which was why I could afford it. It wasn't bad, though. I
had half of the second story of an established-but-not-
dilapidated four-story building just off Dupont Circle. My
three front windows were up where most passersby never
look, above the storefront first floor. The doorway in the
entry hall at the stairway landing, with its understated
plaque reading *Robert Devaney, Security Services*, led
directly into the office part: very basic, for I had no recep-
tionist, nor any need of one. I'd found it was cheaper to
hire an answering service—this was decades before voice
mail, remember—and return any calls that seemed promising. Stafford and a few others knew the code-phrases to
drop. So the office was really a place to do whatever paperwork I couldn't avoid, not to impress clients. I suppose it
had been somebody's parlor, once upon a time. Behind
the desk was a door leading to the living area, consisting
of three rooms with the usual functions. In addition, there
was what had clearly been a workshop. I'd hired a car-
penter to conceal one wall of it behind a kind of shallow
cabinet. The wall itself held hooks and racks to support

tools. Now they held my tools—two of which I selected the following morning.

Even then, the Colt 1911 A1 was considered old-fashioned almost to the point of obsolescence. I still liked it, for its reliability and for the sheer stopping power of its .45 ACP slug. It went into an armpit holster—it was just barely small enough to carry that way, even under a loose-fitting jacket. Another holster fit around my right ankle. It held a Beretta .25, a gun on which I wasted very little respect. In fact, I regarded it as just the thing for a firefight in a phone booth. But it was very concealable, which covers a multitude of sins in a last-ditch holdout weapon.

In case you're wondering: no, I didn't usually go this heavily armed. But something about Stafford's manner had worried me. That, and the fact that they were hiring me—and even willing to consider a bonus, if Stafford was to be believed—for a job which, from his description, a chauffeur could have handled. This told me there was more to it than he was admitting. I didn't particularly resent his lack of candor—it wasn't like he owed me anything. But neither did I intend to go in blind without taking precautions.

Washington's cozy medium-sized-city ambience in those days had its negative points. One of these was National Airport, the inadequacy of which had long been a staple of local grumbling. It was hard to forget about; all you had to do was look toward the Potomac, at the procession of low-flying planes that had become a permanent backdrop to the Lincoln Memorial. It became even more obvious as you drove over Arlington Memorial Bridge, caught the George Washington Memorial

Highway south, and got into the traffic. Some people actually liked this stretch of road. I didn't, because it took me past the Pentagon, with its unwelcome memories.

The flight I was to meet was a Northwest Boeing 707 from Minneapolis. The crowd was fairly light, and the plane clearly hadn't been full. I had no trouble spotting "Miss Smith."

She was taller than I'd expected, and possibly a little younger, but just as severe as her photo had indicated. Her makeup was minimal, her suit businesslike, and her dark hair pulled back into a tight bun. I stepped forward diffidently.

"Miss Smith?" ("Ms." was yet another linguistic barbarism that still lay in the future.) "I'm Mr. Jones." I extended my hand, even though you were supposed to let a lady do that first, in those days.

She looked me over in a way that wasn't altogether flattering—or maybe that was just my oversensitive nature—and made no move to shake my hand. "Is my transportation ready, Mr. Jones?"

So much for small talk, I decided. "Yeah. Let's get your luggage and—"

"I have everything right here." She indicated the overnight bag she was carrying.

"Oh. Well, then . . ." I extended my hand again, this time to take the bag.

"I'll keep it with me, if you don't mind."

"Okay. Fine. Right this way."

She gave my '59 Dodge an inspection not unlike the one she'd given me. "Hey, it gets me there and it gets me back," I ventured as I held the door for her.

"It suits you," she observed, settling into the passenger's

seat and keeping the bag on her lap.

"Somehow, I could tell you thought so." I got in behind the wheel and pulled out the envelope which I, continuing to play Stafford's little games, had kept sealed until now. I slit it open, curious, and read the address.

Several obscenities were out of my mouth before I caught myself and turned to "Miss Smith" sheepishly. She looked more amused than offended.

"Is something the matter?" she inquired with an economical smile.

"Pardon my French," I muttered. "But . . . well, you see, I don't generally get involved in high-level stuff." In actual fact, I *never* did, and Stafford knew it. *I'm* definitely *gonna demand a bonus!* I thought furiously. I also thought of where I was going to insert Stafford's sealed envelope, rolled up into a tube.

I continued thinking these thoughts as I drove, in sullen silence, back into the District and then northeastward in the direction of the White House.

CHAPTER TWO

The attack came as we were crossing F Street.

Cautious habit, reinforced by my apprehension about this job and crystallized by my first look at the address inside Stafford's envelope, had taken me on a route that was both indirect and very different from the one I'd followed to National Airport earlier. After crossing over into the District, I did a half circle around the Lincoln Memorial and turned right onto Constitution Avenue. As we passed the Ellipse, with the Washington Monument to our right and the White House in the distance to the left, "Miss Smith" gave me a look of arch inquiry, but held her tongue. I affected not to notice as I drove on past the National Archives and turned left on Seventh Street. I intended to continue north past Chinatown, maybe as far as Mount Vernon Square, before turning left again and looping around.

I was silently congratulating myself on my cleverness when the nondescript delivery truck came careening into the intersection from the left, seemingly out of control, and capsized with suspicious precision directly in front of us.

I slammed on the brake, managing to bring us to a screeching stop a few feet in front of that overturned truck . . . which, I could now see, had no driver. I could also see the inconspicuously dressed figures emerging purposefully from behind the buildings at the corner of F Street. Their purposefulness was of a particular kind, which I had learned to recognize: that of armed men. They circled around toward each side of us.

As I brought my raging thoughts under control, one of them would not be suppressed: *How could they have known? There was no way to predict I'd take this route.*

I turned to "Miss Smith" and met her dark brown eyes. They held none of the shocked panic they should have. All I could see there was a resigned, slightly exasperated *Oh, shit.*

I dismissed all of this from my mind as I unlocked the door on my side and opened it a crack. Then I reached under my jacket with my left hand and grasped the Colt. It was awkward as hell, but I'd had practice.

As the first of the nondescript figures approached my side of the car, I kicked the door open, to slam into him. As he reeled back into the man behind him, I grabbed "Miss Smith" by her upper left arm and pulled her behind me as I flung myself out of the car. Simultaneously, I whipped out the Colt and got off a shot that entered the first man's head under the chin and blew off its top in a pinkish-gray shower.

The crowd of sightseers that a traffic accident always attracts began to scream.

I was too busy to notice. I hit the street rolling, still pulling "Miss Smith" behind me. Out of a corner of my eye, I noticed that she was still clutching her overnight bag. I got to my feet, pulling her up with me. In life-and-death situations, you don't pause to worry about trivia like a dislocated shoulder. But she had the feel of a woman in good condition . . . and, praise be, she wasn't screaming hysterically. As she staggered to her feet, I fired off three rapid shots that didn't hit anybody but made all the attackers take cover behind the overturned truck. Taking advantage of that moment, I pulled her around behind the car.

There were no shots. I shifted the Colt to my right hand and risked a peek over the car.

Shots rang out, and bullets whined off the car. But that wasn't what bothered me. As I snatched my gun hand back, something happened to that arm—it felt as though the arm had instantly gone to sleep, but with an added numbness. Unpleasant as hell. I cried out in shock and dropped the Colt.

"Miss Smith" seemed to recognize my reaction, and she went pale.

"Paralysis beam," she gasped. "It must have brushed your arm only fleetingly. They're actually using something like that right here on a city street!" That aspect clearly concerned her more than my well-being.

I scooped up the Colt with my left hand while trying to shake some feeling back into my right arm, and glared at her. "Listen, whatever-your-name-is, I want to know just exactly what the hell is going on here, and who these people are, and how they knew where we'd be, and—"

"There's no time for that now," she snapped. "We've got to get in *there*." She pointed to a narrow alley between two buildings on the right-hand side of Seventh Street.

"What?" A renewed fusillade of shots sent us crouching deeper, and elicited new screams from the bystanders who still huddled behind whatever shelter the sidewalks afforded, too terrified to run. I didn't return fire, not wanting to risk a repetition of what these guys had just done to my arm. Besides, I wanted to conserve the four rounds left in my magazine. It was, I reflected, one of the reasons the police continued to prefer revolvers: in a situation like this, you could spend your spare time "topping up."

"Look," I told her, "what we need to do is sit tight and hold them off. The cops will be here in a couple of minutes."

"*No!* You don't understand. I can get us to safety—I have the means. I just can't use it here, in public, where there are witnesses."

To this day, I'm still not certain why I let her take the lead, when I was supposed to be the professional in charge. Maybe I was just very rattled at encountering things that I didn't understand but which *she* evidently did. Whatever the reason, I reached down and drew the Beretta.

"Do you know how to use one of these?" I asked.

"Not really. You, uh, pull the trigger, right?"

"No, you *squeeze* it." I released the safety and handed it to her. She took it gingerly. "It doesn't have much kick. Just hold it in both hands like this." I demonstrated with the Colt, for the feeling was returning to my right hand. "Empty the magazine in the direction of the bad guys while you're running. Ready?"

She nodded jerkily.

"All right. . . . *Run!*" As I shouted the last word, I rose up and started shooting.

She sprinted gamely toward the alley, firing away. She hadn't a prayer of hitting anything . . . but *they* didn't know that. Also, they must have been stunned by the sheer unexpectedness of this move. They kept their heads down until we'd almost reached the alley. As the shots finally began to ring out behind us, I anticipated the same tingling numbness I'd felt before, only worse. But then we were around the corner and into the alley. "Miss Smith," gasping for breath, dropped the empty Beretta and started getting something out of her bag.

I detached a fresh magazine from the holster belt and slammed it into the Colt's butt. Then I positioned myself between "Miss Smith" and the alley entrance, in firing stance.

That was when the world abruptly went blurry and gray and silent.

I didn't even know how to react. It was too unexpected, and too foreign to ordinary experience. I turned to face "Miss Smith," who was standing very close behind me. She, at least, was still in sharp focus and full color. She was holding an odd-looking device about the size and shape of a paperback book. She clasped it to her belt to free her hand. When she spoke, her voice was the only sound in the universe.

"It generates a field, large enough to encompass both of us, which—" she began. Then the first of our attackers was around the corner of the building, moving like a figure in a silent black-and-white movie in poor focus. I started to raise my gun, but she gripped me by the arm. "No! They can't see us or hear us. Just stand still, close to me."

My jaw dropped. Clearly, she was nuts. And yet . . . the ghostly figures were running past us, looking frantically around. One of them faced me, unseeing, from just a few feet away. Then their leader mouthed some inaudible command, and they regrouped and proceeded on down the alley, checking doorways as they went.

"As I was starting to say," she resumed, "the field bends light around itself a hundred and eighty degrees, thus conferring invisibility. In theory we shouldn't be able to see out of it, either, but a partial compensating feature is built in. Actually, it's two fields. The second one blocks sound waves, both ways."

"Who *are* you?" I managed.

"That's not important at the moment. What is important is that we get moving. Anytime now, they're going to pull themselves together and start looking for us with sensors against which this device is useless. Fortunately, we have a shielded command post nearby—it was lucky you picked this route."

"•'We'?" I queried.

She ignored me. "Come on, and remember to stay close to me." She took my hand to emphasize the last point—a gesture totally devoid of affection—and led the way back out onto Seventh Street.

A sheer sense of unreality kept me inarticulate as we proceeded north past the National Portrait Gallery and then worked our way to the right through side streets, moving in a silent world composed of fuzzy shades of gray, past dim people who could neither hear nor see us as we wended our way into Chinatown.

The Friendship Archway, that exercise in wretched excess, hadn't been constructed yet. There was just a squalidly picturesque district of exoticism and sinister menace that was largely—though not entirely—bogus, the whole effect comfortably cushioned by the knowledge that you were only about ten blocks from the White House. We passed invisibly through alleyways behind restaurants you'd never find listed by the AAA, where the by-products of their kitchens were disposed of. (No, you don't want to know.) As soon as we were inarguably alone, "Miss Smith" touched the little device on her belt. With a suddenness that was vertiginous for me but clearly no novelty for her, colors and sounds beat in on us as the universe returned to normal. She matter-of-factly returned the device to her bag and motioned me to follow her.

She led me to a laundry. (Yes, a laundry. I wouldn't *dare* make that up.) As we entered, the old Chinese guy behind the counter met her eyes. She approached him and said something I couldn't catch. He nodded. She motioned me to follow her to the right, behind a rack of hangers, rich with that freshly laundered smell. We worked our way around behind it, walking sideways to fit through the narrow spaces. She stopped in front of a segment of wooded wall that was distinguished only by a wooden carving of a Chinese ideograph . . . or what looked like one. I'd had some exposure to the Kai, Tsing and Tao scripts in the Army, but I couldn't place this one. She ran the palm of her hand over it. I spotted a faint greenish glow around the edges of her hand.

Soundlessly, a rectangular segment of the wall, large

enough to admit one, moved back a couple of inches and slid aside. She passed through. I followed. The wall closed again.

We were in what looked like an empty closet, barely large enough to accommodate the two of us, lit by a dusty forty-watt bulb.

I was trying to frame a question when I felt a very faint vibration through the soles of my feet, followed by an equally faint sensation of descending, like an unusually slow and soundless elevator.

"Miss Smith" turned to face me. She held a small tubular gizmo, pointed at my midriff.

"Sorry," she said, without any deep conviction.

The next thing I remember was awakening on a cot.

It was a very nondescript cot in a very nondescript room—windowless, walled with some material I thought of as "plastic" in my inability to identify it. The door had a perfectly ordinary knob.

I got to my feet, and almost fell back over. It wasn't nausea, or vertigo, or anything except a stiff sensation of having lain unmoving for too long. I established my equilibrium—Special Forces training has its uses—and walked carefully to the door. I tried the knob. It was locked, of course, but I'd had to try.

I looked around more carefully. There was an obvious— if advanced-looking—video pickup near the ceiling, in the corner to the right of the door. I had no objection to that. Indeed, the ability of whoever I was dealing with to observe me offered some hope that they wouldn't just leave me to rot, now that they knew I was awake. Just to hasten the process, I made a rude gesture with the middle finger of my right hand in the direction of the pickup.

I was considering the pros and cons of mooning the pickup when the door finally opened.

"Miss Smith" entered, dressed exactly as she'd been when I'd last seen her. (Or at least I think she was. I've never been a particularly insightful observer of women's clothing, as all the women in my life have made clear to me.) A youngish man followed her, but stayed in the background, keeping his hand close to the opening of his jacket. I didn't even bother trying to calculate my chances of taking him—not when I had no idea of where I was, or how to get out of it.

"How are you feeling?" asked "Miss Smith" in a tone that passed for cordial with her.

"Never better. And now that we're among your friends, and I'm completely helpless, could you *please* tell me your real name?"

She blinked with surprise. "Well, I suppose it can do no harm. I'm Renata Novak. And I'm as human—and as American—as you, in case you'd wondered."

"Actually, I hadn't." This was true—surprisingly, inasmuch as I was something of a science-fiction fan. If I'd been a real hard case, maybe my mind would have strayed into wild speculations. Fortunately, the completely prosaic aspect of everything about Renata Novak except her hardware had kept me anchored securely in what I still fancied to be reality.

She resumed briskly. "At any rate, Mr. Devaney—"

"Ah, so you know my name."

"Of course. As I was saying, we find ourselves faced with the problem of what to do with you."

"You seemed to know just what to do with me, in that elevator."

"Do I detect a note of resentment? I should think you'd be more appreciative. I could have simply activated the privacy field for myself in that alley, after you had gotten me safely to it, and left you behind to deal with those who were following us."

There seemed no good answer to this, so I contented myself with my best glare. Irritatingly, she seemed not to notice, but continued without a break.

"So you see, Mr. Devaney, we're not without some concept of ethics. But you've seen things you have no business seeing, and become involved in matters whose importance you can't possibly imagine."

"Oh, I think I can imagine the importance of the Presidential succession."

This brought her up short. "What makes you say that?"

"It has to have something to do with the fact that Lyndon Johnson has abruptly become President. Remember the address I was originally supposed to take you to? Besides, something has got George Stafford on the verge of wetting his pants. What else could be involved, at this particular time?"

"Very clever, Mr. Devaney. You're even right, as far as you go. That is the reason for my presence in Washington—and, by extension, for the attack on me. There are, you see, certain things that Mr. Johnson needs to be made aware of. But the problem is the nature of those 'things'—secrets that *must* be kept. The importance of this is such that the assassination of one American president and the accession of another becomes a trivial matter by comparison."

So I can just imagine the triviality of an individual life, I thought. *Mine, for instance.* "You mean," I asked aloud, "the stuff I saw you use?"

"Again, Mr. Devaney, that's just one facet of the secret of which I speak. You shouldn't have seen that 'stuff,' and wouldn't have had it not been for the attack on us. But, through no fault of your own, you *did* see it."

"Hold that thought about 'no fault of your own.'•"

"Unfortunately, that alters nothing. Now," she continued briskly, "our options are limited. There are techniques of memory erasure by which you could be made to forget everything that has happened to you since just before Stafford approached you about this job. This, however, has at least three disadvantages. First, it isn't absolutely foolproof; some residue of memory might remain. Second, some kind of cover story would have to be devised to account for the loss of a couple of days from your life. And third, the procedure is not entirely without risk of permanent brain damage, possibly leaving the subject in a vegetative state."

I got the distinct impression that she had listed the disadvantages in descending order of importance, from her standpoint. I also had the uncomfortable feeling that she'd just dug the hole I was in even deeper, if possible, by telling me about this memory erasure business— something else I had no business knowing.

"You mentioned 'options,' plural," I said carefully. "That's just one option. There must be at least one other."

Renata Novak didn't reply. And her dark eyes, usually so direct, didn't meet mine.

There was, I realized, no need to go into details about the second option.

In spite of everything, I sensed that this woman wasn't evil or bloodthirsty or anything like that. But she had the ruthlessness of someone in the service of an absolute: a cause whose importance transcended all ordinary social rules and moral standards, an end that justified any means.

She seemed to reach a decision. I had a pretty good idea of what that decision was. She opened her mouth to speak.

"Who *are* you people?" I blurted.

She looked surprised. "We're called the Prometheus Project . . . not that that will mean anything to you. And now, Mr. Devaney—"

The door opened. Novak turned with an expression of annoyance at the interruption. That expression smoothed itself out at the sight of the late-middle-aged gent who entered—a tall, lantern-faced guy with slightly receding gray hair and blue eyes whose mildness was, I thought, probably deceptive. He motioned Novak to join him in a corner. They spoke in undertones for perhaps two minutes, while the young guy watched me with a degree of concentration that decided me against attempting any funny business. Instead, I tried to eavesdrop on the conversation in the corner. But I only caught two words, because Novak pronounced them with a startled rise in volume: "Mr. Inconnu."

Finally, she turned back to me. "It seems, Mr. Devaney, that you've suddenly acquired a new option. Actually, it's not even an 'option;' it's simply what's going to happen. You are to be recruited."

"Recruited?" I echoed faintly.

"For the Prometheus Project," she explained, in the tone one uses with a not-terribly-bright child. "That is the decision of an important—a *very* important—individual who has somehow become aware of your case and for some unaccountable reason taken a personal interest in it."

"Mr. Inconnu?" I ventured.

My shot in the dark evidently connected, for she gave me a look of concentrated and distilled venom. "You have an instinctive affinity for things that are none of your business. But then, I suppose it *is* your business now, isn't it? And yes, he evidently insists on it. Very well; you will be transported to—"

"Wait just a goddamned minute! What if I don't *want* to be recruited? Ever think about that?"

"Are you *sure* you don't want to be?" she asked silkily. "Considering . . . ?"

This, undeniably, was food for thought.

The elderly man stepped forward and spoke into the silence. "I tell you what, Mr. Devaney: suppose we take you to the destination Miss Novak was about to describe to you, and there explain to you what the Prometheus Project is all about? If, after hearing what we have to say, you don't wish to participate, then we will make every possible effort to devise a solution that enables you to keep both your life and your sanity, while maintaining inviolate the secret we exist to keep." He raised a forestalling hand as Novak appeared ready to erupt with indignation. "This is Mr. Inconnu's wish. In fact, I'm almost quoting him verbatim." He turned back to me. "Well, Mr. Devaney?"

Did I believe him? To this day, I'm not sure. But, as Novak had put it, my options were limited.

Within twelve hours, I was on the first of a series of planes to Alaska.

CHAPTER THREE

The final hop was by a helicopter we boarded at a totally nondescript little airfield in British Columbia. It took us over the mountain boundary between Canada and southeast Alaska, whose craggy peaks protrude above vast fields of ice and snow. But as one descends to the labyrinthine coastline of Alaska's Inside Passage, the landscape changes dramatically. Indeed, in the summer, few from the "lower forty-eight" are prepared for the lushness of the temperate rain forest—a gift of the *kuroshio*, the Pacific's equivalent of the Gulf Stream.

Our low-flying helicopter was approaching Juneau from the southeast. But Juneau wasn't our destination. Instead, the pilot passed it northward, proceeding over the titanic Mendenhall Glacier and up the Lynn Inlet in the direction of Skagway—which wasn't our destination either.

In later years, we would have looked down on cruise ships off the dramatic fjord coast. But at that time Alaska, nearing the end of its fifth year of statehood, was still out of the way to the point of near inaccessibility. No works of man were to be seen as we passed Point Bridget, and Berners Bay opened out before us. At this point the pilot took a turn to starboard and we headed east following one of the streams that fed the bay, upcountry into regions that would remain remote even in the busiest years of the tourist boom. Soon a small, level valley opened out before us, almost entirely occupied by what was, to all appearances, a military post about as undistinguished as the Canadian landing strip had been.

"Why don't you people just make this whole base invisible?" I asked Renata Novak, shouting above the noise of the descending chopper. She'd said as little as possible, or maybe even a little less than that, in the course of the trip, and I wanted to get a rise out of her. I failed.

"It would be expensive," she explained shortly. "Also superfluous, given the remoteness of this location."

I couldn't disagree with that. I also reflected that the place would soon be practically inaccessible, with winter coming on. These people—the "Prometheus Project," about which I still knew nothing more than the name— could do anything to me they damned well wanted, in total privacy. That didn't bother me as much as you might think. I'd had time to pretty much adjust to being at their mercy. Besides, they weren't all like Renata Novak, if the older guy I'd encountered under Washington's Chinatown was any indication. I consoled myself with the thought as I got out of the helicopter, zipping up my parka against the Alaskan November.

The installation was mostly Quonset huts, but there were a few honest-to-God buildings. Renata Novak led me to one of these, through a chill drizzle that was rapidly turning to snow. Inside, it looked as standard-issue as everything else. There was no magic in evidence, and not even any obtrusive security—it probably wasn't necessary here. Most of the people I saw wore utilitarian military-style dress, but without insignia. This wasn't really a military base, at least not of the military as I knew it.

Renata Novak left me in what was clearly a waiting room, to do what one spends most of one's time doing in institutional settings: wait. I did just that, not even wasting mental energy by contemplating escape. I had no desire to try and traverse the Alaskan boonies on foot—not, I suspected, that I had the slightest real chance of getting far enough to make the attempt.

After a while, Renata Novak returned and motioned me through an inner door. I entered an office so bare of all personal touches and work-related clutter that it clearly had no purpose except interviews. A man seated behind a small desk motioned me to take a chair. My escort sat in another, in a posture of icy primness.

"Welcome to the Prometheus Project, Mr. Devaney," the man greeted, extending his hand. I saw nothing to be lost by taking it. He was well into distinguished-looking middle age. He wore a reassuring smile and the first suit I'd seen here.

"So this is it?" I couldn't keep the skepticism out of my voice as I made a gesture that took in the installation around us.

"Oh, there's more to the Project than this. A *lot* more."

He chuckled. "This is just one facility. It houses Section One, which is devoted to administrative functions, including indoctrination and training. You'll be staying here a while. Oh, by the way, my name is Dennis Dupont. I'm responsible for orientation of newly recruited personnel like yourself. I say 'like yourself' even though your case appears to be somewhat unique."

"Because I was invited here by Mr. Inconnu?"

Dupont gave me a sharp look. "So you know about that. Tell me, Mr. Devaney, how much do you know about Mr. Inconnu?"

"Not a damned thing," I admitted cheerfully, "aside from the obvious fact that it's a pseudonym. I was hoping you'd tell me who he is . . . and what the hell the 'Prometheus Project' is."

"The answer to the second question is bound up with the answer to the first." Dupont appeared to consider his options. "Let me ask you this: what do *you* think the Prometheus Project is all about?"

I considered what I'd seen, and made a wild stab into facetiousness. "Men from outer space?"

"Quite right." Dupont smiled, and spoke into the stunned silence he'd created. "Or, at least, *man*, singular. Mr. Inconnu is quite human, but of unknowable origin. His own explanation—which we have no basis for doubting—is that he is a descendant of humans transplanted from Earth to an extrasolar planet by aliens, for reasons of their own, in the distant past. He himself, he tells us, was able to escape from his people's servitude to warn us of the danger which the Project was subsequently founded to meet.

"And speaking of unusual backgrounds," Dupont

continued, for I was still in no condition to interrupt him, "I've been studying your own dossier, which arrived while you were in transit." He peered at a stack of papers on his desk. "Let's see: you were in the Army, assigned to the Special Forces, until fairly recently, when—"

"I don't want to talk about it."

"Suit yourself. But I can hardly help observing that you were no ordinary soldier—even on the standards of the Special Forces. Your education, for one thing, was such that the Army considered it worth extending still further, particularly in the direction of Asian languages and cultures. All in all, you have quite a variety of skills for a man your age." Dupont gave me an odd look. "A pity for the Army that you didn't stay in."

"I said I don't—"

"Yes, I know. At any rate, ever since your separation from the service you've operated a one-man private security agency, with a rather unusual clientele. Sometimes even a slightly questionable one."

"A man must eat," I philosophized.

"No doubt. But your most regular client has been Mr. Stafford, who was instrumental in getting you your license despite . . . that which you don't want to talk about. As you have probably surmised, he is a member of the White House staff—one of the members unknown to even the knowledgeable segment of the public."

Actually, I hadn't surmised that, although it had always been pretty clear he was something in the government. I didn't let my surprise show, but merely cocked my head as though inviting Dupont to continue.

"Stafford handles clandestine matters, usually through unattached intermediaries like yourself. This has caused him to have contact with the Project. He knows very little of us, and nothing of what we exist to do. But what little he has seen gives him cause to be nervous."

"So I've noticed."

"At any rate, we're now in what I believe is called a 'flap.' The Project's existence is a secret known, in its entirety, only to the President. Therefore, it must be handed down in private from each President to his successor. This has happened twice so far. Unfortunately, as a result of what has occurred in Dallas, the secret can't be passed to Mr. Johnson in the traditional way. We've had to start over from scratch, as it were, and make other arrangements, acting through Stafford. It was for this purpose that Miss Novak was in Washington."

"And should be there now," she broke in with tight-lipped asperity.

"We've been through that," said Dupont mildly, though I caught a note of annoyance. "It's being taken care of. You delivered the . . . exhibits, and that's the important thing."

"Someone else could have been detailed to escort *him* here," she persisted, not deigning to refer to me by name.

"It wasn't just that. You're needed back here. The attack on you brings the Tonkuztra matter to a head. . . ." Dupont came to the halt of a man who knows he's said too much.

"I've been wondering about that," I said with as much casualness as I could muster. "Who were those people who attacked us? And how did they pinpoint us? You mentioned . . . uh, 'Tonkuztra?' That's a new one on me."

"It would be. It's a name I shouldn't have mentioned in your presence. But you'll learn what it means. You'll learn a great many things after you join the Project."

"But I haven't decided whether or not I'm going to join it."

Renata Novak's exasperation surfaced as she addressed Dupont. "Oh, let's not waste any more time with—"

Dupont raised a silencing hand, without letting my eyes go. "As I understand it, Mr. Devaney, we are supposed to make every effort to allow you freedom of choice in this matter. But think a moment: if you don't accept recruitment, you will never, ever learn any more about the things you've only seen glimpses of or heard vaguely hinted at. Aren't you the least bit curious?"

In fact, that didn't begin to describe it. Curiosity was gnawing at my gut like some ravenous animal. Deep down, I knew my coyness was just a bluff—a display of the sheer, habitual contrariness that got me in trouble with depressing consistency. That was why I hadn't wanted to admit to these people my desire—no, my need—to know more. Maybe I hadn't even admitted it to myself . . . until that moment.

I probably let it show, because Dupont smiled. "Besides, assume for a moment that we simply took your word that you'd never speak of these matters, and let you go." Renata Novak made a small strangling noise, which Dupont ignored. He lifted the papers significantly. "What would you have to go back to? You have no attachments. Your professional future is cloudy. After what's happened, Stafford will be skittish about employing you, even for 'normal' jobs. And don't forget, your car was left at the scene of that shoot-out. You're the only person involved whom the DC police will be able to identify. So you'll have to bear the entire brunt of their doubtless considerable curiosity about that incident."

Actually, that last part had already occurred to me. I'd had other things on my mind, but finally the implications came home to me in all their unpleasantness.

"I tell you what," I temporized. "You mentioned something about 'orientation' at this facility. Maybe, if I could be exposed to a little of the basics, I'd be in a better position to make an intelligent decision."

It was just a shot in the dark. I was fully prepared for Dupont to sternly explain that I'd have to make a definite commitment before even the "basics" could be divulged to me. But instead, he simply smiled . . . and I could tell that he knew he'd won. I was hooked, and once I'd heard those "basics" there was no way I'd want to turn back even if I could.

"It happens that we can accommodate you very well. A new group of recruits just arrived earlier today, and they're due for an initial presentation at nineteen hundred hours this evening. We'll just fit you in with them." Dupont stood up. "I'll send for someone who can direct you to your temporary quarters and arrange for you to get something to eat."

"Thanks." I also rose to my feet. "I can hardly wait to learn something about your organization. I mean, so far I really have no idea of what you *do* . . . what you're *for.*"

"Well, let me satisfy your curiosity to this extent: as far as the dominant civilizations of the universe are concerned, we are the government of Earth." Dupont smiled, and extended his hand for the second time. "Welcome to the Prometheus Project, Mr. Devaney."

The "initial presentation" took place in one of the Quonset huts—well heated, thank God. Not until much

later would I learn that there was a lot more to the base—
"Section One" as everyone called it, for lack of any other
name—than met the eye. Most of it was subterranean,
like what I'd briefly experienced beneath a row of Chinese restaurants in Washington, only far more so. But the
newbies were restricted to the aboveground facilities. To
this day, I don't know whether that was a form of hazing
or just a well-meant desire to shield us from an overload
of strangeness.

I filed in and sat down along with a small group of
others, mostly about as young as myself, or nearly so, but
otherwise immune to generalization. At least a third were
women and two or three were nonwhite, which was note-
worthy in 1963. We all gave each other slightly uneasy
side-glances, for no one seemed to know anyone else. No
conversation took place, and there were clearly no cliques.
It began to occur to me that the circumstances of my own
presence might not be quite as out of the ordinary as I'd
assumed. Indeed, the term "ordinary" might be of very
limited applicability here.

In front of us was a slightly raised wooden platform
that you couldn't really call a dais, holding a screen, a
slide projector, and two chairs. Dennis Dupont occupied
one. The occupant of the other was . . . more interesting.

She looked younger than me, and—I ungrudgingly
admitted—a lot prettier. Her figure was maybe a trifle
on the sturdy side, but I'd never been attracted to the
stick-figure ideal of high fashion. (Renata Novak came a
lot closer to that.) Her medium-long hair was light brown,
and framed a heart-shaped, high-cheekboned face with
blue eyes and what I think novelists call a generous
mouth . . . or at least it gave the impression that it *could*

be generous, when she was a little less serious than she currently looked.

Dupont stood up, interrupting my agreeable thoughts. "Welcome, ladies and gentlemen. I won't ask you to call out your names, since you'll all be getting to know each other over the next few months. At present, you're all strangers, having been recruited in various ways and various places. So I thought you might be interested to meet someone who was *not* recruited for the Project. Instead, she was practically born into it. And she can give you a uniquely personal perspective on its origin. I give you Miss Chloe Bryant."

The young woman, who now had everyone's rapt attention, stood up. She was, I finally noticed, wearing a dark gray-brown skirt and a light golden-brown turtleneck sweater which highlighted her healthy figure without any conscious affectation of fashion whatever.

"That's not strictly true about me being 'born into' the Project," she began in a pleasantly husky voice. "In fact, I was five years old when Mr. Inconnu arrived in 1946 . . . and I became one of the first people to see him."

That caused a stir. I did some quick mental arithmetic, and looked at Chloe Bryant with renewed interest. I'd known she was young . . . but twenty-two? She looked older than that. Maybe it was her seriousness, which nonetheless was of a very different sort from Renata Novak's.

She activated the slide projector, and an early-middle-aged man in Naval officer's khakis appeared on the screen.

"My father, Lieutenant Commander Curtis Bryant," she explained. "In the summer of 1946, he was in command of the destroyer USS *Elijah Ashford*. He was bringing his ship back to Norfolk, Virginia, after a training cruise. Off the Virginia Capes, they spotted a castaway in a . . . very unusual life craft."

I studied the image, and reflected on the fact that fathers' looks are not always a reliable guide to predicting those of daughters. Commander Bryant had the kind of face most charitably described as engagingly homely. In particular, the nose was unforgettable, with its bulbous, bifurcated tip. His crew must have sometimes found it hard to maintain proper military decorum, with that proboscis protruding from beneath the bill of the captain's hat.

"As you've probably surmised," continued Chloe Bryant, peering down a nose that bore absolutely no resemblance to the paternal one, "that castaway was Mr. Inconnu. By the time *Ashford* made port at Norfolk, he had demonstrated to my father that he was, indeed, what he claimed to be.

"I think I can be forgiven a little pride in my father— who, incidentally, was killed in the Korean War six years later. The world unknowingly owes him a great debt. If he hadn't been able to recognize the importance of what he was dealing with, and the absolute necessity of keeping it under wraps . . . Well, the consequences simply don't bear thinking about.

"My mother and I were waiting on the pier when the ship docked. Mother had brought a camera to catch Dad as he came ashore." Chloe Bryant paused. "Mr. Inconnu has always . . . discouraged the taking of photos of himself. This is one of the few in existence." She dropped another slide into the projector. It had been made from a clearly amateurish photo. It showed Commander Bryant, nose and all, coming off a gangway. Walking beside him was a taller, leaner man, also wearing khakis but without rank insignia—he'd doubtless been given them to wear aboard the ship. Beyond the obvious fact of his humanity, what stood out most was the hideous, freshly stitched gash on his left cheek.

"And that," continued Chloe Bryant, "was when I saw him. I ran up to Dad for a hug, and then noticed the man with him. I looked up at him. I was frightened at first, partly because of that disfiguring injury, but mostly because of a quality of unfathomable strangeness. But then he smiled down at me." Her voice changed, and she spoke more to herself than to us. "I've never forgotten that smile he gave me—nor have I ever been able to interpret it, except that I could have sworn it held a deep sadness. For a second, I thought he was actually going to cry. But I also sensed a great love." She suddenly remembered when and where she was, and gave a short, self-deprecating laugh. "Merely my imagination, of course. He was probably just trying to be nice to a little girl. And I've never seen him since.

"Anyway," she concluded briskly, "some of you already have a general idea of what happened after that. Dad turned Mr. Inconnu over to his superiors—who, thank God, could also be made to understand what was at stake. All of you will learn the details shortly, as part of your basic orientation. The upshot was the Prometheus Project. It was the beginning of a story you're now becoming a part of. It will be a very different life. You'll know things that the human race at large cannot be allowed to know—including the very existence of the Project, and the work we do. It's lonely. But I can promise you one thing. You'll have something most people will never have, although the intelligent ones wish they had it: the sure and certain knowledge that what you're doing *matters*." Amid a profound silence, she sat down.

And that was the first time I saw Chloe.

Chloe . . .

Chloe, where are you now?

CHAPTER FOUR

Winter settled in, and so did we.

Orientation was exactly that: basic familiarization with things foreign to what we'd always believed to be reality. In a sense, our total ignorance was probably an advantage for the instructors. They had no preconceptions to overcome. It wasn't like, for example, military basic training, where the newbies arrive *thinking* they know something. We had no such illusions.

They roomed us two-by-two, pairing new arrivals with relative old-timers. I think the idea was that the veterans would save the instructors some trouble by passing on information in advance and preparing us for what lay ahead. At any rate, that was how I met Dan Buckley. He was former Air Force, and at one time had been a contender for the astronaut program. Then something had happened. We got along well, for each of us instinctively recognized in the other a kindred disinclination to talk about the past.

One of the first things we learned was the organizational structure of the Project. Dupont himself handled that.

"As you can see," he said, pointing to an organization chart, "we report ultimately to the President—through Mr. Inconnu, who has direct access to him. No one else knows about the Project in its entirety, although there are some presidential aides who sometimes come into contact with us, usually indirectly, and never know anything more than the identities of the individuals they deal with.

"The Project comprises five Sections, each with its own headquarters. Section One, as you already know, is Administration, including personnel matters such as training.

"Section Two is Security. Its job is twofold: making sure the secret of the Project is kept from the general populace, and preventing aliens from learning the truth about how backward and disunited Earth really is. In the first capacity, Section Two operates on Earth; in the second, its personnel often find themselves deployed beyond the atmosphere."

By this point in Dupont's lecture, I had a pretty good idea which Section I'd be assigned to.

"Section Three," Dupont continued, "is Research and Development. It produces new technology from the knowledge Mr. Inconnu brought, and also from what Section Four—which I'll get to in a moment—obtains from alien cultures. It also decides when these technologies can be safely released, on the basis of its projections of their societal effects. In this latter role, it coordinates with Section Two to devise ways things can be 'discovered' or 'invented' without compromising the Project." Dupont chuckled. "Remind me to tell you sometime about Shockley and the transistor. That's always the way it's done: the secret is subtly 'fed' to someone with no connection to us. But that was an early case . . . and, I gather, a particularly important one."

Somebody a few seats down from me raised a diffident hand. "Uh, why is *that* so important, sir? So what if teenagers have those little tiny radios to listen to bad music?"

"I once asked an acquaintance in Section Three very much that same question. He told me that according to his Section's forecasts it's going to change the rules of the game more than they've been changed at any time since the Industrial Revolution. He said we've already seen a straw in the wind. Remember the attempted coup by the French army command in Algeria, year before last? In the past, it probably would have succeeded; the young conscripts would have obeyed their officers and sergeants as they were conditioned to do. But the government had distributed thousands and thousands of simple transistor radios to the troops. So De Gaulle was able to address them directly, bypassing those officers and sergeants. But it goes beyond that. My acquaintance, speaking from the experience of civilizations immeasurably older and more advanced than ours, says the *real* changes will come about when the transistor is wedded to electronic computers and to the kind of communications satellites we're beginning to see even now. He claims that I wouldn't recognize the society that's going to develop after the next three or four decades. From what he's told me, I suspect that if I'm still alive then, I won't like it very much. But I also suspect it will survive my disapproval.

"Section Four is Intelligence. Its job is to supply Section Three with new alien technologies—borrowed, bought or stolen—with which to continue the human race's 'crash course.' This mission requires it to work closely with Section Five.

"Section Five is the Project's Diplomatic arm. It is arguably the most important section of all . . . and certainly the oldest, for the Project's first order of business was to run the most terrifying bluff of all time. Using the knowledge Mr. Inconnu had brought, it cobbled together a false front that convinced the Delkasu—you'll learn who they are shortly—that they were dealing with a unified, not-too-primitive world, and persuaded them to agree to limit their contacts with that world to a 'treaty port' on its satellite." Dupont smiled as he watched our understanding dawn. "That's where Section Five maintains its headquarters: at Farside Base, as its called, on the back side of the Moon. There, it handles all official contacts with aliens. It sends out missions which try to keep those same aliens played off against each other, while seeking out allies and doing everything else you can imagine—as well as quite a few things you can't, at least not yet. These missions naturally have Section Four components . . . and also Section Two personnel to 'ride shotgun.' "

I found myself more and more attracted to Section Two.

Someone else raised his hand, and posed a question

I'd wondered about myself. "Sir, I don't understand. With alien ships coming and going, why don't they pick up radio broadcasts from Earth? Just one newscast and that would be it for the 'false front.'•"

"There are a couple of answers to that," Dupont explained. "First of all, the Delkasu haven't used the radio wavelengths over long ranges for centuries. Their communicators employ specially treated neutrinos." There were blank looks on a number of faces, including mine, even though the elementary particles with zero rest mass had been postulated for a long time, and named by Enrico Fermi in 1933. "In short, they simply aren't listening. At any rate, part of the agreement is that they communicate only with Farside Base."

"But sir, that's another thing," the questioner persisted. "How is this 'Farside Base' on the Moon going to be kept secret from the human race? From what I understand, President Johnson has reaffirmed President Kennedy's commitment to putting men on the Moon by the end of this decade. What happens when people are there on the surface, exploring and colonizing and mining?"

Dupont's face took on the careful expressionlessness of a man who had to take care not to say too much. "I'm not personally involved with that problem. But you're not the only one to whom the question has occurred. As I understand, countermeasures are in the works. But those countermeasures are political and cultural rather than technological in nature."

I suppose we all looked puzzled, because Dupont just smiled and changed the subject. "At any rate, all alien contacts are restricted to Farside Base . . . or at least they're supposed to be. Of late, it appears that Earth is drawing some unwelcome attention from the Tonkuztra."

That got my attention, for I remembered hearing the name before. It evidently meant nothing to anyone else, though, for a puzzled murmur filled the room. Dupont raised a hand to forestall questions. "That's something else you'll learn more about later. For now, I'll just tell you that it is an organization among the Delkasu race I mentioned earlier . . . a criminal organization."

This caused a stir. It didn't quite fit with our preconceptions of alien races.

"•'Organization' is actually too strong a term," Dupont continued. "It's decentralized to the point of being chaotic. But certain of its elements have evidently begun to suspect that Earth is not as they've been led to believe it is. And they have been making efforts to investigate further."

"You mean," someone said, a little unsteadily, "that they're right here on Earth?"

"No. There's no evidence of a direct Tonkuztra presence here. They seem to be working through human proxies—doubtless obtained through the same traitor or traitors who gave them their initial information." Dupont let that sink in for a moment or two before continuing. "Yes: there is no room for doubt that someone within the Project is compromising us. But very cleverly, doling out vague hints that something is not right on Earth. Fortunately, the Tonkuztra are so divided among themselves, and so hostile to the larger interstellar society in which they operate, that the information has gone no further. They have, however, begun to act more overtly, through their human cat's-paws . . . most notably in a recent incident in Washington."

As he said this, Dupont's eyes met mine briefly. I kept

my mouth shut. If he didn't want to go public with the fact that I had been involved, I wasn't about to blurt it out.

The organizational stuff was very interesting, of course, but it wasn't what we had all given up various things to learn. No, we wanted the knowledge that would set us apart from other mortals: what the Prometheus Project was *really* about.

That was reserved for later. But Dan Buckley prepared me for it somewhat, as I'm sure other people's unofficial mentors did for them.

First, we had to get the basic groundwork in what the universe was really like. This started with basic descriptive astronomy—not too different, I gathered, from the conventional wisdom of 1960s Earth—and went on from there.

Our principal instructor in these matters was an Ira Fehrenbach, Ph.D. Knowing him gave me a better understanding of the things that brought diverse people into the Project. He would never have the fame—and the Nobel prize—that certainly would have been his had he stayed outside, for the knowledge he now possessed could not be made public. But that meant nothing to him. Only the knowledge itself mattered.

He made us see a galaxy swirling into form, its primordial hydrogen condensing into whorls whose mass—and therefore gravity—was sufficient to ignite them into the fusion-fire of stars. A small number—not that *any* number in the realm of astronomy was really what I thought of as "small"—were so massive that their fires were too intense to burn for long. They died spectacular early deaths as supernovas, roiling the interstellar medium and enriching it with the heavy elements generated by thermonuclear alchemy in their inconceivable furnaces. But most stars were far less massive—they belonged to the "main spectral sequence." As Dr. Fehrenbach explained, that meant they could burn for billions of years at the steady rate that allowed for the formation of planets, and for the appearance of life on those planets . . . eventually.

"That's the kicker," Dr. Fehrenbach told us one day. He was a lively little guy, and something of a polymath, very different from the overspecialized clam-cold astronomer of stereotype. "How many of you read science fiction?"

A few hands went up with various degrees of hesitancy. Mine was among the more hesitant ones. Most of my science-fiction reading dated back to my adolescence. Since then, I'd seen a few movies like George Pal's *War of the Worlds*, and watched a few *Twilight Zone* episodes, but that was about it. So I felt a bit out of date.

"A lot of those writers," Dr. Fehrenbach continued, "have figured out that certain types of stars—the main-sequence ones of the F, G and K types, the ones not too different from the Sun—can have planets like Earth, and that life can arise on those planets . . . eventually, maybe intelligent life. But they sometimes seem to assume that *all* planets like that must have intelligent life *right now*. That's their fallacy. Suppose you picked a thousand people at random out of the population of New York. What are the chances that all of them would be exactly thirty-two years, seven months and eleven days old? No, they'd be all different ages, from infants to octogenarians. Well, so are stars. They're being born and dying all the time . . .

and the Sun is actually above average in age. Most of them are too young for life to have developed even if the conditions for it are right. A few others have lasted so long that cosmic accident or their inhabitants' folly has scrubbed them clean of life. At any given time, there are only a *very* few intelligent races—no, let's not be snobbish, let's say 'toolmaking races'—in existence in the galaxy.

"And of those few races, the probability of any one of them being technologically advanced is very small."

"You mean," someone queried, "that most of them aren't as smart as we are?"

"No, no, no! To the extent that it can be measured, all civilized races seem to be about equal in innate intelligence. It figures that they'd get that far and no farther. Once a species goes the tool-using route it comes under evolutionary pressure to become a *better* tool user . . . and then a tool *maker*. Our remote ancestors didn't develop tools because they had big brains; they got the big brains because they had already become tool users. As somebody once said, 'Man didn't invent tools, tools invented man.' But once that happens, the race starts molding the environment to suit itself, rather than adapting. And organized societies protect their weaker members. In short, evolution stops.

"No, it's not a matter of brains. It's a matter of social conditions. If those hadn't been just right in Western Europe five hundred years ago, the Scientific Revolution wouldn't have happened. The Chinese were the most inventive people on Earth. But in a unitary empire run by a leisure class that rewarded cultural conservatism above all else, those inventions were like seeds dropped on gravel. Civilizations are a lot more likely to be like

China—or ancient Egypt, or the Byzantine Empire—than like Renaissance Europe. Europe just had a lucky break—although it must not have seemed like it at the time—when neither Justinian nor Charlemagne nor anybody else succeeded in putting the Roman Empire back together again."

I spoke up hesitantly. "Uh, Doctor, this doesn't seem to square up with what we've been told about the galaxy being full of superadvanced civilizations."

"Very good, Mr. Devaney." Coming from some pedagogues, the words might have been sarcastic or patronizing. But Fehrenbach spoke with the unaffected eagerness of a man who'd been given precisely the cue he'd wanted. He was a teacher . . . not to be confused with an educational bureaucrat. The difference is that a teacher wants—no, *needs*—for everyone to know everything he knows, while an educational bureaucrat sees the general dissemination of knowledge as a threat to his status. Unfortunately, there are a lot more educational bureaucrats than there are teachers. (As usual, Shaw got it wrong. Those who can, do; those who can't, become educational bureaucrats.)

"The solution to this seeming contradiction," he continued, "is simple. I've been describing to you what might be called the rules of the game. A few centuries ago, those rules changed. They were changed by a race called the Delkasu.

"You'll learn more about the Delkasu later. Briefly, they drew one of the 'lucky numbers' in the game. They had a Scientific Revolution of their own, and arrived at a political solution which permitted it to become self-sustaining, neither immolating it in a nuclear holocaust nor smothering it under the sociological by-products which our own world is beginning to see in their early manifestations. They then moved on into the realms of what we consider science fiction. They became the first ever to discover the secret of faster-than-light interstellar travel. They began to explore and colonize many worlds. They encountered other, less advanced civilizations, and imparted their techniques to those civilizations . . . which then became secondary centers of the colonization process. All at once, life in the galaxy was no longer a matter of blind, spontaneous chance. Instead, it was consciously extending itself, spreading from world to world and altering those worlds to accommodate itself. Nothing would ever be the same again."

"How can we be sure these, uh, Delkasu were really the first ever to discover interstellar flight?" someone wanted to know. "After all, you've told us that the galaxy has been around for . . . how many billions of years?"

"We can be certain they were the first because if somebody else had discovered it in the course of all those billions of years, we wouldn't be here. Neither would the Delkasu. Neither would any of the other races we know. Those initial discoverers would have filled up the galaxy and foreclosed the possibility of anybody else coming into existence in the future. No, we're living at a unique moment in the history of the universe: the moment when intelligent life becomes a cosmic force."

I spoke, at least as much to myself as to Dr. Fehrenbach. "But we're around, and at the technological level—barely—to do something about it, at precisely that 'unique moment.' What are the odds against that?"

"Incalculable," Dr. Fehrenbach admitted cheerfully.

"They couldn't be expressed comfortably even in powers of ten. But at any given time there are always *some* locally evolved races on some planets here and there. Why not us? Anyway," he concluded briskly, "the point is that while there are other races around, the Delkasu are the ones who count. They're the technological pacesetters, and they dominate the biggest interstellar political units. In short, we have to live with them."

Spring had come, and I'd had my glimpse of Mr. Inconnu, before we got the lowdown on the Delkasu. By that time, we'd graduated to being allowed belowground.

I'd more or less gotten used to what was down there— all the alien-tech items that the world wasn't prepared for yet. I could handle most of them. The only part that still bothered me was the almost imperceptible tingle you got when passing through the invisible last line of security. To me, a computer was something that filled a fair-sized room and cost millions of dollars. The idea of self-directed machines you couldn't even *see*, hovering to form a screen which, if the automated sensors hadn't liked the cut of your jib, would have done things to your cells that I didn't like to think about . . . well, I just wasn't ready for it. Nor for the doors that didn't open but just *appeared* in what had been a featureless wall. Nor for . . . well, you get the idea.

The auditorium we filed into was pretty mundane, by comparison. But the seats, instead of being lined up in rows facing a screen, were arranged in stepped concentric semicircles around a kind of pedestal in the center. Off to one side was a pulpitlike platform, occupied by Dr. Fehrenbach and Chloe Bryant. Once we were seated, they wasted no time.

The holographic images you've probably seen are fuzzy, flickering things. That was what we were expecting. Instead, the being that appeared, life-sized, on the pedestal seemed to be standing there in the alien equivalent of flesh.

"A typical Delkar, ladies and gentlemen," said Chloe Bryant. "That's the singular form; the plural is 'Delkasu.' He's a male, but the species has less sexual dimorphism than ours."

None of us really heard her. We were in shock.

Not that there was anything inherently horrific or terrifying or awesome about the Delkar's appearance. In fact, he was a little guy, slightly less than five feet tall and wiry. He had two arms, and stood erect on two legs. His skin was a brown-black with coppery red undertones. (I would later learn that there were other color variations, but all were very dark.) There was no trace of hair that I could see. His hands had three fingers and two mutually opposable thumbs, one on each side; they were large for his arms, which were thin but sinewy and, I felt certain, far from weak.

His head was big in proportion to his body, but not ridiculously so. It was oddly shaped, tapering forward to a kind of pointed snout with a single horizontal nostril over the mouth. (Or at least I assumed it was a nostril . . . correctly, as it turned out.) The eyes dominated the face. They were very large, and of a dark golden color.

After the initial strangeness had somewhat worn off, I noticed that he was dressed in a sleeveless tunic, and wore something resembling greaves on his legs and slippers on his feet.

Chloe Bryant gave us a minute or so to recover, then resumed her presentation.

"You will note that he has binocular vision. That's typical, as is the upright, bilaterally symmetrical form, and the two sexes. The large size of the eyes is partly a result of evolution under a relatively dim sun—"

"A K type," Dr. Fehrenbach interjected.

"—but they have no difficulty adapting to our own sunlight. As a species, they are exceptionally adaptable, which is one of the reasons they've played the role they have in galactic history. Another is their aptitude for tool making—notice those hands. They are omnivores, which seems to be typical of intelligent species, but with a strong carnivorous tendency. Likewise typical is the fact that they're warm-blooded . . . not that their 'blood' is the same as ours. Similarly, they're the equivalent of 'mammals' in that the females nurture the young live; but the details are different, as you'd expect of a completely alien evolutionary product.

"Some people are surprised that he's wearing clothes, having assumed that it must be strictly a human habit. But it makes sense. Once a species becomes toolmakers, they begin to expand beyond their original habitat, as our ancestors expanded beyond Africa. This brings them into environments from which they need artificial protection. Eventually, the culture of clothing takes on a life of its own, transcending utility. Of course, the clothing varies from culture to culture. This is what they generally wear at Farside Base. However, for a full anatomical picture . . ." Chloe touched a button, and the clothes vanished. The Delkar's male *equipage* differed from humanity's in ways that drew giggles from some of the women in the room. Almost equally obvious were the differences in his skeletal structure.

I continued to stare at the hologram, and I began to realize that what I was seeing confirmed Chloe's words. The Delkasu were not really all that dissimilar to humans, when you considered that they had begun with an entirely different microorganism in an entirely different tidal pool on an entirely different planet billions of years ago, and had begun to diverge at that point, with each chance outcome representing a new opportunity for strangeness.

It was as though Chloe had read my mind. "You must remember that in evolution, as in architecture, form follows function. There are lots of unrelated species of fish in Earth's oceans—not to mention the cetaceans, which aren't fish at all—and they're all the same basic shape. That's because they've all evolved to fill similar ecological niches. Well, the same goes for the ecological niche occupied by tool users."

So, I wondered, why did the Delkar look so *wrong*? In general shape, he was far less unlike a human than was a horse or a dolphin. And nobody thought *they* looked wrong.

But they were *supposed* to look the way they did.

Maybe intelligent squids like H. G. Wells' Martians would have been easier to take.

I recalled Dr. Fehrenbach's words. We had to live with the Delkasu. What we thought of their looks meant precisely nothing.

I saw Chloe any number of times during training. I even spoke to her several times. But only once did I speak to her alone.

It was shortly before I was due to depart from Section One. By that time, I was a regular in the belowground canteen. Dan Buckley had long since departed, and more often than not I ate alone. But one day I noticed Chloe seated at a corner table, likewise eating alone, as she often did. Most of my fellow new arrivals felt inhibited in her presence, for her connection with the Project made her almost the equivalent of hereditary aristocracy. Combined with her slight air of aloofness, it discouraged familiarity.

Generally, I was no more immune to the feeling than everyone else. Today, though, something made me take my tray over to her table.

"May I join you, Miss Bryant?"

She looked up and smiled. She had a nice smile, but it never altogether lost that faint undertone of seriousness. "Of course. Glad for the company. Mr. Devaney, isn't it?"

"Bob."

"I'm Chloe. I've seen you around a lot, but I haven't gotten a chance to talk to you at any length. I hear you had a run-in with the Tonkuztra." (She *would* know about that, I reflected.) "I also understand Mr. Inconnu took a personal interest in bringing you into the Project."

"So I've been told." Feeling flattered by her interest, I told her the story of my recruitment. "But unlike you," I concluded, "I've never met him."

"I wouldn't say I 'met' him, really. I think I might have said 'Hello' to him, but he never spoke to me . . . just looked at me." She took on a look of puzzled reminiscence.

"Anyway," I resumed, "I just wanted to thank you for making so much clear to me about the Project, over the past months. Although . . . there's one thing I still don't understand."

"What's that?"

"The name. Why is it called the *Prometheus* Project?"

"It's a perfect fit. You see, in Greek mythology—"

"Yes, I know. Prometheus was the renegade Titan who stole the secret of fire from the gods and gave it to men."

"Right." She looked at me with mildly surprised interest. "So you can see how appropriate the name is. Mr. Inconnu brought the knowledge that gives humanity a fighting chance to make a place for itself in the galaxy."

"Yeah, to that extent it does seem appropriate. Only . . . you left out the rest of the story. Zeus was afraid that Prometheus' gift of fire might enable mortals to challenge the gods someday. So he punished Prometheus by chaining him to a mountain, where a vulture tore at his guts for centuries."

"Yes, I remember that." Chloe made a face. "Delightful people, those Greek gods."

"Yeah, a laugh a minute. But the point is, Mr. Inconnu isn't being punished . . . at least not so you'd notice. Is he?"

"I see what you mean. And yet . . . I remember Dad telling me once—I must have been about ten at the time—that when the name was proposed, Mr. Inconnu agreed that it was a good fit. According to Dad, he said it with a kind of grim amusement."

"Hmm . . . I did get a glimpse of him once, here at this station. He *does* have a god-awful scar on his cheek. And in the picture you showed us, it looked like he'd only recently gotten it. He must have gone through a lot getting away to Earth."

"True. But I wonder if the punishment he's undergoing is loneliness. After all, he'll never see his own people again."

"I guess that must be it." But somehow, I felt, there had to be more to it than that.

"Well," Chloe said, getting to her feet and extending her hand, "I've got to be going. I'm finishing up my stint of lecturing here, and getting back into fieldwork. You're about to leave yourself, aren't you?"

"Yeah." I took her hand. The handshake lingered a few seconds . . . it seemed she was in no great hurry to terminate it. "I've been assigned to Section Two."

"Really? I'm with Section Five. Maybe you'll get assigned to one of our missions sometime."

"I'd like that."

As she departed the canteen, she looked back over her shoulder at me and smiled. "So would I."

But it was five years before I saw her again.

INTERLUDE

President-Elect Harvey Langston stared wide-eyed. "You mean . . . Men in Black?"

"Actually," said the President with a smile, "the Prometheus Project prefers to avoid that term."

"But," spluttered Langston, "this whole business about posing as the government of Earth . . . ! Why wasn't the whole thing simply turned over to the United Nations?"

The President gave him a look of disgusted exasperation. "Even in 1946, when it was still possible to hope that the UN might develop into something worthwhile, that was clearly out of the question for security reasons. Thank God it was, given the squalid farce the UN has, in fact, turned out to be! Besides, the Delkasu wouldn't have worn it."

"Wouldn't have worn it?" Langston echoed faintly.

"Get it through your head: we're talking about a civilization as politically sophisticated as it is technologically advanced. They wouldn't have accepted something like the UN—as it is or even as it was intended to be—as a planetary government fit to be a player in their power politics. As it was, the best we could manage was to be accepted as a very minor player. Under the circumstances, it's amazing that we were able to bamboozle them into even that."

The words "power politics" brought a perplexed look to Langston's face. "Yes, you mentioned something about that before. I don't understand. Surely an advanced civilization *must* have left primitive attitudes like nationalism and militarism behind and achieved political unity on a basis of peace and equality and social justice! Otherwise, it could never have survived to reach the stars. A civilization that has unleashed atomic energy has only two alternatives: utopia, or extinction!"

The President studied the ceiling of the Oval Office, with its reproduction of the Presidential seal in low relief. "I've heard that theory."

"It's not just a 'theory'! It's beyond controversy among enlightened, progressive thinkers!"

"I don't doubt that for a moment." Forestalling an angry retort, the President leaned forward and spoke with a seriousness which held even Langston's attention. "I've been told, in outline, the political history of the Delkasu, who've set the pattern of galactic civilization, including its geopolitics . . . or 'astropolitics,' I suppose you'd have to call it. *Only* in outline, you realize; their history is every bit as long and richly complex as ours. You'll get the same kind of overview later.

"Briefly, though, their history isn't dissimilar to ours, up to a point. Various civilizations arose on Kasava, the Delkasu planet of origin. One of them played a historical role analogous to our own Western civilization; it had a Scientific Revolution and, subsequently, an Industrial Revolution, and therefore came to dominate the planet. Like our Western civilization, it was divided into a number of competing territorial states—*not* a coincidence, by the way, for in both cases it meant there was no universal state that could stifle innovation to protect the *status quo*. Those states played the same kind of endemic war-game as Europe did in the sixteenth through nineteenth centuries, finally graduating to total war.

"But by that time, one of their nations, called Toranva, had established a clear *primus inter pares* status among the others. From the way it's been described to me, it was as if. . . . Well, imagine that Britain, instead of losing its American colonies, had succeeded in incorporating them into a kind of imperial federation, resulting in a power base that was in a different league from Spain and France and so on. Toranva led a coalition that won the Delkasu's first total war. But that war, like our World War I, resulted in a totalitarian reaction among the losers. So the coalition had to stay together for a 'cold war' that produced—as ours did—forced-draft technological advancement. Toranva led the way in that, acting as the organizer and informational clearinghouse for R&D. Toranva also assumed the official role of 'protector' of certain particularly threatened states, with no diplomatic euphemisms. War finally broke out, just as the Delkasu were developing atomic energy—in fact, it was the threat of a totalitarian state getting nuclear weapons that brought it on. By the time it was over, the primacy of Toranva had achieved overt recognition in their equivalent of international law.

"So what the Delkasu took to the stars with them was a kind of political consciousness different from any human culture's. It wasn't a one-state civilization like China, with just the central empire and the barbarians. But neither did it have the Western legal fiction of equal sovereignties, a holdover of the Middle Ages when all kings were social equals regardless of how many or how few troops they could put into the field. Instead, there was generally accepted recognition of one . . . super-sovereignty, I suppose you'd call it. Other nations had certain rights which they were entitled to have respected. But there was no doubt about the hegemony, nor any embarrassment about it.

"As the Delkasu expansion into interstellar space assumed explosive proportions, this pattern expanded with them. The hegemony of Toranva on the planet Kasava simply extended, to become a 'super-super-sovereignty' among the new nations that were arising among the stars as a result of Delkasu colonization. It worked.

"And then it had the heart burned out of it by a supernova."

"Supernova?" Langston blinked. The word had a dimly familiar sound. He'd once taken an astronomy course in college because it had seemed the easiest way to meet the science requirement for graduation—a requirement to which he objected on ideological grounds. He glanced out the windows behind the President's desk. It was a clear late-autumn evening, and the first stars were beginning to come out. "Uh . . . you mean the sun of the Delkasu home system blew up?"

"No. Main-sequence stars—the kind of stars that can have habitable planets—don't go that route. But some of the more massive stars do. One of those was only about four light-years from Kasava—a little less than the distance between us and Alpha Centauri, the nearest star. It blew, a little over a thousand years ago . . . although it will be thousands of years yet before the light reaches us. The wave front of the blast had almost reached Kasava before they became aware of it, leaving them little time to prepare. Not that they could have done all that much if they had been given time."

"But," wondered Langston, "what harm could it do across such a distance?"

"Plenty. Like electromagnetic pulse, for openers. What do you think would happen to our civilization if all the power grids were wrecked, all the telecommunications networks scrubbed, all the computer databases wiped clean? And that would just start the dominoes falling. Even then, Delkasu technology was at least a century ahead of where we are now. So they were even more dependent on electronics than we are, and hence more vulnerable. Primitive subsistence farmers would have come through better. But even the subsistence farmers wouldn't have been spared the radioactive fallout to follow. Ecological catastrophe followed the collapse of civilization.

"They got as much of the population and as many cultural treasures as possible off Kasava in the limited time they had. Afterwards, of course, no spacecraft were able to operate in the system—at least not with the technology they had at the time. Kasava had to be left to die. Later, as they improved their shielding techniques and the wave front passed on and dissipated, they returned.

Subsequently, Kasava has been resettled, and much has been done to help the savages descended from the survivors: reeducation, and repair to genetic damage. But Kasava will never be more than a shadow of its former self, insignificant save in the realm of sentiment.

"So ever since then, the Delkasu have been in what they consider a state of political limbo. The hegemony is gone. Instead, there are a bunch of interstellar successor-states, all of which agree that the hegemony ought to be reestablished . . . but each state thinks *it* ought to be the one to do the reestablishing. It's been a snake pit for centuries, and it's only getting worse. You see, the Delkasu states are increasingly jostled by non-Delkasu races which have adopted Delkasu technology and become players in the game. Hence, more snakes in the snake pit."

"And," Langston queried, "they consider us one of those 'players?' "

"*Not* a significant one," the President told him firmly. "You must be absolutely clear on that. Think some Third World microstate. In reality, of course, we're not even *that*, on their standards. If they knew the truth, our status would—if we were extremely lucky—be that of a protected hunter-gatherer tribe of the upper Amazon or New Guinea. But the Prometheus Project managed to convince the first Delkasu explorers—who arrived just a few years after Mr. Inconnu's arrival—that Earth had gotten organized in what they considered an appropriate way under an American hegemony, and was just barely advanced enough in a technological sense to have stumbled onto the secret of interstellar travel. By their own lights, this meant we were entitled to the equivalent of diplomatic recognition, including an agreement to respect our funny insistence that all contacts be handled through the 'treaty port' on the back side of the Moon."

"That's something I still don't understand. How has this 'Farside Base' been kept concealed from our lunar orbiters? Yes, I know," Langston partially answered his own question, "you've told me about this invisibility technology. But with interstellar spacecraft coming and going from it . . . ?"

"Very fortuitously, the interstellar drive produces few if any by-products which are detectable by means generally available on this planet. And the Project's own Earth-to-Moon craft are, of course, as undetectable as galactic-level technology can make them. But the real answer to your question is that we have, in effect, abandoned the Moon since the 1970s." The President cocked his head. "Have you ever wondered why that happened?"

"Well," Langston huffed, "of *course* we abandoned such an *obscene* waste of money! With so many problems here on Earth crying out for socially useful spending, how could we possibly afford space exploration?"

The President gave him a look of sardonic amusement. "Yeah. How could we *possibly* afford the one thing the US government has done in the last half century that's actually shown a profit? It may interest you to know that the line you're parroting is one that the Prometheus Project itself insinuated into the popular consciousness, with the eager but unwitting help of the self-styled intellectual elite. A damned shame. But it had to be done."

"What are you talking about?" Langston's anger waxed along with his bewilderment.

"Kennedy *had* to make his famous commitment to reaching the Moon—it was a matter of national prestige, after the Soviet Union had gotten into orbit first. But even as he was doing it, he knew nothing could be allowed to come of it. So the subtle undermining of the whole enterprise began immediately. Even at the time, some people realized that the Apollo crash program wasn't the right way to go about it. A more systematic approach—not putting men on the lunar surface quite so soon, but laying a solid foundation for future development—would have made better sense. But that was the whole point: to discredit it, make it look like just a ridiculously expensive stunt." The President gave a sad chuckle. "Ordering those guys to jump around in low gravity and swing a golf club and otherwise act silly was a master stroke!" The chuckle departed, leaving the sadness. "Yes . . . it was too bad. In fact, it had some unfortunate cultural side effects by seeming to confirm what the twerps of that era were saying about the 'establishment.' But it was necessary."

"Why?"

"Haven't you been listening to *anything*?" The President got his irritation under control and spoke levelly. "If we were swarming over the Moon right now—as, rationally, we *ought* to be—there'd be no way Farside Base's existence could be concealed. The whole secret would be blown, with the consequences I've tried to make clear to you."

"But from what you've been telling me, it's already been 'blown,' as you put it. This, uh, Tonkuztra . . ." Langston struggled to collect his thoughts. Organized crime, like international great-power rivalries, had no place in his picture of what an advanced society was supposed to be like. "According to you, *they've* known the truth about Earth for almost half a century now! Why bother trying to continue the deception?"

"Because as far as we know, the secret's still good as far as the larger galactic society is concerned," the President explained. "You must understand that the Delkasu word 'Tonkuztra' refers to a criminal . . . subculture, I suppose you'd call it. *Not* to any centralized organization. It's divided into a multitude of outfits, originally based on blood ties and to some extent still so based. There's no *capo di tutti capi*. All these families, as we might as well call them, hate each other almost as much as they do the law enforcement authorities.

"So while it's true that one Tonkuztra family apparently learned that something was not quite right about Earth, they weren't about to let it become general knowledge. That would have let their rivals in on it!

"Besides, as far as we can figure it, even that one family doesn't have the whole story. It seems that the traitor was feeding them the information in the form of hints . . . one of them at a time.

"So the Project has continued with its work as though the secret is still intact. That assumption actually holds, as far as the official diplomatic contacts are concerned. But the knowledge that there are, somewhere, entities with an inkling of the truth is something that the Project has to live with.

"In particular, it's complicated the lives of Section Two. Starting in 1963, their job acquired a whole new dimension: combating any further Tonkuztra operations on Earth, through human proxies. Also, it hasn't made their job of riding shotgun for Section Five diplomatic missions any easier. It didn't get easier even after they found out who the traitor was. . . ."

PART TWO:
1968

CHAPTER FIVE

My first trip to the Moon settled one question I'd been wondering about: how the Prometheus Project had been sending its people to and from Farside Base all those years without anybody noticing.

Yes, I knew about the invisibility technology, and I was sure that spoofing radar was no problem. But you must remember that my formative years belonged to the late forties and early fifties. When I imagined going to the Moon, I visualized something like a king-sized German V-2 rocket with portholes, shaking the earth and bruising the eardrums as it rose straight up on a pillar of fire, bulling its way past gravity by sheer, wasteful brute force. (Which, as it turned out, was pretty much the way Project Apollo was in the process of doing it.)

In fact, though, from the standpoint of the Delkasu and the other galactic races, these methods were so primitive as to be barely imaginable. Indeed, one of Section Five's problems was making sure none of the alien visitors to Farside Base ever noticed any of Earth's official Lunar probes. Fortunately, the problem was a minor one; the probes were few, as were the aliens present in the Solar System at any given time, and anyway they simply weren't looking for such things.

Now I understood why they weren't, as I departed for my first assignment beyond the atmosphere.

The craft I rode was rendered invisible and undetectable by galactic technology. But that was a matter of routine precaution, and hardly even necessary. It was no larger than the fuselage of a small airliner, and it belched no flames as it ascended in almost total silence from the well-concealed base in the Montana Rockies. The impellers that drove it converted the angular momentum of the spinning electrons in the atoms of their core elements directly into linear momentum.

Hey, don't look at me! I'm just telling you what I was told. I don't understand what it means, or how it's done, any more than you do. All I know is that I sat in a cabin with a few other passengers, looking at a screen marked "view-aft," and watched the landscape fade into a curved blueness, varied by pale buff desert and swirled with cloud patterns. At some indefinable but unmistakable point, it stopped being "down" and started being "away," a blue sphere amid the starfields. And there was no sensation of motion.

That was another thing about the propulsion. A compensating field automatically canceled the tremendous accelerations that would otherwise have reduced us passengers to a substance resembling chunky salsa covering the aft bulkhead. Another application of the same technology produced an artificial gravitational field that held us to the deck at our usual weight.

It all bore no resemblance to spaceflight as the world behind us knew it. Rather, it was like sitting in a plain but perfectly comfortable room on that world, watching a film of a planet receding at a breathtaking rate. It made it hard for me to feel the proper awe at what was happening to me. It was too effortless, the way I was being whisked to what had always seemed the just barely attainable goal of the ultimate human endeavor.

The thought of that goal made me look in the "view-forward" screen. The Moon was growing at the same immoderate rate at which the Earth was shrinking in the view-aft.

It was only a quarter Moon . . . as viewed from Earth. As we curved around behind it, the face that had been hidden from human eyes until the past few years began to reveal itself.

People often call that face the "dark side of the Moon," but that's a complete misnomer. It's just as likely to be illuminated by the Sun as is the side that permanently faces Earth. This became obvious to us as the great globe of Earth—four times the diameter that the Moon shows to earthbound humanity—dipped below the stark Lunar horizon. The Sea of Moscow and all those Russian-named craters fled below us, illuminated in harsh, airless clarity.

The first Prometheus Project people who had come here over two decades earlier on the wings of Mr. Inconnu's secrets must have been a pretty prosaic lot; they didn't give any fanciful names to the surface features that they were the first humans in all history to behold. So when the Soviets had sent the first Lunar orbiter and exercised their right to name their discoveries, the Project had adopted those names, generally mispronouncing them . . . including that of the crater named after Korolev, the mastermind of the early Soviet space effort.

It was that crater toward which we now descended.

The Project knew as well as everyone else when any of Earth's publicly known space probes could be expected to swing behind the Moon. So there was no need to continuously expend the energy to keep the great opening at the base of Korolev's ringwall concealed. Besides, approaching alien visitors might have wondered why such concealment was considered necessary. We passengers therefore watched the entrance grow in the viewscreen as our craft slowed and descended.

From a distance, it looked like a vast cave mouth, the home of some ogre out of myth. Then, as the ship's finely balanced propulsive forces brought us slowly through it, the smooth regularity of its interior became apparent. A tunnel that could have accommodated an aircraft carrier slanted gently downward, illuminated by our ship's running lights and the glow of the rectangular opening at its far end. We drifted toward that glow, so as to pass through the invisible force-screen that held atmosphere within it but offered only gentle resistance to a slow-moving solid object. We felt a slight vibration as the ship crossed over into atmosphere, and emerged into a harshly illuminated empty space too vast to immediately comprehend. Surely, the mind insisted, the space vessels that cavern held—most of them far larger than ours—must be toys.

Of all the things I had, over the past five years, seen and heard of, this was the one I still found most difficult to credit. Granted, I knew by now about nanotechnology—a word that hadn't yet been coined. I also knew that the Project hadn't needed to have Farside Base completely up and running in time for the first Delkasu arrivals; the essence of the deception was that Earth had only just precociously discovered the interstellar drive, and was still working on the Lunar installation. Yet, knowing all that, I could only stare around me and wonder at the fact that the Project had been able to make even a convincing start at hollowing out this chasm beneath the Lunar surface in the late 1940s. The sickening moment as I stepped out of the ship's artificial gravity field into the Moon's one-sixth G didn't help my mental equilibrium.

"Bob!" A familiar voice brought me out of my rubber-necking. I swung around to see Dan Buckley approaching across that illimitable floor, moving with the gait of one long accustomed to the local gravity.

"So," he exclaimed as we shook hands, "I understand they've finally succumbed to a moment of mental weakness and decided to let you out-system."

"Yeah. Some would say it's about time. But what the hell are you doing here?"

"Haven't you heard? I'm your pilot."

"Oh, God! I'm doomed!"

Shortly after leaving Section One, I had heard that Dan had been assigned to Section Five as one of their interstellar pilots. I'd been reduced to abject envy, for he had been seeing the unimaginable sights of galactic civilization while I'd been stuck on Earth doing Section Two's scut

work. Admittedly, my own little experience on the outskirts of Washington's Chinatown had caused that work
to get more interesting, for the Project's security head-
aches had abruptly expanded to include countering
Tonkuztra proxy operations like the one that had almost
cut short my promising career. Still, it hadn't been what
I'd had in mind . . . until I had finally graduated to escort
duty for one of Section Five's diplomatic/intelligence/
general skullduggery missions beyond the Solar System.

"Come on," said Dan, ever the fount of all enlighten-
ment. "Let's get out of this overgrown hangar and into
the living areas, where the gravity is Earth-normal. I'll
help you get settled in. We've got a briefing at 1900."
Farside Base used Earth's Greenwich Mean Time, which
the ship's brain had obligingly downloaded to the rather
sophisticated device I stubbornly continued to think of as
a wristwatch. It was now a little after 1700. I'd have time
to grab a bite to eat. As for sleep patterns . . . well, I was
used to jet lag.

What with one thing and another, it was a couple of
minutes after 1900 when Dan and I entered the small
briefing room where the head of the mission was to
address us. I started to run my eyes over the assembled
group, looking for familiar faces . . . but then I spotted
the mission head at the front of the room.

"Oh, shit," I breathed.

I hadn't seen Renata Novak for five years, but she hadn't
changed. Our eyes met, and while she showed no overt
sign of recognition I somehow got the feeling that she
remembered me.

"Well, now that we're *all* here, we can begin," she said
with unsubtle emphasis. She stood up and activated a

holographic display. I recognized it immediately, having seen it repeatedly, in various forms, during training and afterwards.

A myriad of tiny lights streamed in three irregular rivers of tiny gleaming dust motes. Those rivers showed a perceptible curvature . . . for they were spiral arms, and the display encompassed a good eighth of the galaxy. I knew, with the part of my brain directly behind my forehead, the immensity of what I was seeing depicted. But I also knew I hadn't a prayer of truly grasping it. I'd learned to deal with the problem by not even trying. Instead, I simply thought of it as a form of geography, for all the world as though I was looking at a map of landmasses and seas on Earth.

The three streams of light were, from top to bottom, the Sagittarius, Orion and Perseus arms. "Top" and "bottom" were arbitrary, the former being defined by the center of the galaxy, which lay outside the scope of the display. The topmost stream was the widest and densest, for the Sagittarius Arm was one of the two principal ones of the galaxy, curving from the galactic core in a complete half circle before fraying out into the darkness of the great void. It also had the distinction of holding the home system of the Delkasu. By comparison, the Orion and Perseus arms were minor ones—"shingles" was the term the astronomers sometimes used. And the Orion Arm had only one, very tiny distinction: an ordinary star, shown as a tiny green dot, around which orbited a thoroughly unimportant planet called Earth.

I reminded myself that the distinction between the spiral arms and the spaces between them was not as sharp as that between land and sea. Contrary to what some people imagine, those interstitial spaces are not empty rifts devoid of stars. Indeed, the density of stars per cubic light-year is only ten percent greater inside the spiral arms than outside them. It is only the short-lived giant stars, and the interstellar medium out of which they coalesce, that are concentrated in the arms, illuminating them and creating a contrast that is more apparent than real.

Thus endeth Professor Bob's astronomy lecture, cribbed from memories of Dr. Fehrenbach's *real* ones. Bear with me, because this stuff is necessary to an understanding of everything that happened afterwards. You see, even that ten percent difference had been enough to make the spiral arms the line of least resistance—or, more accurately, the line of greatest opportunity—for Delkasu expansion. Starting near the upper right-hand corner of this display, near the Carina Nebula, they had spread along their own arm in both directions for many centuries before seriously venturing into the Orion Arm and the Perseus Arm beyond it. That venture had started from the newly settled regions of the Sagittarius Arm to the left (as we were seeing it), with their tradition of pioneering, and had worked its way slowly from left to right along the lesser arms. Thus the "geography" of the galaxy had imposed a certain shape on the developing galactic civilization.

And on top of that shape, centuries of politics and war had overlaid yet another pattern. That pattern showed in volumes of softly glowing color within the display, marking the boundaries of the grand interstellar empires.

Novak pointed a pencil-like implement, and a white dot appeared on an oblong region of yellow in the middle of that stretch of the Sagittarius Arm shown in the display, not far (*Ha!*) from Earth. "Our mission," she began crisply, "is here, to the Antyova system, in the Selangava Empire."

I ran over in my mind what I'd learned of Delkasu history. Which wasn't much, really. Given the unthinkable vastness and complexity of their domains, I doubt if there was anyone—much less any human—whose mind could hold it all. But we in the Project tried to follow the main lines of development.

About a century ago, a military genius named Sakandri had arisen among the Delkasu. A large empire—*really* large, even by their standards—had blossomed into existence with a suddenness that had sent shock waves across the spiral arms. For a moment, it had seemed that the civilization-wide hegemony that was their long-lost political ideal was finally at hand. But only for a moment. The empire had overreached itself to death in a remarkably short time. Sakandri's lieutenants had divided it up before his corpse had gotten cold. The only lasting result had been a slew of successor-states which altered the configurations of the traditional power game without changing its rules. Of these, the largest was Selangava.

"Selangava," Novak continued, "has problems. In fact, you might say that as the principal heir of Sakandri's empire it has inherited the lion's share of the problems he would have had to face if he'd lived longer—notably the Agardir.

"You'll learn more about the Agardir later, on the voyage out. Not that we humans have all that much data about them; acquiring more is one of our mission's objectives. We do know that they are a race that had achieved interplanetary travel in their home system before the Delkasu arrived. By a fortunate set of circumstances, they were able to get galactic-level technology from Delkasu renegades, and adopt it before they could be overwhelmed. Fortunate, that is, for them; not so fortunate for everyone else. They're an oddity: a toolmaking race descended from pure carnivores . . . specifically, pouncers. Their outlook on life—and other life-forms—is what you might expect. And they're embittered about the 'head start' that enabled the Delkasu to fill up so much of the galaxy. It's motivated them into a forced-draft expansion. And they're pressing hard on Selangava, within whose volume of space they live. It's not exactly what Selangava needs right now, on top of its rivalries with other Delkasu powers.

"This, of course, is what puts us in a good position. Selangava needs all the allies it can get . . . even us. Specifically, they have economic interests here in the Orion Arm, and we're in a position to improve their logistics by allowing them additional resource extraction rights in this system."

We all nodded. Nanotechnological industrial processes couldn't change atomic structure; if you wanted the molecular assemblers to make you something out of certain elements, you needed to supply them with those elements. The right to mine for rare minerals in the Solar System's asteroids and satellites was the only thing Earth—meaning the Prometheus Project, without Earth's knowledge—had to offer the galactic powers, aside from a sideline specialty trade in cultural curios.

Looked at objectively, it might have seemed damned peculiar, if not ludicrous, on two levels. First of all, why didn't galactic-level civilization simply transmute rock into rare elements, rather than mining them? The answer was that transmutation involved processes so expensive that it was more cost-effective to mine the stuff in low-gravity environments—especially if those environments were in the regions of space where the stuff was needed, thus saving transportation costs from the few industrial power-houses where "economies of scale" made transmutation a practical proposition.

That left the second seeming paradox: why did societies with such power *need* our permission? Why not just move in and take whatever they damned well wanted? Earth wouldn't have had a prayer in hell of stopping them—not even Earth as they believed it to be, much less Earth as it was.

But this was the whole point of the diplomatic recognition of Earth's existence that the Prometheus Project had finagled. The Delkasu had an elaborate system of interstellar common law, developed over the centuries and formalized since Sakandri's time, which nobody could get away with blatantly disregarding—the other Delkasu powers wouldn't have stood for it. One of that system's cornerstones was the principle that a race which was recognized as sovereign (that's not really the right word, but it comes closer than anything in the human legal vocabulary) held title to all natural resources within its own planetary system and any others it brought under the mantle of its sovereignty by colonization. It was a reflection of the Delkasu political philosophy: some polities were more equal than others, but the less equal ones had certain clearly defined rights.

"The Section Five delegation of which I am the head," Novak continued, "will be conducting negotiations with certain industrial concerns in Selangava, with a view to

giving them a vested interest in the Solar System's integrity and thus making them natural allies of ours. That's
our mission's overt purpose—which, as usual, isn't the only
purpose. We're going to be covertly angling for new contacts. Meanwhile, our Section Four personnel"—she
inclined her heads toward the intelligence types—"will
be seeking new insights into state-of-the-art technology,
and also gathering all accessible information about
Selangava. I expect all personnel to give them every
assistance. Remember, there is no such thing as useless
knowledge! In particular, we need to expand our woe-
fully inadequate data about the Agardir, about whose very
existence we only recently became aware.

"At the same time we are trying to repair our own ignorance of the galaxy, we must also take all steps to preserve
inviolate the galaxy's ignorance of *us*. This should go without saying. Since the early days of the Project, it has been
established operational doctrine that whenever we venture out-system, security considerations are paramount.
I emphasize it now because of the Tonkuztra matter, of
which we are all painfully aware. We must assume that
the Tonkuztra are active in Selangava, as they seem to
permeate Delkasu-settled space. It is therefore possible
that the same 'family' that has gained an inkling of the
true state of affairs on Earth may be operating there. If
so, we are going to be in a vulnerable position. Our Section
Two representative will have a heavy responsibility." Novak
gave me a look that settled the question of whether she
remembered me. "It is—perhaps—fortunate that he has
been well acquainted with the Tonkuztra threat since its
inception. Indeed, he was directly involved in the very incident that made us aware of it." Her expression suggested

that I was somehow responsible for the whole problem. I met it with a smile I hoped was as irritatingly bland as I intended.

"And now," Novak resumed after a chilly pause, "I call your attention to the timetable for our journey—a not inconsiderable one even by Delkasu standards. Fortunately, we have a short time before departure, so I have scheduled a series of briefings on—"

I stopped hearing her. For I had resumed my interrupted survey of the group, and had spotted a head of light brown hair that I hadn't seen in five years.

What with one thing and another, it wasn't until shortly before departure that I was able to speak to Chloe in private. And it was a purely accidental meeting, in the observation dome.

Practically all of Farside Base was subsurface. That was only prudent, on a world with no atmosphere for the meteoric trash of space to burn up in from friction. Also, it simplified the problem of keeping the installation pressurized; zillions of tons of rock spring few leaks. And, finally, it rendered the vast facility invisible to the primitive but perfectly functional space probes from the unsuspecting world on the other side of the Moon.

Still, humans have a psychological need to view the outside scenery from time to time. Even more to the point, the Delkasu share this need and therefore expected Farside Base to have facilities for assuaging it. In fact, the lack of such facilities would have seemed awfully peculiar to them.

So the designers had compromised with a dome of transparent nanoplastic in the center of Korolev, accessible by grav-driven elevator from the base below. It was, of course, rendered invisible every time a space probe from Earth was overhead. My Section Two colleagues were responsible for that. They were also responsible for somehow arranging that no extraterrestrials were in the dome at those times, to see the stars take on the kind of blurriness I'd seen from inside an invisibility field in an alley in Washington, and wonder why. I imagined they probably drank a lot.

One of those extraterrestrials was there when I emerged from the elevator for my first visit to the dome.

I almost didn't notice him (I assume it was a "him") at first, because the spectacle took my breath away. Around the dome, at all points of the nearby Lunar horizon, was the jagged ringwall of Korolev. Overhead stretched an infinity of black velvet, thick with more stars than were ever visible from the bottom of Earth's atmosphere, even on a clear and moonless night in the desert or on the ocean. For an instant I felt the onset of vertigo, as if I was about to fall off the Moon, and go on falling forever. The one-sixth weight—this was outside the living areas' artificial gravity field—didn't help.

So a moment or three passed before I saw the dark, lithe creature in utilitarian gray clothing, walking across the dome's floor with a gait that was not precisely the same as a man's. As he approached, heading for the elevator, I looked into the large dark gold eyes of the first alien I'd seen in the flesh.

I'm sure I stared like an idiot. The Delkar probably recognized me as a yokel just off the boat from Earth. In fact, thinking back, I *know* he did. But at that time I still hadn't developed the ability to read his race's facial expressions—which was just as well. As he passed me, he raised one of his remarkable and rather disturbing hands in what looked like a gesture of stately but casual greeting. I chose to take it that way, and waved nervously back. Then he was gone, and I was left standing immobilized by a mixture of fascination and revulsion and other emotions less easily defined.

"They have that effect on everybody, at first."

My head jerked up at the sound of the remembered husky contralto. "Oh, hi, Miss Bryant," I managed. "At least I assume it's still 'Miss Bryant.' You may not remember me, but—"

"Of course I remember you. Bob Devaney, right? And yes, it's still 'Miss Bryant.' But for heaven's sake, call me 'Chloe.' You're our Section Two watchdog, right?"

"Right. This will to be my first time out-system. I imagine it must be old hat for you."

"It never gets to be old hat." For an instant, the seriousness I remembered, so seemingly incongruous in her, was back. But then she smiled. "Anyway, Selangava will be a first for me. For any of us, in fact."

"Yeah, so I understand." Without even realizing I was doing it, I spoke more to myself than to her. "Not just another star, but another spiral arm . . ." I caught myself, and met her eyes. She was giving me an odd look.

"That's right. The magnitudes involved . . . Well, it's too much to grasp. It doesn't *mean* anything." She shook herself. "Anyway, that was why I came up here. It's probably the last chance I'll get before departure. I wanted a last look at the Moon."

"That sounds pretty ominous," I said, attempting lightness. I didn't want things getting too terribly earnest, not with Chloe standing here with me in the starlight.

She laughed. "Oh, not a *last* look. Just . . . well, you know what I mean."

"Actually, I think I do. But won't we be seeing it—and Earth—in the view-aft as we're headed out?"

"Probably. But that won't be the same thing, will it?"

"No. I don't suppose it will."

So I stood beside her and gazed out, trying to feel what she felt. No question about it, I reflected, it would be a while before I saw this view again.

I never dreamed how long.

CHAPTER SIX

The gravity and the air weren't exactly those of Earth, and the lighting was a little dimmer than humans liked, for this was a Delkasu ship, operating out of Selangava's capital system of Antyova. A combination cargo and passenger carrier, she had dropped off some trade delegates at Farside Base on her return swing homeward, and the Project had negotiated passage for us on her. (I still couldn't help thinking of a ship as female, even though the Delkasu had no such tradition.) Under interstellar shipping law, she was required to take on a local pilot—Dan Buckley, in this case—while maneuvering in-system. It was a regulation we were very much in favor of, as it gave our people valuable experience with up-to-date galactic technology. Of course, it left Dan somewhat

underemployed afterwards. He would be attached to the
Section Four spooks, to help analyze any goodies they
obtained. I knew him well enough to know that would
bore him to insensibility. I also knew it was a price he'd
gladly pay, and throw in his immortal soul, for the opportunity to take the helm of a ship made of dreams, and
guide her ten leagues beyond the wide world's end.

The environmental differences were barely noticeable,
for the Delkasu had evolved on a planet very similar to
Earth. And most of us soon got over the subtle psychological oppression of proportions and decorative motifs
alien to those of any human culture. The main problem
was the scale of things. It wasn't too bad for most of the
women or even for the smaller men. But I was six feet
one and a half. I soon learned from painful experience to
bend down when going through hatches, and I could never
get comfortable on the furniture.

But I forgot to notice the discomfort of a couch too
small for me as I sat in the lounge and watched the Moon's
surface fall away below us until the odd shift in perception occurred and it was no longer "below" but "behind."
Then it was a globe, with the seemingly smaller blue globe
of Earth peeking over its shoulder.

There were no Delkasu in the lounge. Departures like
this one were routine from their standpoint, and this particular departure held no special significance for them.
But I wasn't alone. Most of the other members of the
mission were there as well, forgetting for once to squirm
in a futile search for comfortable positions on the furniture. We watched in silence for a long time. With
increasing distance, Earth and the Moon assumed their
true relative size as they grew smaller and smaller. We

could not take our eyes off that celestial doublet.

After a while, an announcement came over the intercom in the rapid Delkasu speech. A machine-generated voice followed with a translation in perfect but expressionless American English—no great trick for Delkasu computer systems—for the benefit of the human passengers: "Stand by for activation of drive field."

"You can't feel a thing when it happens," said Chloe, who was sitting to my right.

"Yeah, so I've been told."

"But," she continued, refusing to leave well enough alone, "you still know, on some level, that something is *wrong*. And, of course, the visual effects are pretty startling, at least when you're close enough to a planet for—"

Even as she was in midsentence, the ship reached that distance at which the Earth/Moon system's gravity was no longer strong enough to prevent the formation of the drive field . . . and something occurred which Earth's scientific consensus held to be impossible.

It was, naturally, something I'd wondered about from the moment I'd learned what the Prometheus Project was all about. I wasn't a complete scientific ignoramus—almost, but not quite—and I knew what everybody knew, that Einstein's theory of special relativity said you can't travel faster than the speed of light. (To be perfectly accurate, it *doesn't* say that. What it says is that you can't *reach* the speed of light. Beyond that point, there's no problem. It's just that you can't *get* to that point. All of which is neither here nor there.) So how did the Delkasu do it? They might be advanced as hell, but they still lived in the same universe as us primitives. And that universe has a top speed limit.

The solution to the problem is obvious: you just create your own universe.

Okay, now that I've got your full attention . . . no, of course that's not really it. The idea is this: Einstein was right as regards normal space-time, but an area of expanding space-time (as, in fact, space-time *did* expand during the Big Bang) has no theoretical limits to how much faster it can move than the rest of space-time. So you generate an asymmetric field of negative energy around your ship—a bubble in space-time within which the ship "hitches a ride," moving faster than it could in the larger continuum . . . at least as viewed from that continuum.

Once again, don't blame me if you don't understand all this. *I* don't understand it either, so my sympathy for you isn't exactly of the fulsome variety. And don't let your lack of understanding worry you; twentieth-century Earth was generations and generations away from the mere mathematics of the thing. But it explained how the Delkasu and the other races who'd adopted their technology had been able to create a functioning interstellar society—or, at least, one that functioned about as well as human society had for most of history, when messages moved only as fast as ships or horses, for not even the Delkasu had an interstellar equivalent of radio.

It also explained something else I had wondered about. I'd seen all those wonderful old Chesley Bonestell paintings in *Look* magazine: enormous spacecraft of seemingly impossible fragility being constructed in orbit, with no weight to impose limits on their size and no air to require aerodynamic streamlining. Why was it, I'd asked, that the star-travelers used ships that could be fitted into a hangar (admittedly a goddamned big one) under Crater Korolev?

The answer lay in the physics of the drive field, whose power requirements were linked to the size and mass of the ship it was required to enclose. Above a certain tonnage the curve rose sharply to the point of diminishing returns. There were a number of factors involved, but as a general rule the practical limit for an interstellar spacecraft was around fifty thousand tons.

You may well say that something the size of an *Iowa*-class battleship is still a pretty good-sized spacecraft. In fact, relatively few of them—mostly warships—reached this size. Galactic society had made a virtue of necessity where the drive field's limitations were concerned, using lots and lots and *lots* of relatively small ships designed for atmospheric transit, thus avoiding the inconvenience of transshipment at orbital stations. Ours was typical: a twenty-thousand-ton lifting body.

All of which was very fortunate from the standpoint of the Prometheus Project. A hole in the back side of the Moon was easy to conceal; some humongous orbital space station would not have been.

Not that I was really thinking about any of this as Dan Buckley engaged the drive field, nor about anything at all except what I was seeing in the view-aft. I'd been warned to expect it. The warning did no good.

All at once the Earth and the Moon, which had been receding at a rate that was merely awe-inspiring, simply shot away, falling down an infinite well of star-blazing blackness. In an instant of soul-shaking brevity, the world of my birth was lost among the star-swarm as though it had never been. Then the sun followed it into oblivion, dwindling to just one bright star among the multitudes, leaving our eyes and minds with no reference point to

cling to amid infinity. Around the outer edges of the
display, the nearer stars were streaming impossibly past,
visible only by grace of the computer, which edited out
Doppler effects.

Without remembering having reached for it, I realized
I was holding Chloe's left hand tightly in my right. Some
of the other people in the lounge sounded like they were
going to be sick.

"No," said Chloe, speaking as much to herself as to
me, and showing no inclination to let go of my hand. "It
never gets to be old hat."

There was no scientific basis for the idea that time was
in any way distorted within a drive field. And the lights in
the quarters that had been leased for us were set for a
homelike twenty-four-hour day/night cycle, unlike the
thirty-seven-hour-plus period familiar to the Delkasu of
Antyova.

Nevertheless, there was a quality of timelessness about
that voyage that transcended anything science could mea-
sure. In retrospect, it seems too short to recall clearly.
But at the time it was an endless faring into realms beyond
imagination, with stars endlessly emerging from the
starfields ahead to drift past and merge into the starfields
astern. As time went by, the farther stars began to shift
their patterns as well, and the familiar constellations dissolved as though they had never been. For us, each of
those familiar configurations that vanished was yet another
burning bridge.

When we departed our native Orion Arm, the only way
to tell was a slight thinning-out of the procession of passing
stars. Ahead lay a deceptive blackness: the Sagittarius dust

clouds that hid the star-crowded heart of the galaxy from Earthbound eyes. But then we proceeded beyond that veil, into regions of blazing star-birth. There, between the Triffid and Lagoon Nebulas, lay our goal.

Antyova was an undistinguished star, as are all the stars where life-bearing planets can exist. It was a little smaller, cooler and yellower than Earth's sun, and its second planet was, at a slightly smaller orbital distance, a trifle on the warm side for its Delkasu inhabitants but just right for us.

"Don't expect too much exoticism on strange planets," Dr. Fehrenbach had once cautioned us. "The things that make Earth the way it is are the very things that make it life-bearing. If a planet is *too* different from Earth, neither you nor the Delkasu nor anybody else will be able to live on it." From everything we had been told, Antyova II seemed likely to live down to that somewhat dampening assessment.

Or so we thought.

The final approach happened to coincide with dinnertime. (We'd long since used up the food we'd brought, and were eating what the ship provided, with the vitamin supplements that enabled humans to stay healthy on Delkasu cuisine. We were even getting used to it.) So we brought our trays to the lounge with the idea of munching away while observing the proceedings with the blasé detachment of the sophisticates we by then fancied ourselves to be.

The food got cold. It's hard to chew with your mouth hanging open.

True, from a distance there were few obvious distinctions between the blue marble called Antyova II and the one called Earth. The only immediately obvious differences were merely cosmetic. Two small moons instead of one big one, for example. . . .

Only, it wasn't easy to tell those two natural satellites from some of the artificial ones, for those were too big to be artificial, as big as small moons.

The outermost ones were military bases, the smallest of them incomparably vaster than any structure ever wrought by humankind—shell after shell of them, surrounding the capital planet of an interstellar empire. The closer ones had other purposes, not all of which we ever learned. Most of the functions familiar to us—communications, surveillance, and so forth—could be handled perfectly well by small, automated satellites such as our own civilization was beginning to use. And we already knew that the efficient atmosphere transit provided by the impellers, combined with the tonnage limitations on interstellar craft, made orbital stations irrelevant as spaceports. No, these Brobdingnagian constructs had purposes that were incomprehensible or—more likely, and even worse—*frivolous*. We didn't fully appreciate that until the largest of the lot appeared. Its size didn't register at first. It couldn't, surely, be appearing from *behind* the planet. Could it?

"That," came Renata Novak's dry voice, "is the orbital imperial palace."

We all looked around, for we hadn't known she was there. She generally wasn't given to socializing with the troops. But there she was, staring as fixedly as the rest of us at the viewscreen.

Chloe cleared her throat nervously. "Uh . . . *orbital* imperial palace? Does that imply that there's *another* imperial palace?"

"Oh, there are several . . . even here in this system. Most notably, there is one held aloft over the capital city by gravitic technology. It's larger than a small town. We won't be landing there, by the way. Outside this system . . . well, there are several orbital palaces not much smaller than this one in provincial systems, maintained against the contingency—which occurs every few years, at most— that the emperor might pay a visit. Not that they call him or her an emperor, of course, nor Selangava an empire. The *Vanaz* is a constitutional monarch, as in almost all Delkasu polities." Novak never took her eyes off the screen, and her voice remained strangely expressionless. "As a percentage of what we would call the GNP, the cost of these . . . residences is not particularly significant."

We all began to realize that there were magnitudes even harder to grasp than the five thousand light-years of space we had just crossed.

Then our ship began to swing into low orbit. We had approached Antyova II from its current dayside. Next we curved around into the local night, expecting darkness pockmarked by the occasional lights of cities.

What we saw were dense cobwebs of light the size and shape of continents. Only the oceans were dark . . . and even those were spangled with lights that must mark the locations of islands, both natural and artificial.

Novak ran her eyes over all of us, and spoke in a voice as tightly controlled as her features.

"Do you finally get it?"

We barely heard her as we watched the descent. Soon—too soon, impossibly soon—details began appearing as the inconceivable cityscape rushed up to meet us. There was too much to take in: towers that had to be

miles high, transparent domes that could have covered
whole Earthly cities, myriad aircars herded by traffic control into endless, orderly processions of fireflies. . . . Then
we were down, at a field that must be on the outskirts of
an urban center, for in the distance the incredible towers
we had glimpsed from above rose like a wall of light, blocking the night sky halfway to the zenith despite their
remoteness.

We looked hungrily out at an alien world, and wondered when we'd be allowed to explore it.

It didn't take long, really. It just seemed long.

The Project's deal with the shipping line included
permission for us to use our living quarters on the ship
during our planetside stay. Before we could venture off
it, there were various formalities to be taken care of. One
was quarantine. The similarity of human and Delkasu biochemistries was a two-edged sword: if we could eat it, it
could eat us. So while we and the Delkasu could subsist
on each others' food, we could also catch some of each
others' diseases. The microorganisms in question wouldn't
last long inside us, just as we couldn't live indefinitely on
Delkasu food alone. But while they lasted, they could get
revenge by inflicting some unpleasant symptoms. It wasn't
a serious problem, for the first Delkasu in the Solar System
had taken care to tailor wide-spectrum antibodies—mere
routine for them, given their civilization's centuries of
experience in such matters. Still, we had to verify that we
were properly inoculated.

After that, Novak and her Section Five types had a
round of meetings with various local pooh-bahs. The purpose was to arrive at the protocols for her later talks with

representatives of industrial concerns in search of contracts. All very necessary, of course . . . and very frustrating for those of us who were cooped up in the ship.

In the course of those conferences, she learned something unexpected, and unsettling.

"It turns out," she informed us at group meeting, "that there's a delegation here from Khemava."

We all blinked and searched our overloaded memories. It was evening of the long day of Antyova, to which Novak had insisted we start adapting, and we were all feeling something reminiscent of jet lag. Chloe finally spoke up. "Uh . . . isn't that one of the other successor-states?"

"Yes—the one that's second only to Selangava in importance. And their relations have had their ups and downs." Novak activated a small portable display at the head of the little conference room we were packed into. It provided a smaller version of the astrographic display she'd shown us on the Moon. She indicated a three-dimensional yellow expanse. It was in the Orion Arm, but a little ways (*Yeah, right!*) to the left-hand side of the display, so it was at least as far from the Sun as was Antyova, at the other apex of a right triangle. So it was in regions that were relatively new to the Delkasu. But, I finally recalled, they had found a native civilization there—and conquered it. That had been about three centuries earlier, before the unwritten code of customary interstellar law that the Project relied on had fully come into its own. And the locals had only gotten as far as interplanetary flight, of a low-tech sort, although they'd been doing it for quite a while.

"This complicates things," Novak continued, sounding even more testy than usual. "Imagine a trade delegation from Liberia arriving in Washington at the same time one from the Soviet Union was in town . . . and trying to get noticed. It may also complicate our security problems, for we know the Tonkuztra is exceptionally strong in Khemava. Besides, the presence of some of the native Ekhemasu is a new factor; we're used to dealing with the Delkasu, but not with them." She gave me a look as overflowing with warmth as ever. "So, Mr. Devaney, it will probably be advisable for you to accompany me and the other Section Five personnel to the reception tomorrow."

"Very well." I couldn't help basking in the dirty looks I was getting from some of the people who were still confined to the ship. I also caught a look from Chloe, but her eyes were twinkling; she would also be attending.

The *Akavahn* was an official who dealt with foreigners on the level of economic matters (but not military or political ones, which were handled by an altogether different bigwig in the capital city, halfway around the planet in the shadow of the floating palace Novak had described). The reception was at his official residence, and one of the corporations—that wasn't really what it was, but it was the functional equivalent—with which we were dealing supplied an aircar to transport us there.

I remember little of that first trip through an unearthly city. There was too much to take in, and it was too hard to grasp—the mind kept sliding off the strange angles and proportions of an utterly alien architectural tradition. Presently a colossal structure loomed up ahead.

"It has to be big," Novak answered our unspoken question. "The *Akavahn* has to deal with various races, some of which are larger than the Delkasu."

"Like us," someone put in.

"Also some that are larger still. It's considered bad form to make anybody stoop."

We passed through an entrance hall that could have held a fair-sized spacecraft and entered a proportionately scaled atrium. At least that was what it looked like to me, for its lofty ceiling held a skylight, and the walls were lined with potted plants resembling ferns. By that time, I was sufficiently immunized to the impact of strange architecture to be able to concentrate on the beings that thronged it.

The formal dress of Selangava was a good deal more colorful and less practical than the utilitarian garments we were used to seeing on the Delkasu at Farside Base: long tunics and sleeveless robes, whose intricate patterns and combinations didn't always conform to human ideas of color coordination. It was easy to spot the Delkasu from Khemava, for their sartorial tradition was a lot more understated, with simpler lines and a lot of white, although there were some elaborate headdresses, according to a strict hierarchy of rank. (I recalled that this was a "conquest state," overrun by two waves of Delkasu in succession, and class-conscious as such states tend to be.) The outfits were also a little skimpy-looking; their wearers probably felt chilly there.

But most of my attention was on the beings that accompanied those latter Delkasu. All at once, I understood why this building had to be built to accommodate all shapes and sizes.

I'd learned in training that toolmaking races were practically all bilaterally symmetrical, and mostly bipedal, and why. I'd also learned that there were certain exceptions. In particular, on worlds whose surfaces were largely dry land, with landlocked seas rather than oceans, life emerged from the water earlier and often retained more than four limbs—six or occasionally eight and very occasionally more. When beings like that went into the tool-using business, they generally ended up with a configuration not unlike the centaurs of myth.

That was what I found myself looking at now.

The four-legged body was larger than that of a horse, and gracile—I knew enough by then to recognize a denizen of a world with relatively low gravity. Likewise, the upright torso rising from the front like a horse's neck was deep-chested, suggesting a thinner atmosphere than that of Earth or Antyova II. (No surprise; low gravity, low percentages of surface water, and thin air generally went together, although there were of course exceptions.) The skin was cream-colored, although there were individual variations; at first I thought it was covered with very short, fine fur, but it was really a suedelike surface not unlike chamois. Practically all of it was on view, for their clothing consisted only of a kind of harness. The two long, slender arms ended in hands with six incongruously blunt fingers in two mutually opposable groups of three each. The head, atop a graceful neck, had dark eyes even huger than those of the Delkasu in a visage of sheeplike length, although it naturally didn't really resemble the face of any of Earth's animals. . . .

"Good day."

I turned abruptly, and found myself looking up into one of those long, huge-eyed, somehow melancholy faces.

Language was far more of a barrier between species with

differing vocal equipment than it had even been among the various nations and races of Earth. We had been issued earpieces which picked up any nearby voice speaking the Delkasu common tongue—not the only Delkasu language, by any means, but the *lingua franca* of the well educated— and translated it into Americanese in our ears. It could even handle variant dialects of that common tongue, like the one that had evolved in Khemava. I saw that the centauroid torso in front of me wore a pendant with a small speaker. Evidently the natives of Khemava were expected to transform their speech into that of the dominant Delkasu newcomers. It was that artificially generated speech, issuing from the pendant, that my earpiece had picked up—mine and Chloe's, for she had been standing beside me and had also turned to meet those enormous opaque eyes.

"Good day," she replied, speaking slowly and distinctly in the knowledge that her words would be filtered through the miniature computers no human of her generation and mine would ever really get used to. We also had pendants that would provide a translation of our speech for the benefit of the Delkasu. "Am I correct in assuming you have some means of rendering the Delkasu speech my pendant is generating into your own language?"

"That is not necessary." The translators were very sophisticated. Two layers of them could even reproduce nuance—and there was a definite but somewhat wry smile in the voice that sounded in my ear. "I can understand the Delkasu common language, even though my race cannot produce its sounds in a satisfactory way. It is, you see, a required element in our educational system."

"Oh." Chloe recovered quickly. It was, I reflected, natural that she was taking the lead in this conversation. This particular race might be new to her, but she had years of experience at dealing with aliens. I was just trying not to gawk—without success, I was glumly certain. One thing, at least, was helping me regain my mental equilibrium. The translator programs factored gender into their synthetic production of voices, and this one sounded male. So I was able to think of the being as "he" rather than "it."

"Please excuse us for staring," Chloe continued, "but you are the first Ekhemar we have ever met."

"Ekhemar?" The note of bitter amusement I had detected before was back in force. "Yes, that is what you must call me, and my race the Ekhemasu. Actually, those are not our terms. Our own word for ourselves, in our own language, is—" My ears, unaided by the earpiece, heard an alien sound in which a syllable resembling *khem* had a ghostly existence. The earpiece was silent.

"You see?" he continued. "The Delkasu gave our planetary system a name based on our own word for it, then imposed their naming conventions. Those conventions are the only ones that their own computer systems recognize, and therefore the only ones that exist. So by all means call us the 'Ekhemasu.' And my personal name—we have at least been allowed to retain a version of those—is Khorat." That, at least, was the sound that came through the earpiece. It wasn't exactly what my ears heard him say—that was longer, and had at least one syllable that was like nothing a human throat would form. But at least the Delkasu computer systems would accept it.

Chloe gave him our names in return. The stuff we'd been given, having been programmed for English, could handle them.

"A pleasure." Khorat reached into a pouch of his harness with one of his peculiar hands. "It is a custom among us to present gifts to new acquaintances. Please accept these." He held out two tiny items of jewelry, one to each of us. They were shaped like four-pointed stars, of a metal that looked like it could have been an alloy of copper and gold, with a clip behind and a red stone in the center.

"Uh, we have nothing to offer in return," I managed.

"One would hardly expect you to. The custom is ours, not yours. Please accept these nonetheless. I insist."

"Well . . . thank you." I took the trinket. We humans were wearing what would have been appropriate attire for a similar social function in our own culture. Our hosts' etiquette required it, and even if they would have been none the wiser if we'd worn bib overalls, it made *us* feel right. I attached the clip to my lapel.

"Yes, thank you," Chloe echoed.

"Please don't mention it." Khorat glanced across the room. One of the Delkasu from Khemava gave a gesture whose peremptoriness transcended race and culture. "I must go."

"Perhaps we'll meet again," said Chloe.

The alien paused and met our eyes. That long, big-eyed visage wore what I could have sworn was an enigmatic expression. I told myself it probably meant no more than the look of lugubrious mournfulness a basset hound wears even when he's feeling positively giddy. And yet . . .

"I would not be surprised at all if we did," Khorat said slowly. Then he was gone, leaving me and Chloe exchanging puzzled looks.

CHAPTER SEVEN

"Yep," stated Dan Buckley, standing up from the bench. "It's a homing device."

"You're sure?" Chloe demanded, looking past my shoulder.

"No question." Dan turned to the Section Three scientist with whom he'd been paired since leaving the Solar System—and his piloting duties—behind. "Tell 'em, Izzy."

Israel Berman, Ph.D., also stood up, and ran a hand through his prematurely thinning hair. (I've always suspected that excessive brain activity inhibits hair growth. I've kept quiet with that theory since someone pointedly mentioned the exceptional thickness of my own hair.) He and Dan had struck up one of those odd friendships of opposites. I'd asked Dan to recruit him for a bit of after-hours alien-technology analysis, on a strictly unofficial basis. Thus it was that the four of us were squeezed into Berman's quarters, to which he'd brought certain instruments from his working spaces.

"Yes," he affirmed, pointing to the little trinket Khorat had given me. It lay on the bench, gleaming in the overhead lights and the table lamp Berman had trained on it. "It's in the thing that looks like a gem, at the center of the star. Amazing. But there are limits to what you can do even with molecular circuitry. It's an extremely elementary, no-frills beacon."

"What's the power source?" Chloe wanted to know.

"Would you believe a near-microscopic solar cell? Obviously, the device doesn't draw much power. This makes it practically undetectable, unless you know what you're looking for. If you do know, then it's not hard. Of course, I'm not up to actually tracing the circuitry . . . if you can even call it that. I'd need a—"

"That's okay, Doc," Chloe said hastily. "We'll take your word for it. And thanks." She removed her own pin, handling it gingerly with unconscious distaste, and laid it on the bench. She turned to me. "Well, I suppose this settles what we're going to do with these things. . . ." Her voice trailed off as she watched me take mine back. "Doesn't it?"

"Yep. I plan to keep wearing mine. I want you to, as well."

"*What?* But . . . but shouldn't we go straight to Renata and report this whole incident?"

"I never like to bother her with things she doesn't need to know," I said serenely as I reattached the pin to the lapel of my suit. I'd never changed following the reception, for it was later in the same long night of Antyova II.

Dan stared at me openmouthed, which was enormously satisfying. The rare opportunities that present themselves to astonish one's fellow irreverent young with one's own youthful irreverence always have that effect. (Oh, all right, I was thirty-two. But you know what I mean.) "I can't believe I'm hearing this! You're supposed to be in charge of security for this mission. And an agent of an alien power has just tried to plant a bug on you!"

"First of all, Dan," I explained in tones of condescending omniscience, "we don't know that Khorat is an 'agent of an alien power.' I don't know for certain *who* he's working for . . . and I'd like to find out. Secondly, it's pretty obvious that he 'planted' these gizmos on Chloe and me in the knowledge that they'd be discovered. How about it, Dr. Berman? Didn't you say that anybody could detect these devices, given a suspicion of what they were and the requisite technological level?"

"Well, yes," Berman allowed. "And everybody out here thinks we humans have that technological level—with the possible exception of whatever Tonkuztra 'family' has gotten an inkling of the actual facts. And even they must know by now that we've somehow acquired the capability to use galactic-level technology even if we can't produce it."

"Precisely." I nodded sagely. "So a member of a hitherto uncontacted alien race gives these things to me and Chloe, under a pretense that wouldn't fool a child, knowing that we'd be able to deduce what they are." I grew even more studiously inscrutable. "I want to know why."

By now, you're probably wondering why I was being a prick of such monumental proportions. The answer is complex . . . no, correction, it's very simple. Ever since we'd departed the Moon, my job—aside from strictly technical stuff—had consisted of giving lectures on routine security precautions to people I knew I was boring almost as much as I was boring myself. At last, I smelled a whiff of blood. The opportunity to milk the moment for all it was worth tempted me beyond my character—no great feat, according to certain unkind people.

"So," Chloe said slowly, "you think we should to go along with it? Use ourselves as bait for whatever it is Khorat has in mind?" She looked gratifyingly impressed . . . or at least it was gratifying until I realized there was no telling whether she was impressed by my daring or by my insanity.

"I'm not sure 'bait' is the right word. But yes, I want to play out Khorat's little game and see what happens. Something's going on here that I don't understand. That bothers me."

"But Bob," Dan protested, "shouldn't you at least tell Novak what you're planning to do?"

"And if I did, what do you think the chances are that she'd let me go ahead with it?"

"Not very good," he admitted.

"True," Chloe agreed reluctantly. "Renata does have a tendency to be kind of . . . well, you know . . ."

"Anal?" I suggested helpfully.

Chloe looked daggers at me, but didn't argue the point. "She'd probably order you to smash those pins with a hammer, then order all of us to avoid any contact with the delegation from Khemava, then—"

"—Cancel all shore leave," I finished for her.

This caused a glum silence to descend on the room. Novak had announced that she was going to start letting us leave the ship and play tourist. The array of limitations she'd imposed—groups of two or more, no one ever to wander off individually, definite itineraries submitted in advance and strictly adhered to, *et cetera*—had failed to dampen everyone's excitement at the thought of being able to explore this city beyond imagination, like something out of a superscientific *Arabian Nights*.

"Hmm . . . there is that," said Dan thoughtfully.

"There sure is that." I nodded. "Hey, people, don't worry! Chloe and I will just go out on one of these authorized sightseeing expeditions. Novak won't have any worries about giving us permission—I'm the security man, for God's sake! We'll just go around and do a lot of rubbernecking . . . and I'll see if a tail has been put on us. I have some experience in that, you know."

"I suspect," Berman cautioned, "that the means of 'putting a tail' on someone are so different here that your experience will be largely irrelevant."

"Care to lay a bet on it? And even if that's true, I've got some galactic-level countersurveillance stuff of my own. But I don't really expect it."

"What *do* you expect?" asked Chloe. She hadn't, I was pleased to note, protested at my somewhat cavalier inclusion of her in my plans. If she had, I'd been prepared to trot out a theory—doubtless completely spurious—that two of the homing devices were more likely to draw the kind of attention I wanted than one.

"I'm not sure. I just want to get a reaction of some kind. You see, I have a strong hunch that Khorat is acting on his own. Or, if not strictly on his own, certainly on behalf of somebody other than his nominal Delkasu bosses. I think he gave us these doodads so he can track us when we're away from this ship and can be contacted in a more private setting than that circus of a reception. I want to see if he, or somebody else, does try to contact us."

Chloe took on the thoughtful look that was natural to her, as she slipped back into her Section Five persona. "Are you perhaps implying that there may be a power struggle of some kind going on among the Ekhemasu? And that it might offer opportunities for us?"

I noted the way she had pronounced the word *Ekhemasu*. It was sort of like the word *Hawaiian*. As you know if you've ever spent any time in Hawaii, that word can mean any citizen of the state, with no more or less significance than, say, "North Carolinian." But, with a subtly but unmistakably different intonation, it means *native* Hawaiian, the original Polynesian people of the islands. Likewise, "Ekhemasu" (a Delkasu word, as we'd learned) was what the Delkasu rulers of the empire centered on the Khemava system called themselves and all other inhabitants of that empire. But it was also their word for that system's native race, to which Khorat belonged.

Chloe, I could tell, had used the word in the former sense. And visions of exploitable fissures in that empire were dancing like visions of sugarplums through her Section Five head.

"The answer, of course, is that I don't know. We're reasoning in advance of the data, which is a capital error, as somebody—"

"Sherlock Holmes," Berman put in.

"—is supposed to have said. Let's get some facts to work with. We'll send up a trial balloon, and let the chips fall where they may, and . . . have I missed any clichés?"

"Not for lack of trying." But Chloe smiled as she said it.

As it turned out, Novak gave us no real trouble about approving our outing. In fact, she was agreeable to the point of being out of character.

In theory, it wasn't even necessary for us to venture outside the ship to go exploring. Instead, one could simply sit in a recliner, put on a headband, and experience any one of the city's attractions. "Virtual reality" was a term we didn't have then, but I've learned it since. And this was far beyond what that term conjures up for you. It really *was* reality, in all its manifestations, but without reality's irritating little imperfections, and included a guide whose downloaded consciousness would respond to you interactively. I think that last part was probably the reason so few of us went that route; it summoned up too many ghosts and revenants from the tales that still lurked in the shadows amid our mental furniture, however sternly our waking minds might dismiss them in a rationalistic huff. Besides which, we just weren't ready to believe we had actually seen a city until we had actually pounded its pavement.

So the shipping line, as a matter of good customer relations, had put a few aircars at our disposal, programmed to accept verbal commands in English. Not that we were in a position to give any but the most rudimentary commands, given the awesome extent of our ignorance concerning the city. But the software—another term that, for us, still lay in a future when Earth's culture had soaked up more of the galactic technology the Project had doled out—was quite sophisticated enough to interpret the intent behind our fumbling, self-conscious attempts to make our wishes known. Thus it was that Chloe and I were whisked away toward the central plaza that Novak had decreed to be the beginning- and end-point of all sightseeing junkets.

The aircars were low-altitude vehicles, using under-powered versions of spaceships' impellers on a principle that was analogous to vectored thrust. As we passed through the urban canyons, I found that on this second outing I was able to absorb details in a way I hadn't on the way to the *Akavahn's* reception, when I'd been stunned by an overload of strangeness.

Then, with an abruptness that would have been unsettling for anyone with agoraphobic tendencies, we emerged from between the walls of towering buildings and swooped over the plaza—I suppose I have to call it that, even though the word has a cozy connotation, suggesting something far less vast than that expanse, like an artificial valley surrounded by equally artificial cliffs. The artistry of its pattern of alternating walkways and gardens was obvious even across the gulf that yawned between two species' artistic precepts. It was circular, and wide avenues radiated away from it like the spokes of a wheel—sort of like Pierre L'Enfant's original design for Washington, but on an incomprehensibly grander scale.

The aircar set down beside a kind of kiosk that was a subsentient artificial intelligence more or less on the level of the aircars. It was a guide to the city's transportation systems, programmed to receive verbal questions and respond in kind. With our earphones and pendants, it was an oracle waiting to reveal the wonders available to us. But I hesitated before consulting it, content to stare around at the plaza itself . . . and the beings that walked among the intricate arbors of vegetation the Delkasu had brought from their unimaginably remote homeworld, filling the galaxy with it as well as with themselves.

Most of those beings were Delkasu, of course, but by no means all. This city (whose name I never learned, nor even if cities had the kind of personalized individual identity among the Delkasu that they do among humans) was the port of entry for shipping from outside the Selangava Empire. So even among the Delkasu majority, there were various styles of dress . . . and also physical variations among the wearers of those styles, barely discernible to us but doubtless charged with ethnic significance in Delkasu eyes. And, here and there among the crowds, there were others . . . enough sorts of others that Chloe and I weren't particularly noticeable.

As Dr. Fehrenbach and others had repeatedly drummed into us, the number of toolmaking races was limited. And so was their exoticism. The more outré science-fictional speculations about extraterrestrial biochemistries—silicon in place of carbon, chlorine or fluorine in place of oxygen, and so forth—were all very clever, but for various reasons they just didn't work. For one thing, they required planetary environments that were either flatly impossible (planets around blue giant stars) or vanishingly unlikely (massive concentrations of uncommon elements). Still, that left a lot of room for variety, quite a bit of which was on display in the plaza. I saw a biped even shorter than the Delkasu but seemingly almost as broad and thick as he was tall, with thick wrinkly brown skin and a snouted face currently wearing a device that compressed the air of Antyova II to the density to which he was accustomed on his own high-gravity planet. He walked in the careful way one adopts in low gravity. In contrast, a group of tall, attenuated, deep-chested beings with pale-gold skin and crested copper-colored ruffs of something that was neither hair nor feathers were walking laboriously and seemed to be experiencing some discomfort from the air pressure. Maybe, I thought, they thought it undignified to wear respirators that would reduce the pressure for them—or maybe I was just anthropomorphizing again, reading aristocratic superciliousness into the smoothly aquiline curves of their features. There seemed three varieties of them, and I wondered if they were one of the very rare races Dr. Fehrenbach had mentioned that possessed three genders—and, I imagined, very complicated lives. . . .

I felt a tug on my sleeve. Chloe pointed wordlessly at another group of beings—in this case, beings we both recognized, for our briefings had included holograms of the Agardir.

Despite a certain number of "incidents" in out-of-the-way frontier systems, there was—so far—no official state of hostilities between them and Selangava, of which they were still technically a dependency. To date, their aggression had been limited to the spheres of colonization and commerce. (Although one heard complaints that their tactics recalled the old saw about how to tell a pirate from a merchant: if you're armed, he's a merchant.) So there was no reason for them not to be seeing the sights like the rest of us. But I don't think it was entirely my imagination that the local Delkasu shied away from them as they moved through the plaza with their distinctive sinister gait, half-loping and half-prowling, as though prepared to instantly sprint at prey.

They were bipeds approximately the height of tall men. The resemblance to humanity stopped there. There was something odd about the way their limbs were jointed. Their forms were covered with an off-white integument resembling flexible bone, if that makes any sense at all. The faces were long and narrow, reflecting the whipcord leanness of their bodies, and the heads high and flat-backed. The hands had three long, multiply jointed, mutually opposable fingers, which didn't look all that well adapted to tool-using, although the Agardir evidently got along. The feet, likewise, were three-toed, with nasty-looking claws that they kept unconsciously extending. The latter were visible beneath the saronglike garments they wore under a short jacket, in angular patterns of muted colors.

There were three of them, all male. Agardir females, I recalled, were kept almost completely secluded. They glided (no, that's not quite the right word, for the motion was quicker than that) through the crowd, which parted for them. Their heads swiveled from side to side, taking in the sights like any other tourists. . . .

Only, as I watched, it seemed as though those tiny, glittering black eyes kept coming back to Chloe and me, only to swing away as my own eyes met them.

"Come on," I heard Chloe say. "We haven't got all day, and I want to see this 'Museum of Worlds' we've heard about."

She evidently hadn't noticed the Agardir's surreptitious attention. I decided not to trouble her with it. "Yeah, sure," I replied, and began to ask the kiosk for directions. By the time I was through looking at the holo display that obligingly appeared in midair, the Agardir had moved away. But, I noted, not too far away. And their route seemed curiously aimless, as though they had no particular destination, and no purpose except to keep us in sight.

"Okay, let's go," I said to Chloe, and struck out at a pace that drew complaints from her.

Public transport in the city was designed to be usable by a multispecies clientele. Everything was coded with a simple set of symbols. (*Not* color-coded, for not all races saw in exactly the same range.) We found our way without difficulty to the moving walkway we wanted.

Those walkways were wide, and moved at a rate that would carry you to your destination at a rate that was just short of being unsettling . . . at least in their central segments. But stepping onto one of them from the adjacent pavement to either side wasn't hazardous at all, for what you stepped onto was moving at a bare crawl. As you moved closer to the center, the speed rapidly but smoothly increased, in bands marked out by brightly colored laser light-strings. And no, it wasn't a series of parallel tracks. It was continuous. It just happened to move at different rates depending on where you were. And it was all perfectly solid—it was like walking on hard plastic.

No, of *course* I don't know how it was done. I'd been told about a substance which could be made solid in the vertical plane but fluid in the horizontal, in the presence of an electromagnetic field. Izzy Berman claimed to understand it, but his explanation, full of words like "anisotropic," had left me more confused than ever. Still it was a very convenient way of getting around, if a little disconcerting at first. Chloe was obviously appreciating it to the hilt. I might have done the same, if I hadn't been constantly looking back over my shoulder.

We saw wonders beyond imagination in the Museum of Worlds, presented in holographic vividness. We saw the galaxy's blazing core, seen from inside the Sagittarian dust-veils. We saw beings of every possible form life could take. We saw the remains of a long-dead race's attempt to build a Dyson Sphere . . . and also working, contemporary orbital constructs not too much less impressive than that, far beyond even what we'd seen there in the Antyova system, beyond even what seemed the ultimate limit of engineering possibilities. We saw other things less easily described—*many* other things.

If only I could have concentrated.

We finally left, dazed. Chloe shook herself and found her voice. "Well, let's see . . . The next item on our list is—"

But I wasn't hearing her. I'd retained enough presence of mind to scan the crowds as soon as we emerged into the Antyova light. In the distance, vainly trying to be inconspicuous among the shorter Delkasu, were three familiar tall, rangy forms.

"Right," I interrupted suddenly, grabbing Chloe by the arm. "Let's go!" I set out at a pace that required me to practically drag her.

"*Will* you slow down?" she demanded. "What's the matter with you? For God's sake, you're pulling my arm out of its socket!"

"We're being followed," I muttered into her ear. "The Three Agardir Stooges. Don't look back. Just keep up with me." I speeded up, as heedless of her struggle to match my stride as I was of the dirty looks I was getting from the Delkasu pedestrians I was making our way through with my superior mass.

This wasn't going as I'd expected. Not that I'd really known *what* to expect. But one thing I certainly *hadn't* expected was Agardir. What connection could they possibly have with the Ekhemasu Empire, or anybody in it? Unless, of course, the Ekhemasu—or some faction of them, for whom Khorat was working—were trying to use them to weaken Selangava from within. Yeah, that might make sense. Only . . . what the hell did it have to do with *us*? That part made *no* sense.

Chloe fumbled at her little star-shaped pin. "Let's get out of sight of them somewhere and ditch these things," she gasped.

"No. I still haven't learned a damned thing. I want to play this out a little further. But," I continued, seeing the moving walkway ahead, "getting out of their sight isn't a bad idea in itself. . . ."

Without further warning, I pulled her forward in a lunge that took us onto the slow-moving outer segment. Farther in, our fellow passengers—almost all Delkasu—streamed past us at varying rates of speed, up to about fifty miles an hour in the center. As Chloe and I steadied ourselves, I risked a backward glance. Our three shadows, moving in their usual predatory way, had gotten on behind us.

I put my lips beside Chloe's ear and whispered what I planned to do. Her eyes widened. "When I say 'Now,' " I repeated.

She opened her mouth to protest. I didn't give her the chance.

"Now!" I snapped. I grasped her arm, bunched my legs

under me, and leaped across several of the speed bands. Gamely, she leaped with me. Expostulations exploded from the Delkasu we were bowling over, who had been ignoring us with the blasé indifference of the urban sophisticate. Of the comments my earpiece picked up, "barbarians" was the mildest. But then we crashed to our hands and knees on one of the innermost bands. From the standpoint of the nonplussed Agardir trio, we must have shot away from them like the Road Runner from Wile E. Coyote.

Of course, I had no illusions that they'd stay nonplussed. They'd deduce which band we were on, using whatever it was they were using to track us, and get on it themselves. So they'd be ready when we started to cross the low-speed bands to get off. We needed to get off before they could do that . . . which meant immediately.

I led Chloe across the walkway to the opposite side, and we darted away toward a narrow side street. At least I darted; she did more of a fast hobble, favoring her right leg as she'd been doing ever since we'd landed so ungracefully. I had no idea where I was going. I just pressed ahead, telling myself that we'd eventually be able to find one of the kiosks and ask the way back to the central plaza. At random, I picked another corner to turn. It was a quiet street of relatively small establishments, with a kind of down-at-heels look about it that made it less intimidating than most of the city . . . not that I noticed any of that at first.

Face-to-face is the wrong term, for the long, pensive-seeming face atop the centauroid body was too high for that. But the being stood directly in front of us, clearly waiting.

"You!" I blurted. Even with my limited familiarity with the Ekhemasu, I was somehow certain which individual this was. When he spoke, the voice in my earpiece confirmed it, for the tiny brain assigned individual voices. And this was the voice I'd heard at the *Akavahn's* reception.

"Come with me," said Khorat.

We goggled at him. "You've *got* to be kidding!" Chloe blurted.

"Yeah," I chimed in. "Why should we follow you when we just got through shaking your Agardir friends?"

"They are hardly my friends. A little thought will cause you to realize that there are any number of reasons why they are not . . . only one of which is that my species is purely herbivorous, and we therefore tend to feel somewhat ill at ease around carnivores. And you should come with me because that is the only way to get all the questions in your minds answered." Without further ado, Khorat turned and walked away with a horselike motion that might have been amusing in other circumstances.

Chloe and I exchanged a look. She said nothing, but I could tell she was as mystified as I. Wordlessly, we set out after Khorat.

CHAPTER EIGHT

As Khorat led the way along the street, the leisurely pace he was setting began to worry me.

"Hey, Khorat," I called out, "I know we've only got two legs apiece, but we can move faster than this! And I somehow doubt if those Agardir have given up."

"You need not concern yourselves with them," the Ekhemasu replied over his shoulder. "You did a quite effective job of losing them. My compliments."

"Thanks. But they shouldn't have much trouble picking up the trail again, with these little 'gifts' of yours. Of course, I suppose we could throw them away—"

Khorat stopped abruptly and turned to face us. "Oh, don't worry about that. The Agardir have no idea that those devices exist. They have been following you by conventional means, as well as unconventional ones of their own,

involving olfactory sensors. They're quite good at tracking, you know. Being descended from predators, their
heritage predisposes them to it." The translator software
faithfully reproduced the shuddering distaste he couldn't
keep out of his voice. "And they were awaiting your arrival there in the plaza. They've been doing so for some
time, in shifts, on orders from their Tonkuztra employers."

"*Tonkuztra?*" Chloe exclaimed, bewildered.

I shared her bewilderment. In fact, I excelled it. Unlike
her, I was used to thinking in terms of multilayered
intrigue . . . and Khorat had just added a whole new layer.
"Are you saying the Tonkuztra and the Agardir—?"

"Not 'the Agardir' in any collective sense. These individuals are . . . 'renegades' is too strong a word. Say, rather,
'freelancers.' But everything will be explained in good
time. For now, come with me. The Agardir might
reacquire your scent by a stroke of luck." With the first
motion I'd ever seen him make that suggested impatience,
Khorat turned and continued down the street. There
seemed no viable alternative to following him.

The street opened abruptly onto an open square . . .
except that it was more like a single building enclosing a
square, for the space was too vast to be thought of as a
"courtyard." Khorat struck out across the expanse without hesitation, heading toward the building that closed
off the square's far end.

That building, though long and low compared to this
culture's soaring norm, was far taller than those that
enclosed the square's other sides. It rose in tier upon tier
of terraces and loggias, with the combination of massive-
ness and airiness that galactic materials technology
permitted. We passed through the hangarwide portal into

a space that architectural artifice caused to seem even vaster than it was—rather like St. Peter's in Rome, although there was absolutely no resemblance beyond that. All around were the indoor faces of the tiered exterior, with lift tubes based on an application of artificial gravity rising through many levels of galleries. Everything was proportioned on a larger scale than the Delkasu needed, in a way that reminded me of the *Akavahn*'s establishment.

I finally realized where we were. Delkasu cities were dotted with such establishments—a recognized municipal utility, provided by the government, affording space for a wide variety of functions, both commercial and civic. This one was unique because its interior spaces were adaptable to any of the races that frequented this cosmopolitan city. Anybody could rent premises there, and the building—a near-sentient entity in itself—would provide environmental conditions to the tenant's specifications.

I'd wanted to see the place ever since I'd heard about it. Now, as Khorat led us to one of the lift tubes—freight-sized, on Delkasu standards—I realized I was going to get a more in-depth look than tourists normally got.

We drifted upward—a sensation I'd never gotten used to, and still haven't—to an upper level which afforded a dizzying view of the hall or concourse or whatever. But Khorat was disinclined to let us rubberneck. He led us on, along the galleries with their storefrontlike facades behind which were suites of rooms. Each was identified by a set of the universal Delkasu ideographs floating immaterially in midair before the entrance. He reached one such portal, which slid open in obedience to a tiny remote-control device he carried.

Inside was a featureless chamber that could probably have held three Ekhemasu, and so was ample for us. Khorat turned to us, and my earpiece conveyed an apologetic tone. "There will be environmental differences."

I came to the realization that what we were inside was an air lock. "Uh, how pronounced are these differences?"

"Enough to be noticeable. Possibly even a trifle uncomfortable at first. But not hazardous to your species, I assure you."

"Well . . . let's go."

Khorat used his remote, and led us forward. The comfortably Earthlike atmosphere of Antyova II moved forward with us, expanding through the second portal to dissipate into the thin dry air beyond.

I wasn't altogether unfamiliar with transitions like that. I had spent most of my youth at low altitudes, and then lived for a while in Denver. At first, I'd found myself getting winded easily, as well as experiencing dry sinuses and excruciatingly chapped lips, but I'd adjusted. So this wasn't alarming. To tell the truth, it was barely noticeable compared to the abrupt transition from weighing a hair over one eighty to weighing a little less than one twenty-three. I learned that figure later. At the time, it seemed less than that.

I shot Chloe a glance. She looked less disconcerted than I felt, being more accustomed to the profoundly unnatural sensation of stepping into or out of an artificial gravity field. And Khorat was positively prancing. We'd previously seen him in the gravity field of Antyova II, only fractionally different from Earth's and almost half again as strong as that of his homeworld. Now his walk, while still vaguely equine to our eyes, differed from what we'd seen before as much as the gliding gait of a Tennessee walking horse differed from the trudging of a plow horse pulling too heavy a load. I now understood why his pace had seemed so unhurried. In fact, he'd been hurrying as much as possible.

He turned back to face us. "I apologize for any discomfort. But this is the one place I am certain we can talk without fear of eavesdropping." He spoke a few words in what must have been his own language, for my Delkasu translator remained silent. "I have instructed the environmental controls to add to the humidity. And would you prefer that the view be turned off?"

"Oh, no, that's all right," Chloe assured him hastily. I nodded in agreement, forgetting that the gesture probably didn't mean the same thing in Khorat's culture. Like Chloe, I was taking in my first view of the world of Khemava.

At least I assumed that was what we were seeing, by grace of holographic projections that made the room seem a colonnaded portico open on three sides to the landscape. Overhead, the sky was a deeper blue than Earth's, shading almost to royal blue, although judging from the position of the sun it was midmorning or afternoon. (Afternoon, I was certain, without knowing why.) That sun loomed larger in the sky than Earth's did and had an orange tint, suggesting a star dimmer and less massive than Antyova, let alone Sol. A shallow ramp—the Khemasu didn't use stairs, I was later to learn, although they'd learned to get up and down them in the course of dealing with their bipedal Delkasu rulers—led down to a wide canal. It ran arrow-straight to a horizon that seemed a trifle closer than Earth's, although that was probably just my imagination. (Dr. Fehrenbach had told us not to expect noticeable differences in this on any planet in the habitable size range.) That horizon was flat and unclut-tered where the canal vanished into it. But around us, all was monumental artificiality, a cityscape that seemed to blend into the desert beyond it in a reddish-tawny con-tinuum, with bluffs and cliffs of architecture rising above the canal, all in an austere style shared by the phantom building behind us, in whose wall the air lock door appeared to be set.

It looked like a cross between ancient Egypt and Mars—not the real Mars, of course, but the Mars of Bradbury and Burroughs, before the space probes ruined the Solar System. There were a few jarring touches, of course, like the streams of aircars that passed between the buildings and over the bridges that spanned the canal, and the whip-slender trees. And the lights that criss-crossed the sky overhead were, I was pretty sure, not the hurtling moons of Barsoom but artificial habitats in low orbit.

"I'm glad you don't mind the imagery," said Khorat. "Without it, this room is drearily bare and functional, like all these rooms. Those who make use of them are expected to provide their own familiar environments by means of the holographic projection equipment that is made avail-able." He led us to the center of the "portico," where there were a large pile of cushions and two small benches. He lowered himself onto the cushions with obvious relief. They, at least, were real. "We do not use any equivalent of your chairs. These—" he indicated the benches "—were the best I could find."

We perched on the benches, which were also real—

altogether too real, in their hard discomfort.

"So this," Chloe inquired, looking around at the holo show, "is your 'familiar environment' on Khemava?"

"To a certain extent. It bears little resemblance to the capital city, or any of the other major centers. They have, by now, been largely made over to suit the needs and tastes of the Delkasu. In fact, certain districts would seem to you indistinguishable from the city around us. No, this is a representation of the areas that have gone relatively unaffected by the changes the Delkasu have brought." Khorat looked around, and with my increasing confidence in my ability to read his expressions I thought to perceive a trace of sadness. "In truth, this is an idealization—or, perhaps, an accentuation—of those areas: the 'Old Khemava' as it once was, or might have been, or *should* have been." I found myself thinking of *Mrs. Miniver* versus the real post-Industrial Revolution England.

"So," I queried, "this suite is leased by members of your own species alone, as opposed to the diplomatic mission from the Ekhemasu Empire to which you belong?"

"Yes. The local authorities in their munificence provide this facility for the use of non-Delkasu transients, at a nominal fee. Our own Delkasu superiors naturally expect us to provide ourselves with quarters here, to refresh ourselves with a nostalgia-reinforcing simulation." There was a perceptible pause as Khorat brought his already well-controlled emotions under even tighter rein. "But yes, this is a kind of private retreat for those of us who arranged to have ourselves attached to this mission—"

"•'Arranged' to have yourselves—" I began.

"—and therefore is a secure locale for us to discuss

matters openly," Khorat hurried on smoothly. "Including any questions you may have."

"Like why you planted these homing devices on us . . . in accordance with your 'old custom' of gifts to new acquaintances."

"Ah, yes. That. Actually, inventing folk customs isn't much of an art. I'm ashamed to admit that we do it all the time on Khemava, whenever we want to 'put one over' on the Delkasu."

"I don't doubt that for a minute," I said. My mother had been from the South, and I remembered Uncle Remus. (That was before our rulers had declared those tales "demeaning to African-Americans," which would have left the creator of Br'er Rabbit chuckling over yet another confirmation of his estimate of the white man's intelligence.) "But we're not Delkasu. In fact, our race has never even come in contact with yours until the last few days. Which leads to the question of your motives for wanting to track us—"

"Although," Chloe interjected, "now you seem to be telling us that there's no connection between you giving us the devices and the Agardir following us today—"

"Agardir you say are working for the Tonkuztra," I said, picking up the thread.

Khorat waited patiently, then spoke with equal patience. "Actually, there is a connection between the devices and what happened today . . . but not the one you previously imagined. The opposite of it, in fact. You see, I gave them to you because I was certain the Tonkuztra— using either the Agardir or other hirelings—would be following you the first time you ventured out into the city. When that happened, I wanted to be able to locate you promptly so I could get you out of harm's way and explain certain matters to you. The first turned out to be unnecessary. I am now doing the second."

"But . . ." Chloe was having obvious difficulty in deciding which question to pose first. "But surely you knew we'd be able to recognize these things for what they are."

"Of course. That was to assure that you would wear them. My reading of your species suggested that you would be too intrigued concerning my motivations to do otherwise."

My head was whirling so fast I forgot to be irritated by Khorat's accurate—and apparently effortless—prediction of my behavior. "Uh . . . maybe you ought to just begin at the beginning," I said, in a burst of originality.

Khorat settled himself more comfortably onto the cushions his race evidently preferred to more rigid forms of furniture. "The matter is complex," he began, making me feel somewhat better about my own level of brilliance. "As a starting point, the Tonkuztra have stolen something very important from the Ekhemasu."

"Excuse me," I interrupted diffidently, for my earpiece wasn't up to the level of nuance I needed here. "Do you mean from the Ekhemasu Empire?"

"No. I am referring to the Ekhemasu *people*—the original race, of which I am a member."

My brain kicked into high gear. "So, am I correct in supposing that you—whatever your position in the diplomatic mission your empire has sent here to Antyova—are not acting on behalf of that empire?"

"You are. In this matter, at least, I am acting for an organization of my own race. The imperial authorities know nothing of the theft, nor even of that which was stolen."

"May I further assume that it was this 'organization' that 'arranged' for your presence here?"

"Ah, I see you haven't forgotten that slip of the tongue on my part, Mr. Devaney! Yes, you may so assume. We have ways of . . . influencing the imperial bureaucracy when necessary." The alien face suddenly wore the expression I had learned to recognize as one of amusement. "Dismiss any thoughts of some revolutionary cabal among us, plotting the subversion of the empire and the expulsion of the Delkasu."

"No such thoughts had occurred to me," I declared huffily. My reaction probably had something to do with the fact that that was exactly what I'd been thinking.

"I am reassured." The alien's amusement was unabated. "The fact of the matter is, we do not really disapprove of the empire. Nor of the Delkasu, really, even though we have a deep-seated tendency to feel uncomfortable around meat-eating animals. No offense intended," he added smoothly. "We have adjusted to the concept of *civilized* meat-eaters. And the Delkasu undeniably brought much that was of value."

"You mean their advanced technology?"

"Not so much that as their genius for organization. All the more so inasmuch as we have been able to make ourselves indispensable to their organization, and—as I have intimated—use it for our own ends from time to time. At any rate, our historical sense predisposes us to take the long view of things, inasmuch as it is rooted in a *very* long history. We therefore tend to regard the Delkasu and their 'Ekhemasu Empire' as merely an episode. So while we may occasionally daydream of a world without the Delkasu, I really doubt if many of us would take the opportunity if by some miracle it was offered. At worst, we think of them as somewhat—" Khorat or the translator software or both hesitated over just the right word "—bumptious."

"This is all very interesting, I'm sure," said Chloe in a tone of firm female practicality. "But to get back to what you were saying earlier, may we know what is it that the Tonkuztra have stolen from your people?"

"No." This was stated with a flat finality that came across in the hard monosyllable I heard Khorat utter, as well as in the intonation my earpiece gave the English negative. "The fact that we are dealing with the matter in our own way should tell you that this is something our own government cannot be allowed to know. Still less may you."

"Why?" I demanded. "If the Tonkuztra have already stolen whatever-it-is, then the big secret is blown anyway."

"Say what you will of the Tonkuztra, they are not stupid. They are quite capable of appreciating the unique, no, *transcendent* importance of what they have acquired. Not that they can really understand the full depths of its implications, and not that I am fatuous enough to expect it to awaken in them some heretofore well-concealed sense of social responsibility. But the 'family' in question has proven intelligent enough to proceed in this matter with great discretion, going beyond even the pains they usually take to keep secrets from each other as well as from the authorities. They have made no attempt to use the stolen knowledge themselves, but instead have placed it on the market very circumspectly. They have put out feelers only to those potential buyers they consider likely to be interested in this particular merchandise but too backward to make practical use of it. Thus they exercise their cupidity while appeasing their . . . not 'conscience,' never that. Say, rather, 'caution.'•" Khorat's tone took on a kind of bitter sadness. "I'm sure they believe they are being just too terribly clever for words. It is a pity that they are wrong."

"Are you implying that they've found a buyer?"

"I am. That is why the organization to which I have alluded went to a great deal of trouble to make sure my colleagues and I would be here on Antyova II at this particular time. We are here to prevent the sale from taking place."

I found myself nodding. This was starting to make a kind of sense. "So they're selling it to the Selangava Empire? But no; you said they were looking for 'backward' buyers they think can't do any real harm with it. So who *are* they selling it to? And what's all this got to do with us?"

"I see you have still not grasped the implications of what I said before: we had to be in position here *at this particular time.*"

"You're right; I don't get it." I was growing irritated. "What's so special about this particular time, here in the Antyova system? Who's here now, who isn't normally . . . ?" My voice trailed off.

Khorat hitched himself up on the cushions and looked down at us with those huge dark eyes. "I perceive that you begin to understand."

"You mean . . . *us*?" Infuriatingly, my voice broke in a squeak.

"Someone among you," Khorat specified. "Someone the Tonkuztra have been in contact with. Hence, without doubt, the same traitor of whom you are already aware— the one who revealed to the Tonkuztra the truth about your world." Those eyes seemed to grow even huger, and we found we could not look away. "Oh, yes. We Ekhemasu know all about that."

I have no idea how long the silence lasted. Chloe finally broke it.

"I can't imagine what you're talking about," she said in a perfectly normal voice. I've never been prouder of another human being. That was, I'm certain, the precise moment I fell in love with her.

"We shall proceed far more briskly with this discussion if we do not attempt to bullshit each other." Khorat must, I thought, have used a seriously pungent expression, for the prissy translator software to have come out with *that*.

"But," I managed, trying without success to match Chloe's superhuman equanimity, "what makes you think . . . what gives you the idea . . . ?"

Khorat lowered his head and gave a long, rustling sound deep in his throat, which went untranslated. It was, I was later to learn, the equivalent of a human rolling his eyes heavenward with a sigh of mock resignation. "Never mind how we know. As you have probably gathered by now, the organization to which I belong has ways of finding things out. And you may set your minds at rest: we have no desire to expose the truly admirable ongoing deception your people have been practicing. So let us proceed to consider how certain things, heretofore mysterious to you, now stand explained."

"What 'things'?" Chloe inquired, her busted bluff tacitly shelved.

"For one, the reason for the traitor's initial betrayal. It was, you see, a 'down payment.' The information about your planet's real state of affairs was, if you will, 'earnest money' to establish this individual's bona fides with the Tonkuztra."

"But that was five years ago," I protested, remembering my own involvement.

"These things take time, Mr. Devaney. But to continue: something else that is—or should be—clear to you now is the reason why you attracted the attention of the Tonkuztra and their Agardir minions. You are the mission's security officer. From the standpoints of both buyer and seller, your elimination would mean one less thing to worry about. This was so obvious that I took steps to prevent it."

"These," Chloe nodded, fingering the trinket still pinned to her jacket. "I guess I was included in the deal as a friend of his."

I stood up so I wouldn't have to look upward to meet Khorat's eyes. "I don't suppose you happen to know the identity of this traitor among us humans?"

"Unfortunately, no. I was hoping you would be able to help me ascertain it."

"Nothing would give me greater pleasure than to identify this person, and you can be sure I'll make it my top priority starting now. Only . . . I must have missed the part about why I should share my findings with you."

Khorat took no apparent offense. "We can help each other. I am in a position to expedite your investigation— and, incidentally, enable you to verify the truth of what I have been saying."

"All right. I'm listening."

"We have learned that a face-to-face meeting is to take place. It's the way the Tonkuztra do business, you see. Many of their practices and traditions have an archaic flavor, dating back to their days as a secret society on the prespaceflight Delkasu homeworld. I imagine there are parallels among the criminal organizations with which you are familiar. At any rate, we know the time and place of this meeting, whose purpose is to finalize the terms of the sale and arrange for the actual transfer."

"If you know all this, what do you need us for?"

"By a stroke of ill fortune, my colleagues and I are unable to act on our knowledge. At the time in question, our presence is required for a transaction that is crucial for our government. You two, on the other hand, might well be able to observe the meeting. You could learn both the traitor's identity and the time and place of the actual delivery . . . and pass the latter information on to me, in payment for my having enabled you to obtain the former."

"Aw, gee, and I thought you were being our guardian angel purely out of the goodness of your heart."

"Actually, my species has two hearts. And I do not believe you ever cherished any such notion." As I had already begun to suspect, the Ekhemasu sense of humor had definite limits. "But for a fact we are natural allies. You can catch your traitor. And we can put ourselves in a position to retrieve that which has been stolen from us—or, at least, prevent its sale. Are you agreeable?"

"You know, Khorat, we might be able to work up more motivation if we had some idea of what these stolen goods are, and why they're so important."

"I have already explained to you—"

"Yeah, yeah, yeah." I made eye contact with Chloe. She made a face, but nodded. I turned back to the alien. "All right, Khorat, let's get down to cases."

CHAPTER NINE

Renata Novak's reaction on our tardy return was as per expectations.

"You know the ground rules," she snapped, raking us with her eyes from across the tiny desk in the compartment she used for an office. "These excursions outside the ship are to conform to a strict, prearranged schedule, and—"

"Come on," I protested. "Haven't you been listening? We had to do whatever it took to shake the Agardir who were following us."

"So you've said. But are you sure you were really being followed? People in completely unfamiliar surroundings have been known to imagine things."

I put on a great show of keeping anger under tight

control. The act didn't take much effort. "Do I tell you and the other Section Five types how to dicker with the Delkasu? Then don't substitute your judgment for mine in my area of expertise. Unless, that is, you think you have reason to doubt my competence to carry out the Section Two functions for this mission. In that case, I have a right to demand that you put in writing your—"

"Oh, don't play regulations lawyer with me!" Novak fumed for a second or three. "All right, all right; you know when you're being shadowed. But *why* should the Agardir be taking an interest in us humans all of a sudden?"

I didn't dare make eye contact with Chloe. Khorat had insisted that we keep everything he'd told us to ourselves. I'd agreed, on the general principle of restricting information to those with a need to know. Chloe had contended that Novak had such a need. In the end, Khorat and I had argued her down. But another sound principle is that of keeping one's prevarications to the minimum necessary number. So we'd told her about the Agardir, elaborating our escape from them just enough to account for our lateness in returning, and left it at that, with no mention of Khorat.

"I haven't any idea," I stated. Chloe and I had agreed in advance that I would do the talking, given my more extensive experience in reciting whoppers with a straight face. "I mean to find out."

"By all means try . . . from inside this ship. In light of this incident, I'm canceling all private pleasure jaunts into the city."

"You can if you want." *Well,* I thought, *so much for my ambition to be crowned Mr. Popularity.* "But my interest in this matter is neither private nor for pleasure. I must insist that you allow me to get out and conduct my investigation in my own way."

"No! It's too risky."

"I remind you that I'm in charge of security for this mission. In the face of an unanticipated threat, I have discretion to use my own judgment." This was undeniable, as Novak's silent glare attested. I pressed my advantage. "Furthermore, under extraordinary circumstances such as these I am empowered to co-opt—'deputize,' if you will—non-Section Two personnel. I'll need an assistant. Miss Bryant is already involved, so she's the logical choice."

Novak's glare intensified. "Devaney, don't you have more important things to do than antagonize me?"

"Yeah," I admitted. "But they're not as much fun."

With some people, it would have served as a tension-reliever. Novak, though, spoke through lips that barely moved. "Get out."

As we were exiting the door, my conscience caught up with me and I turned back to face Novak. "You know, I'd really rather that you not cancel everybody else's shore leave. I mean, if we can keep everything as routine as possible, so as not to alert the Agardir that we're on to them—"

"*Get out!*"

"Nice going," Chloe murmured as the door slid silently shut behind us. "El Smootho rides again."

"She'll get over it," I asserted, exuding more confidence than I felt. "Anyway, the point is that we have freedom of movement. And this time we're not trying to attract attention. We'll take precautions."

We proceeded to Izzy Berman's digs to collect those

"precautions." He had prepared a privacy field generator on the same level of sophistication as the one Renata Novak had shown me on that memorable occasion in DC but even more compact, as might have been expected after five years. This was merely one of the widgets he had in his shop as more or less standard items. He'd also been confirming the old chestnut about idle hands by poking into new applications of galactic-level technology. One of the by-products of his little hobby was a device which enabled us to open the outer hatch of the ship— the only hatch that mattered, as the airlock was irrelevant here on dear old Antyova II—without activating the automatic tally of arrivals and departures.

Chloe felt compelled to register a protest. "But you just got Renata to agree that you and I could leave the ship!"

"True. But she never agreed that we could come and go without her knowledge."

"You never asked for her consent to that."

"Of course I didn't. She would have had no reason to grant it, and therefore she almost certainly wouldn't have." I hastened to provide reassurance. "Hey, you just don't have the right mind-set for this sort of thing—"

"Thank God!"

"—so take my word for it: any secret known by more than one party isn't a secret anymore. She talks to other people, you know. And we have no idea who the traitor is." That brought Chloe's splutterings to a thoughtful halt, and I pressed on. "So let's keep it to as few people as possible—meaning you and me."

"Izzy also knows about this hatch-opening gizmo," Chloe pointed out.

"True. And he and Dan know about the homing devices Khorat gave us. But that's *all* they know. Even that is too much for my taste. Let's not let it go any further."

"When Renata finds out we've been keeping things from her—"

"—We'll be delivering the traitor to her on the proverbial silver platter with an apple in his mouth. I think you'll find that covers a multitude of sins—if not with her, certainly with her superiors."

Actually, the problem of the traitor's identity was bothering me more than I cared to admit. Especially worrisome was the fact that I didn't even have a theory as to motive. The ever-popular one of greed had never seemed very likely to me. The Project was a fairly tight-knit little world; it would be awfully suspicious if one of its personnel suddenly came into Croesus-like wealth. So how would the traitor spend it? Unless, of course, he planned to defect altogether and be taken into the sheltering arms of the Tonkuztra . . . but how many people would willingly relinquish all contact with the rest of the human race for life?

In the absence of an intelligible motive, there was no point in sifting through the mission's personnel for suspects, and I forced myself not to do so. It would have been a waste of mental energy, and might have led me into misleading preconceptions. Still, I found myself looking at this face and that in a whole new way: *Is this the one . . . ?*

All I had to go on was what Khorat had said: the traitor had been angling all along for some piece of stolen Ekhemasu property we couldn't be told about.

Chloe and I killed time speculating about the nature

of that item while we waited. We didn't have too long a wait, for the time Khorat had given us was the following night. It just seemed long, and not only because of the slow rotation of Antyova II.

"Some kind of superweapon, maybe?" I ventured, as my umpteenth guess. "So he can make himself Emperor of Earth?"

"Give me a break! You've been watching too many James Bond movies. Besides, if the Ekhemasu had stuff like that, they would never have been taken over by the Delkasu."

"That doesn't necessarily follow." Actually, I could see Chloe's point. But I was being argumentative the way a dog chews on a bone after all the meat is gone. "Maybe they were still working on it when the Delkasu arrived, and have been secretly perfecting it since then in some underground laboratory."

"I take back what I said before; this isn't even good enough for a James Bond movie. Remember, Khorat said his organization isn't interested in overthrowing their Delkasu rulers."

"Don't believe everything you hear! Has it occurred to you that Khorat might have been lying?"

"If you don't trust Khorat," Chloe inquired archly, "then what, pray tell, are we doing here?"

Instead of trying to answer the unanswerable, I glanced down at my watch. "Oops! Time to go."

"How convenient," Chloe muttered as we headed for the air lock.

Izzy's little invention performed as advertised, and we emerged into the night of Antyova II. Except that there was no true night on Antyova II, nor on any highly developed galactic world where the stars had long since been banished by the city lights and the orbital constructs. We had no trouble seeing our way as we crossed the expanse of the spacefield. I sometimes found myself wishing this wouldn't happen to Earth, and knowing that it would.

There were none of the shipping line's aircars waiting— there wouldn't have been at this hour even if Novak hadn't canceled shore leave. We proceeded on foot, like two ships on an empty sea, each of us clutching a satchel.

I had always been blessed with good eyesight, and had never needed glasses . . . and never would, given the technology now available to me. (It was one of the many benefits of membership in the Project.) But I wore contact lenses that had nothing to do with vision correction. Instead, their internal microcircuitry—activated and controlled by a remote-*cum*-minicomputer in my satchel—displayed an ever-unfolding map, oriented on the basis of the direction I was walking. It was one of Izzy's more or less standard items, though not one for which we had any routine use. In my capacity as the representative of Section Two, I had a perfect right to requisition a set. Privately, I'd given Izzy the standard dime-sized computer disc Khorat had given me, so he could download the route to the minicomputer.

Thus I followed the ghostly thread, like a player of one of the computer games that still lay in our civilization's future, except that Chloe and I traversed the actual streets of an alien city. We drew occasional stares from Delkasu unused to seeing aliens abroad at this time of the night and unused to seeing our sort of aliens at all. We ignored them, for by now we fancied ourselves old hands in those streets.

That delusion began to vanish when we reached what appeared to be an almost comically ordinary escalator, going down.

Khorat had explained it to us. Delkasu societies, like all societies—never mind the hypocritical denials of certain human ones—were stratified. And in a megalopolis like this, the stratification was not just economic but physical. The great organism that was the city extended belowground as well as above it, like a tree sinking its root system into the soil. That subterranean (*don't* give me a hard time about that word) domain, which visitors like ourselves seldom glimpsed, held much of the nitty-gritty stuff that made the city run . . . and most of the people who ran that stuff, doing the sort of jobs for which they were cheaper than computers.

Don't visualize squalor out of Hogarth or Dickens. In a society as wealthy and advanced as the Selangava Empire—or any of the Delkasu civilizations—nobody starved. Even the local equivalent of an underclass had amenities beyond the imaginations of lower-tech cultures. As Chloe and I rode the escalator down, we emerged into a cavernous, teeming realm lit by vast holographic images—this culture's "billboards"—between artificial cliffs that were residential on the higher levels and commercial below. Here, where non-Delkasu were a rarity and *our* kind of non-Delkasu unheard-of, the stares we got were more blatant than they'd been in the politer precincts above. I fell into the jump-out-of-the-way-or-I'll-walk-over-you stride I'd always found useful in New York, hoping that the body language involved would transcend species and culture. Chloe must have been emulating me successfully, for the crowds parted for us. I imagine our sheer size helped.

As we proceeded, the streets (they were too vast for
the word "passageways" to be a good fit) frequently took
the form of gently sloping ramps that led farther and
farther down. The deeper we got, the less spacious and
brightly illuminated things became, while a dinginess we
hadn't seen on Antyova II became more and more pronounced. The first-level storefronts included more and
more food shops, from which a variety of odd odors
wafted. The crowds grew more raucous and surly, and
their clothing had a look I could now recognize as both
flashy and sleazy.

This was Tonkuztra country. Their kingpins might be
the tycoons of interstellar-scale illegitimate businesses
nowadays, but this was where they'd come from. Up
above, in order to pass in the Delkasu equivalents of execu-
tive suites and country clubs, they had to take on the
protective coloration of the larger society. Down here,
they were in charge, wherever and whenever there was
no cop in sight. More than once, I saw the crowds cringe
away from some gaudily dressed, physically above-average
Delkar who had "enforcer" written all over him. (Or all
over her. Given the minimal sexual dimorphism of the
Delkasu species, strong-arm types were as likely as not to
be female.)

The ramps continued down and down, switchback after
switchback. I had no idea how far beneath the surface we
were. Most of the hectic, noisy garishness was behind us,
and the cavernousness it had concealed like makeup was
now exposed like an aging whore's raddled face. These,
Khorat had explained, were regions dating back at least a
thousand Earth years, now seldom frequented. The

Tonkuztra bosses came here when they had very secret business to conduct. They and their business associates had more direct and convenient means of access than the one we had followed. I consoled myself for my sore feet with the thought that it meant we almost certainly hadn't been noticed. Nobody had any reason to watch the route we'd taken.

Still, I made sure there was no one in sight when we turned down a certain altogether deserted passageway.

Finally, we emerged into a vast, relatively well lit octagonal open space, extending all the way up into invisibility. (It seemed an awfully inefficient use of space, but then I wasn't exactly up to speed on Delkasu architectural precepts.) At its center was a depressed area of the same octagonal shape, from which a shallow dome with a stepped base rose. The eight angles around the dome held Delkasu-sized entrances from which stairs led downward into antechambers of the domed octagonal room below.

This was what Khorat had described to us. He'd also stressed that we needed to be there before a certain time, but not so much before it that our loitering might attract attention even in this unfrequented neighborhood. We followed his instructions, slipping into one of the stairwells and composing ourselves to wait in the shadows.

It was hard to get comfortable. Fortunately, we didn't have long to wait.

A shuffling sound from below alerted us. I peered cautiously over the edge of the stairway, as several nondescriptly dressed Delkasu entered the hexagonal chamber, moving purposefully.

It's always hazardous to try and superimpose human preconceptions on an alien race, even for someone with more experience at it than I had. But even across the interspecies divide, I could sense the difference between these Tonkuztra and the swaggering thugs we'd seen in the passageways. These were pros. They ran devices whose functions I could confidently guess at over every surface of the large room, then fanned out into the ante-chambers.

But for all their professionalism, there was a perfunc-tory quality about their scrutiny. This place had probably been used for so many meetings that their search for sur-veillance devices, always fruitless before, had settled into the grooves of routine. For one thing, they didn't exert themselves to climb the stairs. They just used their superadvanced sensors on the obvious places, then left.

It was what Khorat had told us to expect. And it was what gave me my opening.

After the last of them was gone, I slipped down into the big chamber carrying a device the size and shape of a thumbtack head. Actually, the business end of it was the size of a pinhead; the rest was plastic with the adhesive backing by which I proceeded to attach it to the inner surface of the dome, reaching up to do so at a height of almost eight feet—higher than a Delkar would normally look. Then I rejoined Chloe, and we reemerged into the open space above the dome. We took shelter—such as it was—against the curve of the dome in one of the angles formed by the eight walls. Then I took a very small readout from the satchel, and activated its screen.

The sweep by the Tonkuztra security types would have detected the nanobug I'd stuck to their wall with ridicu-lous ease. But they didn't expect anyone to be around to attach it *after* that sweep. That had been our window of opportunity. Now Chloe and I gazed at the tiny screen and saw what the bug was recording.

It was also recording sound . . . which, unfortunately the readout couldn't convey to us in real-time. We had to settle for the visual image from that near-microscopic camera—a supremely boring image of an empty chamber, at first.

That soon changed.

First, a group of three Delkasu filed into the chamber, accompanied by a double file of the security people, armed with weapons I recognized as cutting-edge even on the standards of the Selangava military. I was even more interested in those security guards' body language. Unless all my instincts were wrong, these guys (and gals) were responsible for the safety of VIDs—Very Important Delkasu. I applied my knowledge of the race to the trio of big shots, and recognized them as middle-aged, well nourished, and suffused with that indefinable air of authority. They sat down at one side of a long table that occupied the center of the room.

One of them spoke tantalizingly inaudible words to a security guard. The latter performed a hand-to-forehead gesture of respect and opened a door opposite the table.

A single individual—doubtless the prospective buyer—entered, bending down a little to pass through a Delkasu-sized door.

Which, I thought with the calm that so often dwells in the innermost depths of shock, was to be expected. After all, Renata Novak was a fairly tall woman.

CHAPTER TEN

I have no idea how much time passed, as I stared at that tiny screen, before Chloe nudged me in the ribs.

"Bob!" she whispered urgently into my ear. "We've got to get out of here."

I shook myself into awareness and out of shock. It wasn't until much later that I fully appreciated Chloe's achievement in coming out of shock before I did. After all, she'd known Renata Novak far longer than I had, and didn't share the dislike that should have served as a prophylactic for me. When I did appreciate it, I fell even more deeply in love with her. Come to think of it, I did so with each new demonstration of the undeniable fact that she was smarter than I was. In fact, I've come to believe that men only truly fall in love (as opposed to *thinking*

they've fallen in love) with women smarter than they are.
I ought to write a learned paper on the subject. Of course,
I'd have trouble getting it published now, in light of . . .
but all that in its proper place.

"No," I finally managed. "We have to stay until they're
all gone. I've got to go back down there and retrieve the
bug."

"Why?" Chloe kept her voice down with an obvious
effort. "We've seen everything we need to see."

"But we haven't *heard*," I whispered back.

Not for the first time, I heartily cursed the nanobug I
was using, straight off the shelf of Izzy's Toy Store. It could
transmit real-time digital images of everything its pickup
was scanning. But unlike the state-of-the-art Delkasu
models, its audio recording could only be accessed by
putting the bug itself into the appropriate device and playing it. We were watching a silent film with no subtitles.

"We've got to have the audio," I continued, keeping
my whisper as low as possible. "Until we can hear what
they're saying, we won't know the plans for the actual
transfer of the goods—the information Khorat needs."

"To hell with Khorat!" hissed Chloe, who seldom swore.
"With what we know now . . ." She gestured angrily downward toward the octagonal chamber, still unable to
verbalize what we'd seen there. "We've *got* to get back
and tell—"

"—Who?" That stopped her. We had visualized ourselves triumphantly presenting the identity of the
traitor—the solution to the mystery that had baffled the
Project for the past five years—to the leader of our mission. Now . . . well, what we had seen sort of put a new
face on things.

"No, Chloe. We're just going to have to go back to the ship, be a couple of perfect little lambs until we're back on Earth, and *then* take our evidence to Novak's superiors. For that, we're going to need *all* the evidence. Besides, even if we didn't owe Khorat anything, I'd still do my damnedest to help him stop this sale from going through. I don't even have to know what the merchandise is. The mere fact that Novak wants it is enough to put me a hundred percent behind Khorat's efforts to keep her from getting it."

Judging from the look on Chloe's face, I must have let more of my true feelings show than was my habit. But she made no protest. We continued to wait, watching the screen with horrified fascination as Novak talked animatedly. I was a pretty fair lip-reader, and I mentally kicked myself for attaching the bug in such a location as to catch her at the wrong angle for using that skill.

Finally, the meeting ended. Handshaking was not a Delkasu custom, but I could tell from Novak's smile and the general aspect of things that an agreement had been reached. The Tonkuztra bigwigs filed out, accompanied by their guards. Another guard escorted Novak out the way she'd come. I deactivated the bug. We waited a few moments to be sure everyone had gone.

"Wait here," I told Chloe, still speaking in a cautious whisper. I let myself down into the antechamber, and then through the door into the big domed room. I reached up, unstuck the bug, and put it in a plastic safety casing.

I was just slipping it into my pocket when I heard the sound behind me.

To this day, I have no idea why one of the Delkasu security types had come back. Maybe he'd forgotten something. At any rate, when I whirled around he was standing in the door through which I myself had come, leveling a weapon at me. I recognized a pistol-sized paralysis beam projector—the kind of beam that had fleetingly brushed me at Seventh and F Streets in Washington, five years before. I had no desire to repeat the experience in intensified form. I raised my open hands slowly, hoping this would convey the appropriate message to a Delkar. I didn't want to spook this one, in whose face and stance I already read confused surprise at finding a human there.

My hands were still on the rise when Chloe, gripping the ledge over the doorframe with both hands, swung herself down silently into the antechamber behind the Delkar, and continuing the swing, slammed her feet into his back.

The impact sent him staggering forward. He discharged his weapon, but the beam hit the floor, possibly paralyzing some crawling insect or other. At the same instant, I launched myself at him, gripping his paralysis beamer by the barrel and bringing my right knee up into his face.

He released his weapon and fell back against Chloe, who had landed on her feet and was still trying to get her balance. They fell in a heap.

The Delkasu are small but not especially fragile. And this one was combat-trained. He shook his head to clear it, and grasped Chloe around the waist from behind, sensing that I wouldn't beam him if it meant paralyzing her as well.

She jerked her head backwards into his face, smashing him on the pointed Delkasu snout that must have still been sensitive from its encounter with my knee. He emitted a shrill yelp that my earphone didn't translate. Chloe twisted out of his grip, leaving him exposed.

Unfortunately, I wasn't familiar with this model of paralysis beamer. Furthermore, a pistol-type grip designed for a Delkasu hand was awkward to the point of impossibility for a human to use. So I didn't even try. Instead, I put as much force as I could behind a swift, artless kick to his crotch.

I've been saying "he," but as usual with the Delkasu it was hard to tell. I was banking on my initial impression of gender being correct, for Delkasu males are even more vulnerable between the legs than human ones. As it transpired, my instinct was right. With a sound halfway between a gasp and a shriek, he doubled over and lay on the floor, making like a shrimp. Taking advantage of his immobility, I fumbled with the paralysis beamer until I was able to discharge it in his direction. His writhing and groaning ceased.

"Come on!" I snapped at Chloe. Plenty of time later to compliment her on that awesome move. I ran back up the ramp, retrieved my satchel, and reactivated the contact-lens display. It was programmed for a round-trip. We started back the way we'd come.

We were out of the vast hexagonal well and on the upgrade when we heard the sounds of outraged discovery behind us. We broke into a run.

Up and up we went, into the more frequented, brightly lit areas. I began to breathe a little easier, and take only occasional looks over my shoulder.

Then, with one of those looks, I caught sight of the tall, loping figures that loomed over the Delkasu crowds.

"They've brought in the Agardir," I told Chloe. "They're behind us. Stay with me, whatever you do."

Even as I said it, I glimpsed a commotion up ahead. The crowds were roiled like a school of fish at the passage of a shark.

What had happened was obvious. The Agardir trackers had called in our location to their bosses, who had then called ahead and ordered the neighborhood wise guys to converge on our route.

With cold certainty, I knew we weren't going to make it out of those passageways. I saw no purpose to be served by telling Chloe that.

But we'd just about come far enough for me to do one not altogether valueless thing.

I waited until we came to a certain intersection of passageways that Khorat had described to us—he'd even flagged it with a flashing light in the contact-lens display, which activated when we got there. Then I grabbed Chloe's hand and pulled her to the right, down a branching passage.

"Bob!" she demanded. "What are you doing? If we get off the track . . ." Her voice trailed off. She'd been about to tell me what I already knew about the difficulty of getting the display that was guiding us to reactivate after you'd departed from that immaterial thread through the Labyrinth. But then she'd remembered what we'd been told about this last-ditch option.

Our eyes met. She understood what I'd seen no point in telling her before. And I knew she knew it. And there seemed nothing to be said. So nothing was. Instead, we clasped hands more tightly and continued along that side passage, or "alley," as I thought of it.

The flavor was different there. There was the same array of food shops, but the aromas had an even greater variety, suggesting—at least to me—an assortment of ethnic cuisines. There were also other establishments of less obvious function. One of these was a dim little narrow-fronted place with a sign Khorat had told us to look for.

I say "sign," but the legend actually floated immaterially a few inches in front of the door. It was in the standard Delkasu ideographs, which I had learned to read, although doing so was still far from second nature to me. I puzzled these out as *Antiquities of Astogra*. We ducked into the door, passing through the holographic lettering.

The Delkar behind the counter was dark in coloring even for her species, almost a blue-black. Against that backdrop, a silver tracery of tattoos showed in striking contrast. Khorat had mentioned that this kind of body-art was characteristic of the Delksau of Astogra, a culturally eccentric colony world lying within the Ekhemasu Empire.

She stared at us. (Yes, she; I was getting better at Delkasu genders.) "May I help you?" my translator rendered the Delkasu, without the quaver my ears picked up.

I did as I had been instructed. "An old friend sent us," I said carefully. This was how my earpiece had interpreted what Khorat had told us to say, and I trusted that the software would faithfully retranslate it. As I spoke, I reached into the satchel and withdrew a complex silver medallion with a purple jewel set in its center.

The shopkeeper's large Delkasu eyes grew even larger, and glowed dark amber in the dimness. She said nothing, and I thought it would probably be good form if I didn't either. Instead, I brought forth the nanobug in its plastic casing and slid it across the counter.

The Delkar swiftly palmed it out of sight. "I'm sorry. I think you must have the wrong shop." Body language that transcended species and culture screamed at me: *Get out! Quick!*

I needed no urging. If we were sighted here, linking this shop to us, all was for naught. I turned away, leaving the satchel whose contents would have revealed the kind of equipment we'd been using. The shopkeeper evidently understood, for she grabbed it and stuffed it under the counter. Chloe and I made a hasty exit and headed back for the main passageway.

As we approached it, the crowd thinned out abruptly, revealing a trio of Agardir blocking our way out of the side passage our lingering scent had led them to.

They weren't carrying paralyzers, or any other weapon that I could see. But they were products of a culture whose males were presumed to be warriors, and their species was a lot more physically formidable than the Delkasu. And they—and their anatomy—were new to us, so I'd never gotten any pointers on unarmed combat with them.

Of course, by the same token, they surely hadn't gotten any such pointers on us.

One of them stepped forward and made an unmistakable *Come!* gesture.

I motioned Chloe back, and shuffled forward, doing my best submissive number. I hoped it had a soothing effect on the Agardir, but I couldn't tell. So without further ado I pulled in my right leg and launched a flying sidekick at the Agardir's midriff.

It rocked him back, but seemed to have little effect beyond that. A second Agardir gave a thin, high-pitched cry and leaped at me like his remote predatory ancestors:

leading with his feet, their three knifelike claws fully extended.

I went to the ground (well, floor) to get under that soaring attack, landing on both hands and bringing my legs around in a hundred-and-eighty-degree sweep that cut the Agardir's descending legs out from under him. He crashed atop me. He was heavier than he looked, and his body odor was acrid. I heaved him off me, into the path of the third Agardir. This gave me time to get to my feet and back into fighting stance.

"Enough."

I swung around and saw the source of the voice, to which my earpiece had imparted a tone of testy impatience. A Delkar with the physical indicia of middle age was approaching, with several of the security guards behind him. He motioned two of them forward. I saw the weapons they carried.

To say that my blood ran cold would not only be a cliché, it would also be misleading, for it implies a state of icy calm. In fact, all I felt was a panic-stricken desire to grab Chloe and run back down the alley from which we'd come.

But it would have been useless, and it might have carried a risk of linking us with that eccentric little shop. So I held still as the Agardir—who also recognized those weapons—scrambled to their feet and got out of the way with ludicrous haste.

"Raise your hands slowly," I managed to say to Chloe. "And look as harmless as you can."

It did no good. The Tonkuztra boss gave the guards another curt gesture.

At once, I ceased to have a mind or a soul. All I had

was pain. In any meaningful sense, I ceased to be human; I was nothing more than a vessel of agony.

The neural pulsers, as Section Four had dubbed them, were a very different application of the technology that had produced the paralysis beamer. They, too, acted directly on the nervous system, but in such a way as to stimulate it into a state of transcendent pain. Every Delkasu government outlawed them . . . which, of course, meant that outlaws had them.

Above the sound of my own throat-tearing screams I heard Chloe's, and since I am trying to give as honest an account as possible, I will say that *I didn't care*. The capacity to care about another being—even Chloe—no longer existed in me. Love, like pride and dignity and honor, had been crowded out, leaving only the unendurable pain that allowed no room for anything else.

But some tiny part of me somehow clung to what I had been told: that the pain really *was* unendurable, and that the body would soon shut down rather than endure it.

Chloe's screams stopped just before shock took me.

No actual physical trauma caused the pain of the neural gun, so when I awoke it was gone. And my mind was already setting about the blessed process of forgetting how it had felt.

My brutalized nervous system was another matter. Any attempt to move my hands—the only movement I could even think about, for I was strapped down on a hard bed—resulted only in a spasm of twitches. I lay still, managing to slowly turn my head to the right, from which direction I could hear the sound of groans. Chloe was strapped into an identical bed, still in the grip of nightmares. Like me, she was naked. They'd doubtless done a very comprehensive search of our clothing, which naturally would have turned up Khorat's little trinkets. At least they'd attached catheters to prevent us from soiling the beds.

Delkasu technicians came, examined us and drugged us, all with impersonal efficiency. Time began to lose its meaning as I drifted in and out of a chemical haze.

Once, one of my lucid periods coincided with one of Chloe's. "Where are we?" she rasped dryly. She was blushing down to below her neck in her nakedness.

"I don't know," I replied on my second try, after swallowing the miniscule quantity of saliva I could summon up. "Have you told them anything?"

"No." A pause. "Not that I know of."

"Neither have I." I didn't bother to repeat her qualifier. We both knew that we could have already blurted out everything—including Khorat's involvement—in our sleep, under the irresistible compulsion of truth drugs that did not require the subject to be awake.

But then again, we might not have. So I said nothing further, given the near certainty of our room being bugged. Chloe must have figured it out as well, for she also kept quiet.

After a while, the drugs ceased, and time resumed its accustomed pace. At the same time, we found we could move our hands without inducing an uncontrollable fit of trembling. Water was brought, and some kind of tasteless food.

Soon after that, the door of our bleak little chamber slid open to admit the Delkar who had ordered the nerve pulsers used on us, followed by a quartet of his goons.

Abject terror gripped me by the guts, before I noticed that they were unarmed except for the leader himself, who carried one of the pistol-sized paralysis beamers.

"You are to be questioned," he stated without preamble. They had left us our translator earpieces. "You can go willingly, or paralyzed."

"Can't we at least have some clothes?" I demanded. Sudden inspiration: "It's a, uh, cultural imperative with us. We won't be able to give intelligent responses to questions otherwise."

Smocks were brought—even more dehumanizing than the kind you get in human hospitals, since these were scaled for Delkasu dimensions. The goons unstrapped us and helped us to our feet . . . only to have us collapse from the weakness of hunger and the sheer stiffness that had set in while we'd lain immobilized. The head Delkar impatiently sent for his culture's equivalent of wheelchairs, which floated a few inches above the floor on extremely powered-down impellers. They wobbled alarmingly under our human size and weight, and the seats were a damned uncomfortable fit for us, but we managed to get settled in, after which the goons pushed us along the featureless corridors of wherever it was we were.

We came to a small room with a table in its center. The goons maneuvered us into two chairs on one side of the table. They were modern Delkasu chairs, which meant they tried valiantly to adjust to us, but without success. The goons departed, but their boss remained, his paralysis beamer trained on us.

"The individual who is to question you will be here shortly," he informed us.

That turned out to be an understatement. Before I

could even frame a question about the nature of this individual, the door slid open to admit Renata Novak.

CHAPTER ELEVEN

At first Novak ignored us, turning instead to the Delkar with the paralysis beamer.

"You know the agreement," she said coldly. "I am to be allowed to question them alone, with no eavesdropping."

"An agreement made against my advice." The surliness came through my earpiece.

"Still, Tosava'litan made it, on behalf of the *gevroth*. Are you prepared to defy her?"

The Delakar stiffened, but spoke mildly. "No, of course not. You know how to summon assistance if you should need it." A note of sheer malice entered the translation. "You recall, of course, that the agreement on which you are relying specifies that you release us from all responsibility for your own safety and comfort if that 'assistance'

185

should become necessary." He departed, motioning to the goons to follow him.

Novak continued to ignore us as she sat down and took a small device out of her handbag. She studied its read-outs, while I considered and rejected the idea of trying anything. Clearly, it would accomplish nothing but our own deaths. Judging from what we'd just heard, Novak's hostage value would be limited.

"All right," she finally said, to herself more than to us, "they really *aren't* bugging this room." Only then did she acknowledge our presence by addressing us directly. "Well, Mr. Devaney, I see your tendency to meddle in matters that are none of your concern is unabated."

The breathtaking injustice of this overcame my resolve to just glare at her in jut-jawed silence. "In case you've forgotten, I'm the security officer. What could be more my concern than tracking down traitorous slime?"

Novak's eyes went cold and narrow, but she spoke levelly. "You also haven't lost the habit of being resentful when you ought to be grateful. If it wasn't for me, you two would be dead by now—and it wouldn't have been a nice death."

"Don't give me that. The Tonkuztra want information, not corpses."

"That's just it. The truth drugs they tried on you don't seem to work on humans—something about the body chemistry. And they had reason to believe that the drugs they *hadn't* tried would kill you. I gather the Tosava *gevroth*—that means, approximately, 'family'—has had opportunities to experiment on humans. So they were all for using old-fashioned torture on you. I persuaded them that I could get you to confide in me."

I gave a harsh laugh. "You're no damned good at this, you know. You should have told us we sang like birds under their drugs, and that you're just here to get clarification of a few details. Afterwards, you could have turned us over to your Tonkuztra masters."

Novak's jaw muscles twitched with the effort of sustaining her primness in the face of my second attempt to get a rise out of her. "They're hardly my 'masters.' At most, they're business associates—and I have every intention of terminating even that relationship as soon as the current transaction is finalized. I'm talking to you privately because I want to know how you learned of that meeting. If you'll gratify my curiosity, I'll do my best to convince them that you just got lucky, and have no knowledge worth the trouble of extracting from you. You have my word on that."

· "*Your* word?" Chloe's voice was rich with scorn. "What a joke!"

"Except that jokes are supposed to be funny," I put in. "And by the way, I don't believe for a second that little act about this room not being bugged."

"It's true. Why should I want to sell you out to the Tonkuztra?"

"Why should you want to sell out the entire human race?" Chloe's question started out defiantly rhetorical, but by the end of the sentence it had become something closely resembling a cry from the heart.

For the first time, Novak's facade cracked. "Sell out the human race? Good God, Chloe, is that really what you think I'm doing? I'm *saving* the human race!"

At first, we simply stared.

"Saving it from what?" Chloe finally ventured.

"You know perfectly well!" All the strained self-control was abruptly gone as Novak leaned forward, face flushed as though heated from within by the fire that blazed through her eyes. "The Delkasu and the other races that have learned from them have foreclosed the future. You've heard Dr. Fehrenbach's lectures about life in the galaxy: the instant one race discovered the secret of interstellar travel, it was as though a movie film had been frozen on a single frame. I suppose it could have been worse. If the Delkasu or somebody else had colonized Earth a few million years earlier, the human race wouldn't even exist, just like God knows how many unborn intelligent species that have been consigned to limbo. But that might have been more merciful. As it is, we're trapped in a universe that has no place for us. We were just a *little* too late."

"We all know this, Renata," Chloe said carefully. "It's the very problem the Project exists to cope with."

"Ha! All the Project has done is trick the Delkasu into letting us exist on sufferance."

"Isn't that a little strong? The Project has also worked to bring Earth up to the galactic technological standard so we can—"

"But we *can't*! Why am I the only one able to see that? In the long run, humanity is doomed to dwindle away into extinction in a Delkasu universe. We'll never have the scope for greatness that we need to be truly human. We're not *meant* to be insignificant! As impotent spectators of the great Delkasu epic, we'll have no incentive to go on living. But all you and I have been doing, all these years, is trying to wheedle the Delkasu into allowing us a slightly cushier state of dependency. It was all we *could* do, given the way history has worked out." With strange suddenness, Novak halted, as though afraid she'd said too much.

I stepped into the pause. "So just what is it you think you can do about 'the way history has worked out?' "

"And whatever it is," added Chloe, "how does it justify betraying the Project—and, by extension, the human race—to vermin like the Tonkuztra? If you really do think you've happened onto something that will dramatically change humanity's status, why haven't you gone to the Project's leadership with it?"

"The leadership! They're nothing but a bunch of old fogeys, hopelessly locked into the approach the Project has been using for the last twenty years. It's the only approach they know, or can imagine. They're incapable of recognizing that it's a dead end. They'd probably all die of heart failure if anyone suggested a radically new solution. No, it was up to me. I had to act on my own."

"You haven't answered Chloe's first question," I pointed out. "The one about why you've been playing footsies with the Tonkuztra. But we all know the answer to that, don't we? Your big idea requires something that the Tonkuztra have got." I kept enough presence of mind to not say *something the Tonkuztra stole from the Ekhemasu.* Khorat's involvement was the one bit of knowledge Novak didn't have, and therefore the one card I was holding. So I spoke in my most reasonable voice. "Let's make a deal. I'll tell you how we found out about your little game." (I risked a small jab to Chloe's thigh under the table, but not a side glance to see if she'd gotten the don't-act-startled-at-anything-I-say message.) "In exchange, you tell us just exactly what it is you think is so valuable it's worth buying at the price of letting the Tonkuztra in on the truth about Earth."

"You're hardly in a position to be bargaining, Devaney." Novak's trademark stiff formality was back, closing like shutters over the startling passion she'd allowed us to glimpse. "And no, you're not ready to be told the subject of this transaction. You wouldn't believe it anyway. I will tell you this much, however: you're only partly right about why I was willing to dole out some of the truth to the Tonkuztra. You see, if my plan works, it *won't matter* that the Tosava *gevroth*—or anybody else—has the information I've given them. They'll have accepted payment in worthless coin. So in the end I won't have *really* sold anyone out."

"It's a dangerous game you're playing," I remarked. "Sane people don't gamble for stakes like these."

"I take no offense at that remark because it is rooted in ignorance. The 'stakes' involved are totally beyond the comprehension of a lowlife like you."

"Maybe. But unless I'm misreading the signs, Chloe and I have thrown a monkey wrench into your plan. What happened? Did our presence at the meeting spook this Tosava mob and sour the deal?"

Novak glared. "It is only a temporary inconvenience. I was able to confirm that no other humans were missing from the ship, so you two were acting alone. And a search revealed that you had no surveillance devices. So Tosava'litan, the boss of the *gevroth*, has calmed down, and the transfer of the merchandise will proceed on schedule." She stood up abruptly. "If being told the nature of that merchandise is your price for telling me how you learned of the meeting, then I'll just have to swallow my curiosity and let the Tonkuztra question you in their own way." She started to leave, then paused. "I truly wish I could spare you this, Chloe . . . and even you, Devaney. But this is bigger than all of us. Individuals must sometimes be sacrificed to the greater good."

"Now where have I heard *that* before?" I wondered out loud. "Oh, yeah, I remember: every lunatic zealot who's ever lived."

"Renata, you know you can't get away with this," said Chloe in a tight voice. "How are you going to account for our absence? Nobody will buy an unexplained disappearance. There'll be an investigation."

"That's right," I nodded. "They'll dig and dig. And you know what's at the back of Section Two's mind whenever we investigate *anything* these days: the traitor who's been our bugbear for the last five years."

Novak looked at us, and even now I still think her look held a genuine sadness. If it didn't, she was a better actress than I believe her to have been. "Oh, no. They won't be thinking in those terms. Because, you see, they'll already know the identity of their traitor: *you*, Chloe."

Chloe and I were temporarily without the power of speech.

"I've taken the necessary steps, and prepared the necessary evidence," Novak continued, expressionless. "It will be generally believed that you betrayed the secret of the Project back in '63. I'd hoped it would be possible to tie you in, Devaney," she added as an afterthought. And, I swear to God, I could detect no trace of personal malice in her voice. "But there was no getting around the fact that the Tonkuztra had their information before you were recruited into the Project. So that incident in Washington, which was intended to exculpate me by casting me as the target of an operation of theirs, had the unintended

side effect of exculpating you as well." Her face clouded.
"Also, there was the matter of Mr. Inconnu specifically
ordering your recruitment. I still don't understand the
reason for his interest in you. But it put your actions and
motivations before that point off-limits." She turned back
to Chloe. "So it seems, Chloe, that you seduced him after
his induction into the Project. Only then did he become
an accomplice in your treason."

"You contemptible bitch." Unless my memory is completely at fault, I said it without heat, as a simple statement
of fact.

Novak ignored me. "Again, Chloe, I genuinely regret
this. I wish there was another way. You must believe that."
She turned to go.

"Whatever bogus 'evidence' you've manufactured will
never stand up," I called out after her. "Not in the long
run."

She stopped just short of the door, and her face wore
an odd, unreadable smile. "You know, Mr. Devaney, you're
almost certainly right. But it won't *matter* in the long run."
On that puzzling note, she departed. The Tonkuztra good-
humor men returned and took us back to our room.

We didn't have long to wait, which was just as well.
The food was the same unappetizing glop we'd gotten
before—doubtless some Delkasu bioengineer's idea of
what humans needed to stay alive. Admittedly, we did.
We didn't even get sick. The effect on our morale was
another matter. Come to think of it, that might just possibly have been intentional.

Worse than the food was our inability to talk openly. I
knew that silence about Khorat was more important than

ever, and I couldn't even tell Chloe why. I could only hope she had figured it out for herself. (She had, as I need hardly add.)

The transfer of the merchandise will proceed on schedule. Those words of Novak's were all I had left to hold on to. They meant that all we had been through hadn't been for nothing. The information we'd left with the shopkeeper was still good . . . as long as Novak and her "associates" didn't find out we'd left it there, and change their plans accordingly.

So we passed our time in a state of strained awkwardness, unable to speak out loud what we both knew. In our ignorance of the capabilities of the surveillance we knew we were constantly under, we dared not even risk an exchange of whispers in the ear.

Then, with startling lack of warning, our door slid open to admit a unit of armed Delkasu, who ushered us out and led us down a series of corridors and up a lift tube. We finally emerged into the Antyova-light of what looked like—and quite probably was—a public aircar port. In a place like this, non-Delkasu were no novelty at all, and our escorts attracted no attention as they herded us across the tarmac with somewhat more subtlety than they'd heretofore displayed. I considered the idea of making a conspicuous public escape attempt, only to reject it. As you may have gathered by now, I am not the stuff of which martyrs are made.

We were taken to a large aircar—airbus might be a better term, except that it means something altogether different to you—and locked into a rear compartment that could have held six passengers. We squeezed into two of the Delkasu-sized seats . . . none too soon, for the vehicle lifted off without warning. The compartment had two small windows, and once the aircar leveled off we stood up and looked out avidly.

It was evidently the same city we'd been in all along, for the central plaza and the streets radiating from it were visible off to one side, like a spoked wheel etched deeply into the expanses of towering buildings. But then that comforting bit of familiarity was gone, and we were passing over a cityscape whose awesomeness was gradually swallowed by its endlessness. It began to remind me of driving across Kansas: you drive and drive but feel like you're getting nowhere because the grasslands to either side are exactly like those you saw an hour ago.

Eventually, though, the city began to thin out into suburbs nestled among hills clothed in the foliage of trees imported so many centuries ago from lost Kasava. Not even Antyova II was solid city from pole to pole. Soon, even the suburbs began to fall behind, and the hills grew more rugged.

Chloe and I looked at each other in the silence that had become a matter of cautious habit. By now, whenever we were both thinking the same thing, we knew it without the need for words. And we both had a pretty good idea of what had happened. Novak would hardly have been able simply to ignore our disappearance. She must have had to go through the motions of notifying the Selangava authorities, who in turn would have launched an investigation, if only on the general principle of running a taut ship. The Tosava *gevroth* had decided to move us from the city to some private place where we could be dealt with at leisure.

Not knowing the details of what we were in for just made it worse.

We were thinking about it when the aircar banked sharply, almost making us lose our balance.

"Hang on!" I yelled at Chloe, before my mind had consciously formed the words *evasive action*.

It was too late. The aircar shuddered and lurched, and a deafening clang reverberated through it. We were thrown to the deck. A hard corner of an armrest caught me behind the right ear. A sunburst exploded behind my eyes and dissolved into a shower of stroboscopic stars. As consciousness ebbed, I felt the aircar begin to slant sharply downward.

When I awoke, I was lying on my back, in late-afternoon daylight. Chloe's face was hovering over me. So was Khorat's.

"What . . . what . . . ?" I tried to sit up, only to subside as a god-awful headache flared.

"Lie still," Chloe said urgently. "You took a nasty bump on the head.

"Our time is limited, though," Khorat demurred. "As soon as he is able to move . . ."

"Yeah. I'll be okay." I tried again to rise, more slowly this time and holding my head lest it split apart. I looked around.

We were in an upland valley. The vegetation would doubtless have fascinated the Section Three people. I was more interested in the big aircar we had ridden, now obviously the worse for wear and lying canted on the ground, and the smaller but businesslike aircar that rested close to it. But most interesting of all were the Delkasu figures moving about. I automatically reached for a gun that wasn't there.

"Relax," said Chloe, grasping my arm. "These are the good guys. Khorat brought them."

"But . . ." I gave my pain-ridden head a shake and ordered it to function. "But Khorat, I thought you said your organization was acting without the knowledge of your Delkasu bosses."

"Oh, these are not representatives of the Khemava Empire," Khorat assured me. "They are native to Antyova II." A note of embarrassment entered the synthetic voice. "In point of fact, they belong to a Tonkuztra organization, the Osak *gevroth*."

Chloe saw my expression. "Well, *relatively* good guys," she hedged.

"Perhaps I'd better explain," Khorat began.

"Yeah, that's one way to put it."

"The shopkeeper from Astogra delivered the surveillance device to us, which enabled us to learn when the sale was to be finalized. She also told us of your capture. This placed us under a moral obligation to rescue you if possible, although the recovery of our stolen property had to come first. For both purposes, we used the services of the Osak, a *gevroth* which is also well established among the Delkasu of Khemava. My organization has had dealings with them before, and they owe us a few favors. Furthermore, they are bitter enemies of the Tosava *gevroth*, and were more than willing to act for us in this matter."

I nodded, remembering what I knew about the snake pit that was the Tonkuztra. They'd never had a Lucky Luciano to pull them together into one big syndicate. The various families were still grimly waging vendettas dating back to the times before the Delkasu had left Kasava.

"Did they block the sale?" I asked. "And did they get Novak?" Chloe, I noted, did not react to my second question with the disapproving look she once would have given me.

"The answer to the first is yes. But as for your human traitor . . . no. The Osak operatives struck just before she was to arrive. She must have found corpses and nothing else."

"Must have been a nice surprise for her," said Chloe in tones of deep satisfaction.

"Subsequently," Khorat continued, "our Osak associates used their own sources of information to determine where you were being held. You were unreachable there, and would have been even more so at the place to which you were being taken. So the only window of opportunity was while you were in transit between the two, over this largely uninhabited region. Still, the Osak *gevroth* had grave misgivings; shooting down an aircar is the sort of thing law enforcement authorities tend to take seriously. I am afraid we had to call in almost all the favors they owe us." Khorat paused as though expecting an expression of remorse for all the trouble we'd been. I felt no inclination to oblige him. "And now, they are in a hurry to depart. So, if you are ready to travel . . ."

"Wait a minute, Khorat! What happens to Chloe and me now."

"Admittedly, that presents a problem. You can hardly go back to your ship, where Novak is doubtless in no particularly forgiving mood." I decided the Ekhemasu *did* have a sense of humor, of sorts . . . or maybe the translator software did. "But do not concern yourselves. You have placed us in your debt. We ourselves must depart for

Khemava shortly, but we will arrange for the Osak *gevroth* to keep you concealed here on Antyova II until berths become available on a ship bound for your world."

"You don't understand, Khorat," said Chloe. "We *can't* go back to Earth now. Renata Novak will get there first . . . which means there'll be a shoot-on-sight order out for us."

"Yeah," I agreed. "Novak is setting Chloe up to take the rap for her own treason, with me playing comic relief."

For a space, Khorat was silent and immovable. One of the Delkasu approached, in an attitude of unconcealed impatience . . . only to slink off at an absent gesture from Khorat. I began to suspect that the elderly Ekhemar, either individually or through his mysterious "organization," exercised more authority than he chose to admit to. Finally, he turned his huge, difficult-to-read eyes on us.

"Very well. As I said, you have placed us under an obligation. Obviously, we cannot take you with us when our diplomatic mission departs. I will, however, arrange other transportation for you from here to Khemava, where I will meet you."

"Khemava?" Chloe echoed. "Your world?"

"Yes. It will have to be arranged without the knowledge of my government, of course. But there seems to be nowhere else where I can guarantee your safety. You will not find it the most comfortable environment imaginable, but I have reason to think your species can probably adapt to it."

"Don't ever try for a second career as a travel agent," I groused.

Chloe shushed me. "Khorat, I'm sure your planet is a

marvelous place, and perfectly comfortable, but . . . well . . ."

"You need not attempt to spare my sensibilities." The translator registered amusement. "I know what you're trying to say. You can never be at home there. That is perfectly natural. And of course the long-range objective is to return you to your own world. I am only proposing this as a temporary expedient until such time as a return becomes practical. It is, I am afraid, all I have to offer."

Chloe and I looked at each other. There seemed no scope for discussion. "Okay," I sighed. "Let's do it."

We crowded into the Osak aircar, to the comically evident relief of its crew, who'd been casting anxious glances at the sky for police aircars. As we lifted off, commands were given, and the wreck of the larger vehicle below was consumed in an eye-hurtingly intense explosion.

"Hey, Khorat," I finally broke the silence. "Now that we're going to be seeing a lot of each other, maybe you could let us in on just exactly what this is all about. What *was* it that Novak was trying to buy from the Tosava *gevroth*?" I gave it my best effort at suavity. "I hope you don't think I'm imposing on the 'obligation' that you yourself were gracious enough to acknowledge just now."

"No, I don't think anything of the sort. And no, I won't tell you. You're not ready for that knowledge."

"Renata Novak told us exactly the same thing," Chloe informed him pointedly.

"Then she was, for once, absolutely right. Where she went wrong was in failing to recognize that *she* isn't ready for it either. No one is."

"Except, of course, you and your organization," said Chloe with some asperity.

"Including us. But we unavoidably find ourselves in the position of being its custodians. That is simply a matter of *blank*." The *blank* was just that: dead silence as the translator software rejected a concept as untranslatable. "But," Khorat resumed thoughtfully, "perhaps I *will* tell you . . . later. Perhaps you will come to be ready."

INTERLUDE

Harvey Langston's eyes were like saucers. "Are you saying the identity of this traitor is known?"

"Yes. It's been known since 1968 or '69. It turned out to be someone nobody would ever have suspected in a million years. Came as quite a shock to a lot of people in the Project, I'm told." The President looked thoughtful. "I've often wondered what the motive could have been. I sometimes think it must have been like that guy Hanson who was spying for the Russians in the 1990s. He wasn't like that slime mold Aldrich Ames a few years earlier, who was in it purely for the money. No, he did it for peanuts. Nor was he a fanatical Communist ideologue like the Rosenbergs; he was a very conservative Catholic, and anyway he went on working for the Russians after they'd given the Soviet regime the bum's rush. Instead, by all accounts it was pure game-playing on his part. He was a social zero who was driven to prove he was cleverer than everyone else. Maybe the traitor within the Project who let the secret slip to the Tonkuztra was like that: stringing them along, never telling them everything. But that's all just speculation on my part. No one really knows."

"Why not? If this individual was caught back in the late 1960s—"

"Not 'caught.' Just identified, and never found."

"But . . . that means this traitor could have been taken away by the, uh, Tonkuztra, and told them more. Or, perhaps, been made to tell them more." Langston spoke hesitantly, for he knew nothing about intelligence work, and was incapable of learning because no one ever learns a subject to whose very existence he is philosophically opposed. His campaign promise to abolish the CIA had been heartfelt, even though Sal DiAngelo and Sidney Goldman had taken pains to reassure everyone that Congress would never really let him get away with it.

"True," the President allowed. "Then again, the traitor might also be dead. To this day, the Project doesn't know how much of the truth has been compromised. So it's proceeded on the assumption that there have been no further leaks . . . and so far, that assumption seems to have panned out. There has been no change in Earth's diplomatic status, and no apparent change in the attitude of the various Delkasu governmental and corporate poohbahs. This, in spite of the fact that the whole thing occurred at a moment when the secret was uniquely vulnerable."

"What do you mean?"

"The first Apollo landing was in 1969. Remember what I was saying earlier about the problem of concealing Farside Base from the human race's official space-exploration programs? Well, it worked both ways. Those space programs had to be concealed from the Delkasu, who thought we'd left such fantastically outmoded stuff behind. The Project has always used the excuse of traffic control to make damned sure no galactic ships have been arriving or departing at the right time to observe any howling anachronisms. But if the Tonkuztra or anybody else had been casting a suspicious eye on Earth around that time, the Apollo landing would have stood out like a Spanish galleon in what was supposed to be a modern naval base.

"In short, the deception seems to be holding up. The Project isn't about to look a gift horse in the mouth by questioning it. Instead, they've pushed ahead with the other half of their mission."

"You mean the introduction of galactic technology?"

"Right. In fact, they've accelerated it as much as they dare, taking advantage of what seems to be a reprieve as long as it lasts. They've tried to soften the societal impact as much as possible by releasing concepts into the culture before the actual 'invention' of the technologies. For example, ever since shortly before the turn of the century the neural-net computer has been something 'everybody knows' is just around the corner. Well, it's about to become reality. Unfortunately, there's really no way to prepare people for the revolution in theoretical physics that's coming in a few years. But the average person won't even be aware of it until later, when the practical applications begin to appear. And the Project has been taking steps, for decades now, to get notions like reactionless drives and artificial gravity firmly established in the popular consciousness. By now, they're part of the generic 'special effects' visualization of the future, and never mind that physicists say they're impossible." The President chuckled evilly. "Those Hollywood sleaze-buckets have no conception of how they've been subtly manipulated."

Langston sought to catch up. "So . . . the Prometheus Project has proceeded since 1969 as though nothing had happened?"

"Pretty much. Of course . . . you have to wonder what's been going on since then, out there in the galaxy, in places we don't even know about. . . ."

PART THREE:
1969

CHAPTER TWELVE

The Khemava system was an incredibly wealthy one, even though it consisted of only a few planets huddled around a heat-stingy orange sun.

In part, this was a matter of lucky breaks in planetary formation. The innermost world was like people back home still believed Mercury to be: tidally locked so that one hemisphere permanently faced its sun. It therefore had a "twilight zone" between its hot and cold sides, where mining of its abundant heavy elements was practical. (In reality, according to Dr. Fehrenbach, Mercury is "resonance-locked" into a day precisely two-thirds of its year, a consequence of having a highly eccentric orbit very close to the Sun. A lot of science fiction was due to become obsolete in a few years, when that fact became generally known.) Next outward was the Ekhemasu homeworld of Khemava. Then came a dense, mineral-rich asteroid belt where the Titius-Bode formulation said a third planet should orbit. That planet's gestation had been aborted by the proximity of the actual third planet: a gas giant more massive than Jupiter, glowing with the heat of its own gravitational compression. That heat, though insufficient to ignite the fusion fires of a sun, warmed the great planet's inner moons. One of those moons was bigger than Mars, big enough to hold an atmosphere (complete with an ozone layer to block the radiation that sleeted from the primary planet) and liquid water, in which life had arisen. Minimal planetary engineering had been required to turn that moon into a second home for the Ekhemasu race.

That last gives a hint as to why I said that the system's wealth was only partially a dispensation of cosmic chance. The Ekhemasu had never discovered the secret of interstellar flight; it wasn't the sort of thing their sciences tended toward. So they had remained in their own treasure-house system, and by now that system was as much their handiwork as an accidental by-product of the blind forces of astrophysics. They and their works pervaded it to a greater extent than I could imagine ever being possible for humanity in the Solar system.

This had something to do with their sheer numbers. The Ekhemasu were herbivores, descended from herd animals, and they tolerated—no, enjoyed—a degree of crowding that would have driven humans to the ugliest manifestations of mass psychosis. Planet II was a smaller world than Earth, only about six thousand miles in diameter, with seas rather than oceans, and vast expanses of desert. But it nonetheless held tens of billions of these large beings: a dense, orderly, incredibly productive hive, providing the foundation on which the Delkasu had erected their "Ekhemasu Empire."

But that was only part of it. The other part was the length of time they had been at it—a history stretching back over scores of thousands of years.

You can maybe get some inkling of it if you're an American who's been to the Mediterranean and seen a place like Rome where buildings have arisen on the foundations of earlier civilizations until it's more like a geological formation than a city, or the Greek islands which have been terraced and cultivated so long that they are as much artifacts as geographic features. In such places, the very ground seems to exude an aura of thousands and thousands of lives that have worked, loved, hated, given birth, killed and died for millennia, until every square inch must surely be psychically charged. Khemava is like that, only more so—much more so. Even I could feel it, despite belonging to a different species . . . indeed, to a species that had evolved in a different spiral arm. So long is their history that the giant satellite of Planet III is much the same as Khemava itself, for the Ekhemasu colonized it before the Sumerians dreamed up the idea of keeping records on clay tablets. (At least I'm told it's much the same; I've never been there.)

It wasn't until later that I learned all this. Chloe and I arrived in the Khemava system as concealed cargo aboard a ship belonging to a legitimate front corporation owned by Khorat's Tonkuztra buddies of the Osak *gevroth*. Reasonably comfortable cargo, I must admit, thanks to Khorat's arrangements. Granted, we had to eat computer-formulated human-type synthetic rations. And the ship's brain gradually altered the day/night cycle to the ninety-six-plus-hour one of Khemava—but that was actually a more convenient one for us, as it came to just about four Earth days. And otherwise, the environmental parameters of humanity and the Delkasu were so very similar that it was no worse than the time we'd previously spent in hiding on Antyova II under the sheltering Osak wing. That time had lasted for months, Earth time, and then the voyage to Khemava took weeks. For all that time we had a great deal of privacy, under the incurious care of aliens who were keeping us healthy as part of a business transaction.

So, astute reader, it's probably time to take up a subject about which I just know you've been wondering. . . .

"No, Bob!" Chloe gasped, coming up for air after kiss number something-or-other. She sat up abruptly, swung her legs over the side of the Delkasu-sized bunk, drew her smock (the only term I can think of for the sleeping garment our hosts had provided), and released a gust of breath.

I gave a sigh of my own as I sat up beside her. A bunk the size of a love seat (*ouch!*) made intimacy unavoidable. Soon I had slid an arm around her shoulders and was nuzzling her neck. She started to respond, then stiffened.

"No!" she repeated, and stood up abruptly, shivering. "You know we can't. And you know why."

I fell back on the bunk with a groan of frustration. "Yeah, I know . . . I think."

At first we'd been restrained by the presence of aliens, but our inhibitions had gradually dissolved in the face of those aliens' obvious disinterest in our behavior. They'd finally acceded to our request for separate rooms, without really understanding it. (Social customs designed to protect females—and, more importantly in some societies, their reputations—from the sexual aggressiveness of physically stronger males were foreign to the Delkasu.) But that, too, had been insufficient. In the end, nature had taken its course . . . but not to its logical conclusion.

It had been difficult for both of us—probably more so for me than for her. In the end, she'd granted me physical release in ways that only made the longing for the ultimate consummation worse, but which at least did not run the risk which she was adamantly unwilling to take. And in truth, I really *did* understand.

Now, standing with her back turned, she explained once again, speaking as much to herself as to me.

"I will not bring a child into the kind of life we're looking at. We don't know how long we're going to be on Khemava, where we're going to be the only two humans. We don't know if we'll *ever* get back to Earth. In which case, when we die our child would be alone among aliens. We have no right to make that kind of decision in the name of an unborn human being who never asked for such a life."

"And the nearest human contraceptives are umpty-ump thousand light-years away," I nodded, staring at the overhead. "So where does that leave us?"

"I don't know," she said in a voice that could barely be heard.

I know what you're thinking. Forget it. In those days, abortion had yet to achieve the legal and social acceptance you take for granted. Chloe wasn't Catholic, nor even noticeably religious; she was perfectly willing to prevent conception, had we possessed the means. But terminating pregnancy afterwards was something else again—something she would not and could not contemplate. And I wonder how many women of the oh-so-liberated later generations would have been willing to put their bodies—and the fetuses carried in their bodies—at the disposal of aliens for such a purpose. Especially considering that there was no assurance that the aliens would know what they were doing . . .

So as usual I stood up and quietly left for my own room, pretending I didn't hear her muffled sobs.

So matters stood when we landed on Khemava.

Khorat was as good as his word. He met our freighter at the vast spaceport outside Khemava's imperial capital of Sakandreoun.

It was a completely clandestine meeting, of course. For the purpose of getting us through the bureaucratic rituals of landing, we'd been transferred to a large modular transport unit—the interstellar equivalent of the cargo containers that you take for granted but which in those days were still causing the longshoremen's union to get its undies in a bunch. It had been secretly equipped with life support, but there was no more nonsense about separate rooms. Fortunately, we weren't in it for long. And for part of that time we stayed strapped into the well-padded (but, of course, uncomfortably small) couches that had been provided, sparing ourselves bruises or worse as our container was shunted about, finally coming to rest in a warehouse along with the rest of whatever it was that was being shipped from Antyova to Khemava.

It was only then that a signal light flashed over our

heads, and the access hatch clamshelled open to admit a harsh artificial lighting.

Two beings stood silhouetted in the glare. One was a Delkar—presumably an Osak operative, fidgeting with what I took to be eagerness to wash his hands of us. Beside him loomed an Ekhemar.

"Hi, Khorat," I said, even though I couldn't make out individual features.

"Greetings." My earpiece produced the voice the software had assigned to Khorat. "No discourtesy intended, but we are rather in a hurry. So if you will come this way . . ."

Khorat took his leave of the Delkar and hustled us through the warehouse, which was of enormous extent. He was in a hurry, and only the low gravity enabled us to keep up with him despite chronic shortness of breath in the thin dry air. We boarded an aircar whose ports were closed up lest anyone should observe the likes of us. The cabin held furnishings designed to accommodate both Delksau and Ekhemasu. We sort of fell between the two extremes, and there was no seating that really suited us. So we stood up, held on to stanchions, and watched the viewscreens as the aircar rose from the warehouse floor and soared through hangarlike doors into the protracted late afternoon of the orange Khemava sun, under a royal blue sky.

The cityscape that unfolded beneath us was an interesting contrast to the one we'd observed on Antyova II. Sakandreoun—a Delkasu name—had been founded alongside an immemorially ancient Ekhemasu city with which it had gradually merged, supplanting the original name . . . which, however, could still be heard in certain old districts where the alien rulers seldom ventured. So the gleaming towers favored by the Delkasu reigned unchallenged only in the quarter they themselves had founded. Elsewhere, their works formed a glittery, brittle-seeming encrustation atop an architecture that was difficult to tell apart from mountain ranges until one got close enough to observe its symmetry. Come to think of it, that architecture was greater than the relatively wimpy mountain ranges to which this planet (only about forty percent Earth's mass, hence a smaller molten core and less in the way of plate tectonics) had given birth. It was the kind of monumental masonry we humans think of in connection with our earliest civilizations—pyramids, ziggurats, and colossal sculpture—only on a scale beyond belief. It was as much a part of the planet's structure as anything produced by geology.

Any day, it seemed, the Delkasu additions—artificial, evanescent, irrelevant—might melt away, or crack apart and shiver into a cloud of crystalline dust, and vanish like the rapidly fading memory of a dream.

We flew on, and the works of the Delkasu grew sparser, until our aircar seemed to have taken us backwards in time and we were flying over the Old Khemava. Eventually, even that thinned out, and we entered the outermost outskirts I could now recognize as having provided the inspiration for the holo projection I'd seen on Antyova II, complete with the canals stretching away into the desert.

We followed one of those canals westward out into regions of tawny and ochre desolation, broken only by the canal itself and occasional oases from whose foliage peered buildings of unguessable antiquity, often fashioned into the forms of gigantic stylized Ekhemasu. Then even those grew fewer, and the long afternoon wore on toward dusk. Eventually, we glimpsed a range of mountains against the bloated, slowly westering sun . . . and one mountain in particular.

As I've mentioned, this low-gravity planet possessed relatively few of the mountain-building forces that convulsed Earth and similar worlds. But the mountains it did give birth to occasionally reared skyward to great altitudes, by grace of that same low gravity. Such a specimen grew slowly in the forward viewscreen. It had the look of age and weathering typical on that world, where mountain-formation took place only at very long intervals. But the eons had been powerless to diminish such a titan by very much; it still towered over its fellows in lonely pride.

As we approached, it became clear that the great mountain was part of a spur of the main range, rising above foothills whose bleakness was relieved only by wind-stunted trees very different from this world's tall, willowy norm. The aircar banked to starboard, and we proceeded over that desolation of low hills and rock outcrops, drawing closer to the mountain that was the monarch of this austere realm.

Then we rounded a curving ridge, and with startling suddenness a vista opened up before us which was clearly the work of conscious intelligence but which, like so much of this world's architecture, blended with the landscape in a continuum rendered seamless by the passage of millennia.

It was a kind of box canyon that had been sculpted into colonnaded terraces, rising to the base of the great mountain. Wide ramps led gently up from one terrace to another. We landed on the uppermost terrace, before a facade that had, it seemed, been carved out of the stone of the mountain whose cliff walls reared up above it to the zenith. That facade's architectural motif could not speak to us across the chasm of alienness. We could only stand in awed silence before its soul-shaking monumentality.

"Khorat," Chloe finally said, "you're not going to tell us that you've kept this place concealed from the Delkasu, are you?"

"Of course not. They are quite well aware of its existence, and of what it is: the headquarters of the organization I have mentioned to you before."

I forced myself to ignore the surroundings and think straight. "But in that case, how can this organization be a secret?"

"I never said it was." Khorat was at his most maddeningly bland.

"I don't suppose you could tell us the name of this organization of yours."

Khorat paused. "The name in my own language would mean nothing to you . . . as it means nothing to the Delkasu, who therefore simply use a form of it in their own language." He spoke a word which my unaided ears heard as *Medjavar*. My earpiece was silent, for it was untranslatable.

"But what *is* it?" Chloe persisted. "You've told us it isn't a revolutionary cabal."

There was a long silence in the earpieces before Khorat responded. "We go back rather a long way . . . approximately thirty thousand of your years. At that time," he continued into our stunned silence, "our industrial revolution had reached about the point yours has reached at present, with the first computers making their harmless-seeming debut. Certain of our thinkers recognized with great clarity that specific trends, projected to their logical conclusions, held the potential to transform society into something unrecognizable—and repellent. They organized for the purpose of combating these trends and preserving the world in a natural state—broadly defined to include the natural accretions produced over time by a tool-using race. To a great extent, we have succeeded."

"And thereby made possible that world's conquest by the Delkasu, who observed no such limitations," I said quietly.

Chloe drew a breath and shot me a glare. But Khorat's equanimity was unruffled. "Actually, that would almost certainly have happened anyway. Advanced technology does not, in itself, guarantee military victory. As descendants of herbivorous herd animals, we have no aptitude for war. But even if you are correct, an ephemeral alien overlordship is a small price to pay for averting the future we foresaw." The old Ekhemar's voice took on a tone that sent a tingle up my spine even in cybernetic rendition. "And in the realm of such forecastings, our science is far more advanced than yours, or even that of the Delkasu."

"And the Delkasu permit you to continue to function?" Chloe queried.

"Oh, yes. You see, they have a well-established policy of noninterference with the social patterns of a world which provides the economic underpinnings of their 'Ekhemasu Empire.' It is a case of—"

"—Not killing the goose that lays the golden eggs," I supplied.

I have no idea how the translator software rendered

that. But after a brief pause, Khorat resumed. "Precisely. They think of us as a local religious sect. In this they are mistaken. But it is hardly our responsibility to correct their misconception."

"You mean," said Chloe, in tones of undisguised incredulity, "that they don't even keep tabs on this place? Not even from orbit?"

"No. Oh, naturally their security agencies' satellites maintain a surveillance of the planet's surface. But except when they are actually engaged in an investigation with a specific target, the imagery is merely scanned from time to time as a matter of perfunctory bureaucratic routine. This place receives no special attention. As a matter of fact, our arrival here was planned with some care to coincide with a time period when no such satellite would be overhead to observe the disembarkation of beings with your rather distinctive appearance. That time period is about to draw to a close. So if we may proceed inside . . ."

We passed through colonnades and archways that were vast even on the Ekhemasu scale, and entered a new world.

CHAPTER THIRTEEN

At first, we diligently kept track of the length of our stay on Khemava, multiplying each of the local days by 4.083 to get the number of Earth days with mathematical exactitude. Then we just rounded it off to four. Then we stopped altogether. There seemed no point, living as we were in a dreamlike state where time had no meaning.

It wasn't that we were acutely miserable. Not at all. Aside from a few dehydration symptoms which we soon got over, Khorat's prediction that we would adapt to his planet's environment panned out. And our quarters, in the labyrinthine warren that had been hollowed out of the mountain over the ages, were nothing if not spacious. They were even comfortable—at least after our hosts succeeded in knocking together some human-compatible furniture. Even the food wasn't too bad. We had to continue consuming the nutritionally sufficient glop, since it contained the vitamins we needed. But we could, and did, supplement it with the food products of Khemava, which were often quite tasty in a vegetarian sort of way. And after the Ekhemasu came to understand the effect of ethanol on the human nervous system, they produced a kind of bathtub gin that was more or less passable. (Not passable enough that there was any danger of me, much less Chloe, succumbing to the temptation to overindulge in the stuff.)

No, the problem was the lack of any accustomed reference points. I doubt if I can make you really understand it; you've never been in a place where *everything* was designed by an alien culture for a species of unhuman size and shape. It does odd things to your sense of reality.

Also, there was the matter of language. There was no real communications problem, for when dealing with us the denizens of this place routinely wore the pendants which produced the Ekhemasu Empire's dialect of Common Delkasu. But among themselves, they generally spoke in their own ancient language. So except when we ourselves were being addressed directly, our earpieces remained silent, and the colossal halls and galleries held no sound except incomprehensible alien murmurs

At least Chloe and I had each other to cling to. More and more, I found myself agreeing with her resolve not to put a child at risk of being left all alone in this place.

We also had diversions. The Medjavar had the schedules of the imperial surveillance satellites down pat. (Not that those satellites were really much of a concern, given the cursory quality of the local cops' monitoring.) So there were frequent periods when we could explore outside. We also had unlimited access to virtual excursions around the world of Khemava and also back through its history, and the history of many worlds. Chloe was in her element, though often in an agony of frustration at her inability to share this cornucopia of new knowledge with her colleagues back on Earth. Even I found it easy to lose myself in unimagined worlds and ages.

In addition, we saw Khorat from time to time. He had quite a few demands on his time, what with his official position in the Imperial bureaucracy and his unofficial one with the Medjavar. But he periodically dropped by the Sanctuary, as it was called—the Delkasu-ized Ekhemasu name was unpronounceable—on Medjavar business. To a strictly limited extent, he was willing to talk to us about that business. Thus we began to learn more about how the Medjavar did what they did.

For example, Khorat's imperial employers were well aware of his membership in the Medjavar, which they regarded as simply a picturesque native religious society. They did not know the identities of all the Medjavar members who worked for them, like some of those who had been part of the diplomatic mission on Antyova II. In fact, they had no conception of the extent to which their officialdom—largely staffed by native Ekhemasu, except at the most exalted levels—was permeated by the Medjavar.

It was an old story for the Medjavar. For tens of thousands of years they concealed the full extent of their numbers, activities and influence as they had nudged their own civilization ever so gently in what they considered the right direction. (Even now I'm not sure if I agree with them about that direction's rightness. But my misgivings are surpassingly irrelevant.) For them, the coming of the Delkasu had been merely a historical hiccup, albeit a rather large and noisy one. After they'd learned to play the game by Delkasu rules, they'd played it with a skill developed over time spans the Delkasu had almost as much trouble grasping as we humans did.

All this we learned while conversing with Khorat during his occasional visits. In the meantime, I continued—if only from sheer stubbornness—to try to draw him out concerning that which had been stolen from the Medjavar, and which Renata Novak had wanted so much.

"So, Khorat," I drawled to him one day, with a studied casualness to which I doubted the translator software would do justice, "I don't suppose you've heard any more about Novak?"

He gave me an unreadable look. We were on the uppermost terrace of the Sanctuary's stepped facade, sitting beside a balustrade on the Ekhemasu cushions to which I'd adjusted but would never really grow accustomed. We were alone, for Chloe was inside, absorbed with some new marvel Khorat had brought back from unknown stars. A few especially bright specimens of those stars were visible overhead against a late-afternoon sky that was shading toward ultramarine. The thin air held the seductive quietness of Khemava's desert regions, and I fancied I could hear rushing water in the canal on the far side of the mountain.

"Why do you ask?" he finally inquired.

"Oh, just curious. After all, she's an old friend . . ."

"Not for the first time, I find myself doubting your sincerity."

I didn't bother to dispute the point. "Besides, I can't help wondering how sure you are that you've really put paid to her little deal with the Tosava *gevroth*."

The hushed afternoon seemed to grow even quieter. "What do you mean?" asked Khorat, in a tone whose expressionlessness was not due to a deficiency of the translator.

"Well . . . blame it on my background, but I can't help but wonder. It's pretty clear that what she was buying from them was some form of information—diagrams or instructions or something. You say you got the computer disc or whatever on which it was recorded. But wouldn't the Tosava have made copies?"

Khorat's body language eloquently displayed relief from sudden tension. "Oh, do not concern yourself with that. One of the terms of their arrangement was that Novak was to get the original, and that no copies were to be retained. Otherwise, it would have been no use to her, insasmuch as—" The Ekhemar halted so abruptly that his flat herbivore's teeth almost clicked together.

I pretended not to notice. "All well and good. But where I come from, types like the Tosava aren't exactly noted for keeping their word."

"Actually, the Tonkuztra families have a certain tradition of living up to the letter of bargains that have been finalized according to certain prescribed formulas. Otherwise, they wouldn't be able to do business at all. And in this case, our sources of information suggest that the Tosava were quite willing to comply. As I previously intimated, they had some inkling of what they were dealing with, and felt a certain relief at knowing that it would never become common knowledge, but rather would be the exclusive property of a culture they deemed too primitive to do any harm with it. They therefore wrote a condition of their own into the contract: that Novak would never let the secret go any further. She, we understand, was entirely agreeable to this."

I leaned back on my cushions. Clearly, after his one small slip—which told me nothing I could make use of—Khorat was not about to let any information be wormed out of him. "So," I mused, "the information is now securely back in your hands . . . unless, that is, it gets stolen again."

"The probability of that is small." A note of complacency entered Khorat's tone.

"Still . . . it happened before."

"Once. We had fallen into laxness. It will not happen again. The material in question is here at the Sanctuary, where it can be kept under tight security at all times."

I considered this. "Still, it would be simple for you to eliminate all possibility of its ever being compromised again."

"What do you mean? How?"

"Destroy it! You know: wipe the database clean, make a bonfire of the blueprints or whatever. . . ." My voice died as I saw the effect my words were having on Khorat.

I had made some progress toward being able to "read" the Ekhemasu in general and Khorat in particular. But now he was in the grip of an emotion I had never seen before. I can only say that if I'd been looking at a human I would have sworn he was making a physical effort to control his visceral revulsion at a suggestion so indecent as to lie beyond the pale of obscenity. Of course I know that's like translating German by the if-only-it-were-English system. But whatever it was, it was so different from Khorat's usual *persona* as to be alarming.

"Uh, Khorat," I ventured, "I hope I haven't inadvertently given offense."

The old Ekhemar gave a final shudder and took a deep breath. "No, I suppose I am not really offended. You cannot be expected to understand the philosophy which the Medjavar have followed for several times longer than the entire recorded history of your race. Let me try to explain.

"As you know, we have always sought to influence— and, if possible, control—the dissemination of dangerous knowledge, in order to steer society away from undesirable paths—"

"As defined by yourselves."

The software must have accurately reproduced my tone. Khorat's huge eyes held an unreadable expression. "You've never been altogether comfortable with that, have you?"

"No, not altogether." Something in those eyes compelled honesty. "Maybe it's just that I grew up in a society which makes something of a fetish of freedom of information." *And which takes a dim view of people playing God*, I retained enough tact not to add. "But has the possibility ever occurred to you people that you just might be wrong sometimes about what knowledge is 'dangerous' and which paths are 'undesirable?' "

"As a matter of fact, we are most sensible of our own fallibility. It is for that very reason that we have always observed an inflexible rule: knowledge may be concealed, but it must never be *obliterated*. We regard ourselves not as the proprietors of knowledge but rather as its custodians, holding it in trust in case later events or discoveries prove us wrong. Thus any mistakes we make need not be permanent in their effects." Khorat paused, as though seeking for words to express something which, for him, required no words. "Whenever any item of knowledge is lost, a potential aspect of the future is foreclosed forever. To do this deliberately would *truly* be to play God!"

I blinked in surprise, for without any prompting from me Khorat had come out with a Delkasu phrase the software had translated by that particular English expression. Maybe, I decided, he wasn't as insensitive as I'd supposed to the kind of concerns that had been bothering me.

"So," I asked quietly, "you're prepared to run the risk of leaving . . . whatever this is lying around?"

"If you must put it that way. However, the 'risk' is so small as to be ignorable." Serenely: "Nothing can go wrong."

Why was I even surprised when, the following night, the Sanctuary was raided?

By "the following night" I mean the next twenty-four-point-something-hour night of Khemava. For me and for Chloe, it was simply a "day" that, like every fourth one, was dark.

However, by sheer coincidence, it was our "night" as well—the time period we arbitrarily set aside for sleep. So I was dreaming the disturbing dreams that had troubled me since coming to this place, when the first explosion wrenched me brutally out of them.

Drilled-in reflexes took over for me. I rolled out of bed, fumbled out of habit for the gun that wasn't there, and simultaneously reviewed all my senses.

Sight wasn't much use in the dark, and hearing had already been alerted. Feel reported the impact of the hard floor as I fell on it, and taste was irrelevant. But smell . . .

Gas! shot through my mind.

I held my breath, stumbled to my washbasin, grabbed a wad of paper towel, soaked it, and clasped it across the lower part of my face before allowing myself to inhale. Then I switched on the light and stumbled to the connecting door to Chloe's room.

The door opened before I reached it, and Chloe tumbled through.

"Bob!" she gasped. "What's happening? And . . . what's that smell?"

The fact that she was still functioning told me a great deal. I flung away my makeshift gas mask and drew a breath. The odor was unabated, but I could perceive no physiological effects. It wasn't until later that I learned the raiders were using a chemical agent effective against the Ekhemasu species but not, fortuitously, humans. At the time I merely assumed some such explanation, and acted accordingly.

"Come on!" I grabbed her by the arm and pulled her through the door into the corridor, illuminated by dim emergency lights. There the gas was faintly visible and the smell was stronger, but we still felt no ill effects. From the distance came the noise of chaos. I dragged Chloe after me, past the fallen, unconscious form of an Ekhemar. My idea was for us to get outside and sprint into the desert night, where we couldn't be cornered, and worry later about finding our way back.

I was thinking about it when reality wavered in a curious way. Before I had time to realize that I was passing through an invisibility field from the outside, I crashed into the short wiry form of a Delkar, losing my grip on

Chloe's arm as the alien and I went over in a heap.

He and I grappled clumsily in our private world of blurred shades of gray. He had a paralysis beamer, but it was long-barreled and useless at close quarters. And he obviously knew nothing about human anatomy; he went for my upper chest, where the equivalent of a solar plexus would have been if I'd been a Delkar. I, on the other hand, had a pretty good theoretical grounding in unarmed combat with his species. I used my superior weight and strength to immobilize him and, working one arm free, used the elbow to shove his oddly shaped head sideways, exposing the neck. Having no hand free, I bit him just below one tiny ear—not to break the skin, but to pinch a certain nerve. He went limp.

Getting to my knees, I took time to notice details. The Delkar wasn't wearing any sort of gas mask; evidently the stuff the raiders were using didn't affect his species either. He did have, attached to a belt around his black coverall, a device I remembered from an alley in Washington. I switched it off. The world, including Chloe, snapped back into focus and full color. She recovered quickly, being familiar with the field, and moved to my side as I fumbled to get the control pad free.

I had just about succeeded when the black-clad figures popped soundlessly into sight around us, their invisibility fields ceasing to exist with the suddenness of pricked bubbles.

Chloe and I froze into immobility, bracing ourselves for the touch of the paralysis beams.

Instead, to my amazement, one of the Delkasu merely gestured with his weapon, motioning us along the corridor. We felt no inclination to argue.

They herded us around several corners, deeper into the warren of the Sanctuary. They obviously knew where they were going—probably from interactive contact-lens displays, I imagined—but I soon grew bewildered.

Then they hustled us around a final corner, and I suddenly knew where we were. Not that I could have found my way back to our quarters unaided, for I'd only seen the monumental doorway looming ahead of us once, and that only in passing. It had been in the course of a quickie tour we'd gotten of the Sanctuary shortly after our arrival. We'd been ushered past it before I could frame a question, with a haste that made pretty clear that it was not a legitimate subject for curiosity.

But now it stood open, and Delkasu forms were moving in and out of it. Standing amid the litter of equipment that, I supposed, had been used to open it, were more Delkasu . . . and, looming among them, three humans.

The leader of our captors approached one of the humans, who turned toward us. Renata Novak's face wore as little surprise as I felt.

"I told them to be on the lookout for humans," she said without preamble. "I had a feeling you two might have been brought here, after that fiasco on Antyova II."

I was determined to match her coolness. "Who are your friends? The Tosava *gevroth* again?"

"Of course. They were as eager as I was—well, almost as eager—to see our mutually beneficial deal come to fruition. Also, while they might possibly have let meddling by the Ekhemasu go unanswered, the involvement of their old enemies of the Osak *gevroth* made it something they couldn't ignore. So they and I had a mutual interest in a solution."

Chloe glanced at the motionless form of an Ekhemar. "Yes," she said coldly, "you certainly seemed to have murdered your way to a solution."

"Don't be ridiculous, Chloe! We haven't murdered anybody. We used a nonlethal nerve agent specific to Ekhemasu body chemistry, which induces unconsciousness. Your friends will be awakening before too long, with no significant ill effects. The Tosava insisted on it."

"What peachy guys," I observed absently, while I covertly sized up the situation. The Delkasu had moved on. But the two other humans—male, nondescript, unfamiliar to me—both had paralysis beamers trained on us, and looked alert.

"They insisted on it," Novak continued, ignoring me, "because they don't want to antagonize the Medjavar any more than necessary. They cherish hopes that this whole business can be just written off as quits between them. For the same reason, they also insisted that there be no unnecessary looting of what is in here." She gestured in the direction of the great doors, through which the last of the Delkasu had departed, carrying mysterious burdens. Then she gave us a shrewd look. "You don't know what's in here, do you?"

"I didn't . . . but I think I do now," said Chloe. "It's the Medjavar's storehouse of knowledge. Their hall of records."

I stared at her. As usual, she'd succeeded in surprising me.

Novak nodded. Then, abruptly, she turned on her heel and strode through those doors. After a fractional second's hesitation, we followed her.

It was hard to believe we were inside a mountain, for

this was too vast to be called "cavernous." It stretched away into indefinite distances, under a lofty ceiling upheld by forests of massive columns—rows and rows of them, marching off into the shadows. And everywhere, between those columns, were racks for computer storage media, in various forms from various cultures.

Novak was some distance ahead of us, standing with her hands on her hips and looking around. She radiated an intensity that somehow allowed her to dominate all this giganticism, which should have reduced her to a visual zero.

"God," she breathed. "I'd love to plunder this place! But for now I have to stay on good terms with Tosava'litan. And she seems to think the Medjavar could be inconvenient people to get *seriously* mad at you. So we're not allowed to take anything except what we came for."

"About which," said Chloe, "I suppose you still won't tell us."

Novak turned to us, looking surprised. "You mean your Ekhemasu friends haven't confided in you?"

I had a sudden attack of shrewdness. "No. It seems us primitive humans can't handle the knowledge. You know what they told us? They weren't really worried about you getting it. Being a human, you're too stupid to understand it, much less do anything with it." Strictly speaking, of course, this was what the Tosava *gevroth* had thought—incorrectly, in the opinion of Khorat and his colleagues. But I pressed on, inventing freely. "They said recovering it on Antyova II was just sort of a routine precaution. They were worried that a crummy human like you might screw up and lose it to somebody else—somebody smart enough to be dangerous."

Novak's face took on a look of tight control, like a mask

with festering bitterness oozing out from around the edges. "So they said that, did they?" she asked, very quietly. She looked around. The Delkasu were all gone. We five humans were alone amid the echoing immensity. All at once, her expression cleared. "Well, I don't suppose it can do any harm now, can it?"

One of her men fidgeted. "We've got to get out of here. Tosava'throvor said—"

"You take your orders from me, not him! And we've got a few minutes." She turned back to us, and her first words were completely unexpected. "Have you two ever read Orwell's *1984*?"

We both nodded, wondering what the relevance could possibly be.

"He said that whoever controls the present controls the past . . . and whoever controls the past controls the future. Of course, what he was talking about was the way the Communist regimes of our world falsify history and thus control the *perception* of the past. The Project's sociological forecasters tell us that he was too pessimistic, and that those Communist regimes are soon going to be living on borrowed time—and not for very long. But in a way he could never have imagined, he was absolutely right. The way to change the future—the dead-end future the human race is looking at—is to change the past. Not the memory of the past, but *the past itself*."

"What are you talking about?" I demanded, exasperated.

"We're in the position we're in because the human race was just a little late—"

"Yeah, right, we've heard this from you before," I interrupted. "But so what? Nothing can be done about it now."

"Yes, it can."

We stared at her, wondering if she'd lost whatever marbles she possessed.

Novak stared back, then shook her head. "So it really *is* true, isn't it? The Medjavar haven't told you they have time travel."

Looking back, I have no recollection of how long the silence lasted. I do recall what finally broke it: a whoop of derisive laughter from me.

"Time travel!" I finally gasped. "So *that's* what this is all about? *Time travel?*" I couldn't continue, for another uncontrollable spasm of laughter took me.

"Renata," said Chloe, in the carefully reasonable tone one takes when dealing with a borderline nutcase, "time travel is fantasy. The whole concept is a logical absurdity. It would allow for paradoxes like—"

"I haven't got time to argue the point, Chloe. So I'll just suggest that you ask yourself this question: would a Tonkuztra family take the trouble to steal a *fantasy*? And if they did, would the Medjavar go to great lengths to get it back?"

I discovered I'd stopped laughing.

"I found out about it back in early '63," Novak resumed, talking with the rapidity of someone who's spent years holding a story inside for want of an audience. "It was indirect. I learned of it through one of the legitimate Delkasu commercial contacts that Section Five was dealing with. Her organization—'corporation' as we'd call it—was one of those to which the Tosava had put out feelers. They weren't interested. But they'd been given a list of other potential buyers they were authorized to approach. It's the way the Tonkuztra families do business.

Anyway, I was the Project's only point of contact with these people. I was the only one who knew of it. I kept it that way, secretly recruiting a few trustworthy people. In the meantime, I used my contact to get in touch with the Tosava *gevroth*, through the usual Tonkuztra channels."

"And the rest, as they say, is history," I concluded. "All right. Let's assume there's some truth to all this. Now that you've finally got what you paid for—paid by selling out everyone who's ever trusted you—what do you intend to *do* with it?"

"Isn't it obvious? I'm going to do what the Ekhemasu were too cowardly to do, even though they held the means in their decadent hands. I'm going to change *reality itself!*"

Neither Chloe nor I was able to form words.

"I'm going to go back to the early days of the Industrial Revolution," Novak went on, ignoring us. "I considered earlier periods, like the Renaissance or even Classical Greece. But going that far back isn't really practical. And dealing with those societies would involve a whole new set of problems; I'd have to introduce a whole new mind-set, in addition to leapfrogging too many technological revolutions. But in early-nineteenth-century England they even had the concept of the computer, thanks to Babbage. I'm going to take back the whole compendium of galactic knowledge that Mr. Inconnu brought, and which the Project has been gradually doling out. I'm going to have to be even more gradual . . . but I'll be starting a lot earlier. And even more importantly, I'll bring the knowledge that the Delkasu are coming, and that the human race must prepare.

"By the time the little vermin arrive in the mid-twentieth century, Earth will be ready for them. There'll be no degrading subterfuges, no truckling to alien slime! We'll meet them as equals. No, more than that! With the kind of momentum I'm going to impart to Earth's technological progression, we'll eventually surpass them and take our rightful place as the dominant race of the universe!"

By this time, Novak's voice had taken on the fiery intensity of a prophet. From the rapt look her two underlings wore as she poured forth her crazy dream, I could see that for them she was precisely that. She'd known just the kind of people to recruit. Unfortunately, they weren't looking rapt enough for me to try anything. These guys might be true believers, but they were also pros.

"Renata," said Chloe, still superhumanly calm and patient, "if you succeed, what happens to *our* reality, in which none of this has happened? Does it vanish? And if so, where will *you* have come from? That's what I meant about paradoxes."

"There's a difference of opinion on that." With disconcerting abruptness, Novak was back down from Mount Sinai and talking matter-of-factly. "Maybe our timeline *will* vanish. But if so, there is an excellent probability that those of us who travel backwards in time and cause the change will be unaffected—we'll exist in a sort of overarching 'super-reality.' Another possibility is that the present reality will continue to exist, working out its own tragic destiny, while a parallel reality will come into being at the point at which I change history. That way, there'll at least be *one* universe in which events turn out right."

I could only stare at her. I started to speak, but then realized the pointlessness of anything I could say.

I also realized that I had nothing to lose.

"You're mad as a hatter," I said wearily. "And talking to

you is a waste of air. Just do what you're going to do and get it over with."

"Mad? Then don't take my word for any of this. Ask your Ekhemasu friends, when they wake up."

"You mean you're not going to kill us?" Chloe blurted before Novak's words had fully registered on me.

"Of course not, Chloe! What do you think I am?" Before I could collapse in a fit of hysterical laughter over *that* one, she continued. "No, I'm going to leave you here. Why shouldn't I? There's nothing you can do to stop me now."

One of the guards looked worried. "Shouldn't we . . . ?" He gestured in our direction with his paralysis beamer.

"No, there's no need. Besides," Novak added, to us, "it's a fairly unpleasant sensation. I don't know if they have insects, or the local equivalent, in this place, but if so you don't want to be lying around, completely immobile but fully conscious, while they crawl over you . . . and into you, through your nose and your mouth, if it was open at the instant the beam hit you. So just behave yourselves until after we leave. And do ask these Ekhemasu if what I've said is true. I think you'll find they haven't been altogether candid with you."

With that she departed, followed by the two guards, who kept their weapons trained on us as they exited. We were left alone in the midst of the vast chamber, looking at each other and not trusting ourselves to speak.

CHAPTER FOURTEEN

We didn't have a whole lot to do, waiting for the Ekhemasu to awaken. We couldn't even get breakfast, not knowing how to find our way back to our quarters and their stock of human-type rations. So we spent our time looking for Khorat, examining the features of every unconscious Ekhemasu we encountered.

We finally found him, after what were probably fewer hours than it seemed at the time. He was in a gallery-like space that was evidently a kind of office suite, looking out through broad windows over the Sanctuary's terraced approach, beyond which the slow dawn of Khemava was breaking over the desert. We rolled him over—remember, this was low gravity—and tried to arouse him, using every ploy our limited knowledge of his species' physiology suggested.

Our amateurish ministrations must have had some effect. He came around before his colleagues, despite his advanced age.

"Have you contacted the authorities?" were his first words. They came out of our earpieces in the same imperturbable computer-generated voice as always, even though he was speaking in the rustling croak that was his equivalent of a whisper.

"No," said Chloe. "We didn't know how."

"Of course you didn't." With an alarmingly visible effort, Khorat heaved himself upright from where he'd lain sprawled across his cushions. He tottered over to a console and began making connections and talking to various uniformed Delkasu.

"It is probably just as well you were not able to reach any law enforcement agencies," he observed after cutting the last connection. "There will of course be questions, which I will need to deal with. This touches on extremely sensitive matters."

"Yeah, we know," I said shortly. I'm not a morning person, and hunger never improves my disposition.

The translator must have conveyed the hard flatness of my tone, for Khorat stopped what he was doing and turned the unreadable regard of his enormous eyes on us.

"We talked to Novak before she and her Tonkuztra allies left, Khorat," Chloe explained.

"And she told you . . . ?"

"Everything."

Something seemed to crumple up inside the old Ekhemar. He closed his eyes tightly as though in physical pain, and from deep in his throat came a low sound that my earpiece did not translate.

"Khorat?" said Chloe, alarmed. "Are you all right?"

"Quite." Khorat seemed to take command of himself. "There is much to do. We must awaken as many of my fellows as possible before the security forces arrive. We must also return the two of you to your quarters, as your presence here is not generally known and would be awkward to explain."

"Yeah, sure," I nodded. "Not for the world would we cause trouble. But Khorat . . . after the cops are gone, we're going to have a long talk."

"A long, *frank* talk," Chloe amplified.

I heard a rustling Ekhemasu sigh. "Very well. You have my word on it. But at present, there is need for haste."

We spent a boring time as Delkasu officials and their Ekhemasu flunkies swarmed over the Sanctuary. What Khorat had told us about their regard for native Ekhemasu religious sensibilities must have been true, for they stayed away from areas the Medjavar told them were off-limits— like the area where our quarters were located. It even made sense, I reflected. The Medjavar were the victims in this crime. What reason would they have to withhold information?

Finally, the investigators departed and Khorat conducted us to his office. It was a smaller version of the suite we'd found him in, spacious to our eyes but probably the Ekhemasu equivalent of the stereotypical small, book-lined, pipe-smoke-smelling study of some equally stereotypical professor. Except that it was pretty much open to other similar offices; the Ekhemasu, descendants of herd animals, didn't altogether share our human ideas of privacy. But the three of us were alone.

"What did you end up telling them?" I asked Khorat, as Chloe and I settled gingerly onto the cushions that had to serve in the absence of human-adapted furniture. "I mean, about what this raid was aimed at?"

"Nothing. We insisted we had no idea what could possibly motivate such an act. I could tell they were not satisfied. But they will still pursue their investigation vigorously. A crime involving violation of air traffic regulations is one which the imperial authorities take seriously, however vague its motive. And they will enjoy the full—if covert—cooperation of the Osak *gevroth*, who will be livid over a Tosava intrusion on a planet they consider part of their turf." (My respect for the translator software went up yet another notch.) "But it will all come to nothing, of course. They will know nothing of what is involved. Nor may they be told."

Chloe leaned forward in a way that was oddly beseeching. "Khorat, help me understand this. Novak told us that this is all about the secret of . . . well, of time travel." She gave a nervous little laugh, as though desperately inviting Khorat to share her amusement at something so ludicrous, and beseeching him to explain to us what Novak had *really* meant.

Instead, the great dark eyes remained expressionless. So did the voice in our earpieces, as he snuffed out Chloe's hope. "Yes. I see there is no point in denials. It is now time for you to learn the whole story.

"It dates back to shortly after the Delkasu conquest. Actually, I must go even farther back than that, to our beginnings as a race and our fundamental orientation as a culture.

"First of all, you must understand that we are not

particularly good tool users." Khorat held up one of his strange, clumsy-looking hands, so oddly at variance with his race's overall look of highly evolved gracefulness. "Not nearly as good as the Delkasu. Not even as good as you. Your single opposable thumb is a far more efficient arrangement."

"But," said Chloe, puzzled, "you colonized this system, and—"

"Oh, yes, we can do anything you or even the Delkasu can do. It just takes us longer . . . especially in that particular case. Given our species' body mass, interplanetary colonization using reaction drives was a problem whose solution required thousands of years, not hundreds. Only the incentive of this system's potential wealth induced us to do it at all."

"But," I argued, "surely your natural tool-using equipment didn't matter after you'd developed cybernetic technology to do it for you."

A smile entered Khorat's voice. "I am reminded of your culture's folk saying about a certain avian life-form and its egg. You see, before we could reach the stage of robotic manipulators, we first had to painfully work our way through all the earlier levels of technology. By that time, our feet were set on a pathway rather different from those of most tool-using races."

"With the help of the Medjavar." I knew I probably wasn't succeeding in keeping the sourness out of my voice.

"No doubt." Khorat was serene. "I am sure that this is the real reason we were as successful as we were; we were simply guiding the culture in the direction it was predisposed toward in any case. Also, unlike you or the Delkasu, we never experienced total war, with its pressure toward a certain kind of technological development, requiring a certain kind of mind-set.

"You already know some of the consequences. We never discovered the secret of interstellar travel, for example. And our entire material culture has a somehow anachronistic look in your eyes." ("Retro" hadn't become part of the slang yet, so the translator didn't have it.) "At the same time, we advanced into fields of which you are barely aware, and which you would regard as branches of philosophy rather than science."

"Like the ultimate nature of time," Chloe stated levelly.

The Ekhemar didn't have eyebrows to raise, but that was the effect. "You are very perceptive. Yes . . . that, and the kind of dimensional shifting whereby the flow of time can, within a strictly delimited locality, be reversed.

"So matters stood when the Delkasu arrived—the *first* Delkasu, a couple of your centuries before Sakandri incorporated them, and us, into his empire." Khorat began to look uncomfortable. "You may recall what I said about the Medjavar's attitude toward the Delkasu. For the most part, the rest of the Ekhemasu shared it. But there were exceptions, especially in those early days. You see, one of our oldest and most primal terrors was that of meat-eating animals endowed with high intelligence and superior technology. Even after it became clear that the Delkasu did not think of us as a food source—and, indeed, were revolted by the concept of sentient meat-animals—the old fantasy still took a while to release its hold on us. One of those who never escaped its grip was a great scientist named Imhaermekh. His loathing of the Delkasu caused him to pervert his genius into a monomaniacal quest for a way to expel them from our system. His researches led him deeper and deeper into the realms of dimensional physics, for he saw with extraordinary clarity that the only way historical inevitability can be fought is by changing history itself." Khorat subsided into a brooding silence. Chloe and I waited with all the patience we could muster, for even I had the sensitivity to recognize a being struggling to overcome agonizing embarrassment.

Finally, Khorat spoke. "Like most individuals who want a thing badly enough, Imhaermekh finally achieved it. He never actually sent an Ekhemar back in time, but he succeeded in sending inanimate objects back into the recent past—they appeared seconds *before* the experiments. He had to be stopped." The artificial voice trailed off into silence again.

I like to flatter myself that I'm not a total clod. Still, as you may have noticed by now, my sensitivity has limits.

"Well, Khorat," I began hesitantly, "what was the big deal? I mean, the Medjavar had already been suppressing dangerous technological innovations for thousands of years, right? So why was this any different?"

Khorat gave me a somber regard. "Influence, manipulation, concealment, suppression . . . yes, we are no strangers to these things. But only once in our entire history have we resorted to murder."

"Imhaermekh?" Chloe breathed.

"He had to be stopped," Khorat repeated, as much to himself as to us. Then he spoke more briskly. "The saying that 'the end justifies the means' is, of course, nothing but self-serving rationalization. But when an end assumes an importance that is *universal* in scope, debate about means becomes irrelevant."

Chloe spoke earnestly. "Khorat, I don't doubt your sincerity. But . . . but . . . *time travel*? The notion involves so many impossibilities I hardly know where to begin. First of all, it violates the conservation laws of physics."

"How so?"

"Suppose a, uh, time machine goes back to the year X. When it appears out of nowhere in that year, it's adding matter to the universe."

"But," Khorat explained, "the same amount was subtracted in the year in which it departed. The sum matter/energy total of the universe must, indeed, remain constant. But that total may balance out over time. The problem of 'extra matter' which worries you does not exist if the temporal dimension is taken into account."

"But," Chloe insisted doggedly, "even if that's true, what about relativity? Anything traveling backwards in time would be traveling faster than infinity!"

"Yeah," I put in. "Talk about swimming against the tide."

Khorat looked bewildered, and I belatedly recalled that his race, and their language, had developed on a planet with no moon, and hence no tides in its small landlocked seas. He pulled himself together, though.

"It is difficult to explain. You must understand that time travel depends on transposing one's vehicle to a dimension isolated from the time-flow of our own." I sensed that this was the translator software's inadequate best effort at expressing concepts for which English simply lacked the terminology. "Under these conditions, travel into the past is relatively easy. It involves simply separating oneself from the continuum. You are not so much traveling as standing still and letting the time-flow pass

you by, leaving you farther and farther behind in the past."
Khorat visibly struggled to express himself. "To borrow
the terminology of spaceflight, think of it as 'going into
free fall.'

"However, while it is easy in terms of energy requirements, it is *not* fast. Most certainly it is not instantaneous.
This is an image from your world's popular culture of
which you must disabuse yourselves."

"How do you know about our world's popular culture?"
I demanded sharply.

"I have made it my business to inform myself of it since
it became obvious that the Tosava *gevroth* had found a
buyer among your people. I soon discovered that time
travel is a familiar fictional device . . . and that your writers
have many misconceptions about it.

"A significant amount of subjective time must be spent
inside a field which allows large material constructs to
enter the dimensions of which I have spoken. And time
inside that field passes at the same rate as in the outside
universe; there is no equivalent of 'relativistic time dila-
tion.' The apparent length of the voyage is directly linked
to how far back one wishes to go."

"Novak said something about going back to our early
Industrial Revolution," Chloe mused. "About a hundred
and fifty of our years. Her idea is to get forced-draft technological advancement started so early that by the time
the Delkasu arrive we'll be in a position to deal with them
as equals. She also mentioned the possibility of going back
even farther than that, to periods about five hundred years
in the past, or even twenty-five hundred. But she said
there were 'practical problems' with going back that far."

"There are indeed, in terms of sheer tediousness. Even

her plan of going back a hundred and fifty years will involve a somewhat lengthy journey. Exactly how lengthy is difficult to know, as the amount of subjective time that passes inside the field is dependent upon which dimension the ship has been shifted into. There are more than one, you see. As a general proposition, the more difficult they are to access, the shorter the time that must be spent in them. The information at Novak's disposal . . ." Khorat stopped himself, clearly not wanting to pursue the subject. "But that is another matter. For now, suffice it to say that her objective is attainable."

"But . . ." Chloe sought to rally her thoughts. "All right: let's suppose you're right, and that time travel is technically achievable, despite all the physical laws it seems to violate. That still leaves the *philosophical* objections to it. It destroys the whole concept of causality! If you go back and change the past in such a way as to foreclose the possibility of your own existence—shoot your own grandfather in his boyhood, say—then where did you come from in the first place?"

"Novak mentioned," I recalled, "a possibility that it might not change *the* future, but rather create a parallel time track—"

"She is wrong," Khorat interrupted me bluntly.

"Uh, Khorat, that *is* something our thinkers have speculated about. The idea that all possible outcomes of any given interaction are equally valid, mathematically speaking, and—"

"Then *they* are wrong," Khorat stated with even greater finality. "You must accept my word on this. As I said earlier, our civilization has explored the basic nature of reality more deeply than yours. The theory of many parallel time tracks is an ingenious intellectual construct. But in fact there is only the one linear reality, in which there is only the one actually realized outcome to each interaction."

"Well, then," declared Chloe, almost angrily, "we're back to the 'Grandfather Paradox' I mentioned earlier. If the universe that produced Novak never comes into existence, how can she have gone back and—?"

"That, too, is a fallacy. A time traveler really *can* murder his grandfather—a meat-eater's concept if ever there was one!—because his own existence is a product of a reality which preexists the one which his own time-meddling creates after he dimension-shifts back into phase with the normal universe and begins affecting it."

"I'm getting a headache," I complained.

Chloe ignored me. "But Khorat, assuming that Novak carries out her plan, what happens to the reality we ourselves are living in? And *when* does whatever-it-is happen?"

A transcendent somberness seemed to radiate from every detail of Khorat's expression and posture, until it filled the room. "I will attempt to answer those questions in reverse order. To repeat, subjective time spent in temporal transit passes at the same rate as it does in the outside universe. Novak must return to Earth, prepare her ship—"

"You used the word 'ship' before," I interrupted.

"Yes. Time travel will only work in proximity to a spinning body of planetary mass. But for any number of reasons it is quite impractical on the actual surface of such a planet. Therefore, a 'time machine' must be a space vehicle in orbit. But to continue: Novak must make her preparations, then make the actual temporal journey, and land on Earth in the year of her arrival. Whether or not her plans succeed is immaterial; her mere arrival would, in itself, be an event of such magnitude as to immediately begin altering history. So at that moment, in terms of her own subjective existence and ours—"

"*Blooey*," I said, wondering how the translator would render that.

"I doubt if there will be any noise," said Khorat, confirming my opinion of his sense of humor. "I do not know, and cannot visualize, what will happen to us. But I can find no theoretical basis for assuming our continued existence. From our standpoint, I imagine our consciousness will simply stop."

After a while, Chloe felt a need to break the silence in the room. "Uh, Khorat, what you're saying has some disturbing theological implications. I mean, most of our religions assume that the consciousness—the 'soul,' as they put it—survives after death, either by entering into an afterlife or by being reincarnated into another life-form."

"Yes, we ourselves have devised religions with similar beliefs. I myself am an agnostic—which has always struck me as the rational position on the subject, whereas atheism is a particularly breathtaking form of arrogance. But in the eventuality we are contemplating, the question becomes almost moot."

"You're taking this very calmly, Khorat," I observed.

"If I give such an impression, it is because my own personal survival, and the survival of my familiar world, is a trivial matter compared to the truly serious consequences of Novak's meddling in matters of which she has no understanding."

"The *truly* serious consequences?" Chloe echoed faintly.

"Consider: in the world that Novak will create, time travel will belong to the realm of the possible. Even if she retains enough sanity to destroy the knowledge of how she did it, it will not matter in the long run, for the *possibility* will be common knowledge." Khorat studied us gravely. "One thing I have learned about your species in the course of my studies: if humans know for a certainty that a thing can be done, they will not rest until they have devised a way to do it. And there will be plenty of others with motives as strong as Novak's or Imhaermekh's for changing history— causes as compelling, and grievances as intense. So even if she succeeds in bringing about the kind of world she wants, she will have doomed that world in the long run. This will happen again . . . and again . . . and again. And beyond a certain point, theory suggests that the very fabric of ultimate reality will begin to fray, and unravel. The consequences are literally incalculable, for they lie beyond the capacity of any finite mind to grasp.

"Now, perhaps, you understand my seeming calmness in the face of the question of survival after death. If our very universe is canceled out, then one must entertain the assumption that its God is canceled out as well."

Khorat's voice had dropped to a whisper that the trans- lator could barely pick up. Then he fell silent, and this time I felt no urge to break the silence. And, being the least religious person you'd ever hope to meet, I wondered why I had to contain a shudder.

Chloe had more courage. "Khorat, what can be done?"

"Oh, it is already being done. We foresaw this possi- bility. And, contrary to our usual practice, we kept the relevant data in duplicate. Indeed, our duplicate includes at least one crucial bit of knowledge that Novak does not possess."

"What—?" I began.

"No. There will be time for detailed explanations later. The point is, we can—and *must*—take action to prevent this. And I must ask for your help."

"*Our* help?" Chloe, visibly annoyed with herself, brought her voice back down from the squeak to which it had risen, and spoke in her customary husky contralto. "I can't imagine what help we can be, Khorat. But assuming that there's any truth to what you've been saying, and you're trying to stop it from happening, then we *have* to help you. If there's anything useful we can do, we're under an ultimate moral imperative to do it."

"Yeah," I chimed in. In fact, I was a good deal less wholehearted about this than Chloe seemed to be. But she had made an unconditional commitment, and there was no way I could hold back and continue to live with her—or inside the same skin with myself.

Hey, I never claimed to be smart, did I?

CHAPTER FIFTEEN

Even now, I still sometimes find myself wondering how far and how deep the excavations under the Sanctuary went. God knows, Chloe and I never found out.

The last cavern we got to see was on the day of our departure. It was a hangar, extending far into the depths of the mountain against whose base the Sanctuary nestled. It lacked the vertigo-inducing vastness of the one beneath Crater Korolev, for it wasn't intended to accommodate interstellar ships. Indeed, the biggest vessel it held was the one toward which Khorat conducted us.

"An interplanetary shuttle only," the old Ekhemar explained, indicating the sleek, lifting body.

"It looks pretty small, for your species," Chloe observed. In fact, it wasn't all that huge even on human standards.

"True. But the journey will be too brief for the cramped quarters to grow unbearably tedious. And it has compensating virtues . . . most notably its capability to conceal itself from all forms of observation."

"How do you manage to keep it secret from the imperial authorities?" I wondered. "I hope you're not going to try to tell us that they don't mind somebody other than themselves having that kind of capability."

"Oh, they're well aware of it. Private ownership of space vessels is not illegal. And we have a perfectly legitimate use for it, as our organization has many members in the satellite system of the third planet. And normally we put it to just those legitimate uses. It is only in emergencies that we activate the . . . special features we have had installed."

"And about which you somehow neglected to inform them?" Chloe inquired archly.

"We prefer not to bother them with things they don't need to know," replied Khorat, unconsciously anticipating certain human political operatives of a few years later.

We'd barely settled into the passenger cabin when the shuttle rose gently from the hangar floor on the wings of its impellers, and a great door slid open to reveal the desert and the canal that bisected it in the distance. As we swept through that portal and soared aloft, Khemava receded below us and soon became a globe, less blue and more buff than that of watery Earth. It was a spectacle Chloe and I had been denied on our heavily concealed arrival at Khemava. We saw it now by grace of the viewscreens with their outside pickup. Viewed directly through portholes, it would have been blurred and color-washed by the invisibility field.

Time passed, and the planet shrank to the size of a soccer ball held at arm's length . . . then a tennis ball, then a ping-pong ball. I considered inquiring as to the exact purpose of the trip, but Khorat had grown uncharacteristically taciturn. So I contented myself with watching the receding planet in the view-aft.

I was watching it when Khorat and Company engaged another of the shuttle's "special features." With the kind of sickening suddenness I'd experienced on the occasion of my departure from the Solar System, Khemava shot away from us.

I was still gawking when Chloe touched my arm and indicated the view-forward.

A furnace-colored boulder was careening toward us.

The shuttle's illicit field drive was not the sort that could attain the incredible multiples of the speed of light which brought other stars and even other spiral arms within fairly easy reach. One of *those* drives couldn't have been squeezed into a craft so small, and it would have been useless within a planetary system, where not even computerized controls could have prevented it from overshooting any possible target. No, this was an underpowered version, so wasteful and inefficient as to be justifiable only when one needed to cross interplanetary distances in a *great* hurry.

Thus it was that we saw the titanic third planet of the Khemava system hurtling toward us at a rate that orthodox physics declared impossible, like a more-than-Jupiter-sized stone from a war god's sling.

I think I may have cried out.

Then the field was disengaged, and the planet came to an instantaneous halt in the view-forward. Well, not a complete halt, for it continued to swell as the impellers brought us into its orbit. It just seemed that way.

I wiped my brow and stared at the slightly oblate globe. It was like Jupiter, only more so. Its surface—banded by the rapidity of its rotation and swirling with storms into which Earth could have been tossed, unnoticed—glowed in sullen shades of red rather than Jupiter's orange and yellow. And it had a ring. Not a spectacular array of them like Saturn, but something more conspicuous than the thin, narrow, ethereal kind that the space probes were due to reveal in a few years around Jupiter, Neptune and Uranus, composed of little more than ice particles.

Several moons were visible. Off to the right, we could glimpse the bluish life-bearing one that I had been assuming was our destination. But it slid behind us as we proceeded on a hyperbolic course closer to the planet, approaching the ring, which soon lost the optical illusion of being a flat plane of dirty glass and resolved itself into a myriad of rocks, the rubble of a moon which had once spiraled too close to the monstrous planet that now filled most of the viewscreen

"Uh, Khorat," said Chloe nervously, "doesn't a planet like this one—almost a 'failed star'—put out a lot of radiation?"

"Oh, yes. We'd all be dying by now, were it not for the ship's force screen."

"Khorat," I said firmly, not wishing to pursue this cheery topic, "I don't suppose you could tell us just exactly what all this is about?"

"Everything will become clear in due course."

There was nothing I could do in the face of Khorat's maddening serenity but compose myself and watch the show. In spite of myself, I couldn't help but get caught up in the unfolding spectacle as our ship nosed its way cautiously into the ring. It looked, I thought, like the science-fictional vision (quite false, Dr. Fehrenbach had assured us) of the Sun's asteroid belt, thickly strewn with rocks of all sizes. Our pilot, in the control room from which our passenger cabin was quite isolated, was proceeding slowly, fending off the orbiting chunks of rock with deflector shields, an application of the same technology that provided the deck beneath our feet with a steady one Khemava G of gravity.

As I watched, the picture began to waver.

"What—?" Chloe began. Then she gasped.

For once, I caught on to something faster than she did. But I had an advantage, for years before I had gone through an invisibility field. So I wasn't as shocked as she when the picture in the view-forward restabilized . . . and was mostly filled with an interstellar space vessel that hadn't been there before. The few stars we could see, and the limb of the giant planet off to the side, were blurry and colorless, for our craft's sensors were "seeing" them through the larger field that now enveloped us as well as the ship that was generating it.

I studied that ship as we drew alongside her and a tubular passageway extruded itself from her side, seeking our air lock. Although she dwarfed our shuttle, she wasn't particularly large as interstellar ships went—especially ones designed to accommodate Ekhemasu. And she was undergoing some modifications; I could recognize the indicia here and there on the hull, and I spotted an Ekhemar doing an EVA. A centaur wearing a vac suit in free fall is something you don't see every day.

Then there was a soft clank through our hull and a

hissing noise as the access tube made contact and air pressures were equalized. Khorat led us through and into the big ship, where the work of renovation was more obvious in the bustling activity and clangorous noise.

Chloe spoke up. "I didn't know the Medjavar owned interstellar spacecraft, Khorat."

"Actually, this is our only one. Such vessels are very expensive. And private ownership of them is *very* closely regulated. So this one is . . . unregistered."

"Illegal, you mean," I said flatly. "And I have a feeling that whatever goodies you're adding to it are even more illegal."

Khorat didn't pretend to be surprised that I'd noticed. "Arguably, they are not. After all, a government cannot outlaw something which—" He stopped himself abruptly.

"You were saying, Khorat?" I prompted.

"Ah, here is my colleague Nafayum!" said Khorat in the slightly too eager way of someone who is anxious to change the subject. He stepped forward and exchanged ritual greetings with a female Ekhemar who looked even older than he. She studied us as Khorat made introductions.

"Ah, yes. Of course. The humans." The translator gave Nafayum the voice of an elderly woman. It also conveyed a tone I wasn't sure quite how to take, as it suggested curiosity tempered by distaste. I got the feeling Nafayum hadn't forgotten that the only *other* human of their acquaintance was the source of all their troubles. "At any rate, Khorat, all is in readiness for them."

"Uh . . . all of *what* is in readiness for us?" My anxious question was lost in the hustle and bustle as Nafayum led us through the passageways to a compartment with a large, curving viewscreen—a sort of observation lounge which also served as a meeting room. We all reclined on cushions surrounding a circular, surprisingly low table.

Khorat took charge at once. "As the two of you have surmised, this ship is reserved for special emergencies. Normally, when we of the Medjavar need to get about in interstellar space, we make arrangements through ordinary channels—"

"Like when we met you on Antyova II," I cut in. I knew I was probably being rude—in fact, I probably would have been aware of it even without the glare from Chloe I could glimpse out of the corner of my eye—but I was growing impatient with all this. "Let me guess: in the present situation, you can't take the time to bamboozle the imperial bureaucracy into transporting you wherever it is you want to go. Which, I somehow suspect, is Earth."

Khorat exchanged a brief eye contact with Nafayum before speaking in his trademark unruffled way. "Yes. Our thinking is as follows. Novak and her confederates have almost certainly returned to Earth and are in the process of preparing to equip a spacecraft with temporal displacement capability. This will no doubt take time, which provides us with our window of opportunity. We must proceed to the Solar System without delay."

"And do what, once we get there?" inquired Chloe. "Bring the matter to the attention of Novak's superiors in the Project?"

All four of Khorat's reclining legs jerked simultaneously. I suspected it was the equivalent of a human staggering backwards and clutching his chest above the heart. "By no means! Have I not explained that humans cannot, under any circumstances, be allowed to learn that time travel is possible? This applies to your Prometheus Project just as strongly as to the larger society of your planet."

"Well, then?" I queried. "You must have *something* in mind. Otherwise, we may as well stay here and devote ourselves to serious drinking until our universe goes *poof.*"

"We do indeed have a plan, for which we are fortunate to have your cooperation. Our intention is to depart at once, so as to arrive in your native system in time to infiltrate the two of you into Novak's organization, for the purpose of sabotaging her attempt from within."

Sheer absurdity can prevent a statement from registering on the mind, at least at first. So a moment passed before I began to wonder what had gone haywire, the translator software or Khorat.

Chloe, as usual, recovered first. "Khorat, I must remind you that Novak knows both of us."

"We are aware of that. But you are the only human operatives available to us. That is why Nafayum is here." Khorat hesitated until the pause grew awkward. "Are you familiar with the concept of genetic nanoviruses?"

Chloe and I exchanged a glance. We were, in fact familiar with it, which was why our earpieces used the term. Earth in general was still years away from being able to grasp it. Not until the 1970s would the discovery of restriction enzymes open the door to recombinant DNA. And even that was only the first step on the road to tailored genetic viruses, injected into the body and able to resequence DNA and stimulate cell growth in new directions.

"Yes," said Chloe. "The Project knows of them. We also know they have to be custom-tailored for a particular species. The Project lacks the requisite knowledge to do so for humans. And, of course, no one else has had any reason to."

"We have," said Khorat with uncharacteristic succinctness. Before either of us could manage a response, he pressed on. "As soon as we became aware that humans were involved in this affair, we commenced the needful work, against some such contingency as this one."

"But . . . how?" Chloe sounded bewildered.

"We were able to obtain the necessary data on your species through our Tonkuztra contacts. And the technique is a well-established one." Khorat looked uncomfortable. "Our organization has always been, at best, highly ambivalent about this type of biological manipulation. Its benefits—the 'editing out' of genetic defects—are undeniable. But we have made it our business to restrict its use to those benign uses, subverting all investigation of dangerous applications by subtly deflecting them into dead ends. At the same time, as I explained to you before, we preserved the knowledge ourselves even as we suppressed it. Nafayum is our leading expert in the field."

Nafayum spoke up, and the translator conveyed the patronizing enthusiasm of the fanatical specialist. "Given your culture's unfamiliarity with this form of genetic engineering, I should perhaps explain that the changes it makes are quite undetectable, for they are determined by your genetic code—your *rewritten* genetic code. For the same reason, they are permanent, unless you should at a later time have them reversed by the same technique. Thus, for example, if we change your hair color, the hair will continue to grow in the new color. Likewise—"

"Yes, we understand," Chloe cut in testily . . . though

just barely accurately, in my case. "But what *you* don't seem to understand is that Novak knows us very well. You could give me flaming red hair and she'd still recognize me."

"We have taken that into account," said Khorat, with a smugness which didn't last, for his tone grew troubled. "Earlier, I spoke of dangerous ramifications of this technique, the knowledge of which the Medjavar have preserved while suppressing them. Let me be more specific. An extremely advanced, sophisticated form of nanovirus can actively alter and rearrange existing cells, and induce new ones to grow, so as to produce gross changes in the subject's anatomy—not merely modifications of body chemistry, or cosmetic alterations of such things as coloring. Taken to extremes, an organism can actually be metamorphosed into a member of a different species. The potential for abuse is so obvious that the Medjavar's task has been relatively easy, for on this point galactic society agrees with us, and bans all uses of the technique except officially sanctioned, rigorously controlled ones. Its enormous expense simplifies the problem of enforcement. Misuse of it is encountered only among the most decadent Delkasu circles, producing grotesque sexual playthings and exotic servants for the superrich."

I tried to imagine the possibilities. *Outré* genetic tampering hadn't yet become a staple of science fiction in those days. But I recalled a line from the classic film *Bride of Frankenstein*: "Gods and monsters . . ."

Nafayum took up the thread. "The technique has limits, of course. For example, total body mass cannot be increased significantly. I could not, for example, transform you into an Ekhemar—"

"Aw, phooey!" I deadpanned.

"—however great an improvement it would represent," Nafayum finished without a break, confirming my opinion that the Ekhemasu sense of humor was either nonexistent or very, very dry. "I could—given a great deal of preparatory work—turn you into a Delkar, with a residue of excess cells left over in a rather unappetizing form."

"Uh, that's okay," I said hastily. "Don't put yourself out on my account."

"What I am prepared to do now, however, is modify your bone structure so as to alter your facial features and, within limits, your body size and build. I can guarantee that your own parents would not recognize you."

Chloe looked from one Ekhemar to the other and back. "So you're asking us to submit to this . . . treatment?" Her voice held the same reservations I was feeling at the thought of letting aliens futz with my genetic code.

"We should perhaps explain," said Khorat, evidently taking our assent for granted, "that there are certain complications."

"Surprise, surprise," I muttered.

"First of all, after the single injection that is required, it takes time for the biological nanomachines to replicate and perform their tasks. Even for the more elementary forms of genetic surgery, this takes a period of days. For the type of metamorphosis we are contemplating, which places a great strain on the subject's metabolism, it takes still longer, and requires rest under medical supervision—in this case, that of Nafayum, who is not accompanying us to Earth. So we would have to remain here beyond the 'window of opportunity' of which I spoke."

"Well, then, if the whole thing is impractical, why are

we even discussing it?" I was starting to get annoyed.

"It is possible, with great difficulty, to produce a fast-acting version of the nanovirus, which reduces the time required by a factor of at least twenty. Nafayum has done so. We have, as you can see, spared no expense."

"And what's the catch?" Chloe asked point-blank.

"Yeah," I chimed in. "Didn't you say something about a 'great strain on the metabolism?' "

Khorat's self-satisfaction began to show a certain strain itself. "Well, you must remember that the cells are having to keep the body alive at the same time they are doing the work of the metamorphosis. This is why rest and close observation are required. And . . . I believe I forgot to mention that there are certain side effects, including cramps, fatigue, ravenous hunger, chills, sweats and fever, culminating in a comatose state which is accompanied by unpleasant secretions from the various bodily orifices."

"Yes, you *did* forget to mention that," said Chloe pointedly. I contented myself with an eloquent glare.

"When the process is accelerated, these phenomena are unavoidably intensified," Khorat continued. "However, the chances of survival are, we believe, within acceptable parameters."

"Survival?" and "Acceptable parameters?" Chloe and I echoed respectively.

"Well, it is possible for such an accelerated process to run out of control, so to speak. Various possibilities then arise. The overworked cells may overheat, so that the subject is, in effect, cooked from the inside. A more serious problem is the randomization of the nanomachines' directing of cell growth, to produce effects analogous to cancer but affecting all cells in the—"

"All right! That's it!" I surged to my feet. "You want to kill us, Khorat? Fine. Shove us out the airlock without vac suits. But when we volunteered to help you, we were *not* volunteering to become seething, shapeless blobs of cancer cells! You can take your 'acceptable parameters' and—"

"Fortunately, there is a way around these problems," Khorat said hastily.

"We're listening," said Chloe, before I could erupt.

Nafayum took over. "The difficulties Khorat has described can be avoided if we place you into biological stasis, with full life support including intravenous nourishment. Under these conditions, you are being kept alive externally and your own body cells, under the 'supervision' of the nanomachines, can do their work of transformation without endangering your lives."

"Hmm . . ." I thought about it. "Suspended animation, in other words? So we'd be unconscious and totally helpless."

"And totally at your mercy for the entire procedure," Chloe added. Looking back, I can see how one might argue that we had been at their mercy ever since coming to Khemava. But damn it, there's a difference!

Nafayum leaned forward, visibly perplexed. "But have I not explained—?"

Khorat motioned her to silence. "It is your option of course," he said suavely. "Ethics forbids us to compel you." Then, as an afterthought: "A pity, though, that our secondary preparations must go to waste."

I held out a couple of seconds before the primate curiosity on which Khorat was counting triumphed. "Uh . . . 'secondary preparations?' "

"Yes. You see, since we were planning a moderately radical metamorphosis, we naturally looked into certain relatively trivial modifications that could be made in the course of the procedure."

"Such as?" queried Chloe, also hooked.

"Oh, this and that. Things that almost all galactic cultures use as a matter of course—things not even the Medjavar find objectionable. For example, permanently correcting any genetic defects. And . . . oh, yes, life span extension. What were you telling me you thought you could achieve, Nafayum?"

"Starting at their age? Oh, probably a total life expectancy of about a hundred and thirty of their years, plus or minus five. Of course, you know how these things work. They would start exhibiting their species' superficial indicia of aging at only about twenty years later than normal. But they would retain full physical and mental vigor well past the century mark. Still, as you say, it's their option." Nafayum was a bit too casual. She really wasn't as good at this as Khorat. But by that point, she didn't need to be.

Chloe wasn't very good at it either. "Khorat . . . you *did* say you could reverse the changes in our appearance later if we don't like them, didn't you?"

I'm sure I don't need to recount the rest of the conversation.

The things they put us into had obviously been custombuilt for humans. They resembled high-tech coffins—a resemblance I didn't permit myself to dwell on.

They were set up in the interstellar ship's sick bay, which could just barely hold them and their accessory equipment. We got into them under Nafayum's fussy supervision, on opposite sides of a curtain the Ekhemasu had rigged up lest they violate any human nudity taboos. After we were settled in, the curtain was removed and each of us was fitted with various IV ports and other kinds of connections, for we would in effect be cyborgs for the duration.

Chloe raised herself up and spoke to Nafayum. "Are you going to make us unconscious *before* you close the lids of these things?"

"Why, yes. That is part of the standard procedure."

"Good," said Chloe, and our eyes met. She, clearly, had been thinking the same thing I had about coffins. For a long moment we looked at each other, each memorizing the other's face. Then we settled back down.

An IV tube was inserted in one of the ports. I heard a humming, chugging sound. . . .

I blinked a few times. Then I noticed that the overhead I was staring at wasn't the overhead of the sickbay. Then I noticed I was lying in a bed, in a small, featureless cabin. Then I noticed Khorat.

"There is no sensation of the passage of time," he explained.

I tried to speak, but my mouth was very dry. I swallowed and tried again. "You mean—?"

"The procedure was a success. Nafayum has already departed for Khemava with her equipment. We will soon be getting under way for Earth."

I started to sit up, but I was very stiff. I raised my right arm, so that it came into my field of vision.

It wasn't my right arm. The wrist was longer, the hand narrower, the hairs darker, the skin tone sallower.

Khorat read my expression correctly. Without being

asked, he handed me a mirror. I stared into it for a long time.

I had wondered if Nafayum was going to make me Black or Asian or something. She hadn't, but the face in the mirror didn't seem to fit any familiar ethnic category. I'd always been a square-faced, blunt-nosed type. Nafayum and her swarms of microscopic little helpers had made my cheekbones grow higher, while narrowing and lengthening the jaw, and producing a snoot Caesar wouldn't have been ashamed of. To my relief, she'd left my hair as thick as ever, but instead of being wavy and medium brown it was now straight and brown-black. My complexion was likewise darker, and my hazel eyes had turned deep brown. A dark stubble shadowed my lower face; evidently I'd been out of stasis long enough for my beard to resume growing, in its new color.

"Your fingerprints, retinal pattern and blood type are also changed," Khorat informed me. "Nafayum was quite proud of her work."

I managed to sit up and swing my legs over the side of the bed. Very carefully, I stood up. There seemed something very slightly wrong with the angle at which I was seeing Khorat. I later learned that Nafayum, by some overall skeletal lengthening and narrowing, had added a little over an inch to my height, making me almost six feet three.

I stood up, and almost fell back onto the bed as a dizzy spell took me. I felt stiff and awkward as hell, but as soon as my head stopped spinning I found I could walk.

"Chloe . . . ?" I queried. My voice sounded a little odd to me: not quite as deep, and with a slight nasal quality.

"The metamorphosis was likewise a success in her case,

and she is also awake. Would you like to see her?"

"Very much." Cautiously, I stepped through the hatch into the passageway. The next hatch down opened just as I was turning toward it. A figure emerged.

What's another woman doing here? I thought stupidly, before realization hit.

Chloe's hair had been lightened to a tawny blond. The vivid blue eyes that were probably her most distinctive feature were now a less memorable gray-green, and they flanked a snub nose. Her cheekbones, in contrast to mine, had been lowered to make her face oval rather than heart-shaped. Her overall bodily type, like mine, seemed to have been very slightly lengthened and narrowed. (Could this have reflected an esthetic bias of the low-gravity-dwelling Ekhemasu, who probably saw all humans as disproportionately stocky?)

Then she walked toward me and smiled . . . and I wondered if maybe Nafayum was kidding herself about our parents not recognizing us. The Chloe I knew was still in there—the Chloe that had been moving and gesturing and smiling in certain ways for a lifetime. But then, I *knew* this was Chloe, so I knew what to look for. Someone who didn't—Renata Novak, say—would never dream it was she.

I wondered if some such ghost of me still lived inside the character I'd seen in the mirror. I hoped so.

"Bob!" she greeted, "You look . . ." As she spoke, and looked up into my face, her smile faded into a frown of puzzlement. Then her mouth fell open in a gasp, her eyes widened, and the perplexity in her face changed to something indistinguishable from horror.

"Hey, Chloe, I know I need a shave, but . . . Chloe? *Chloe?*"

In fiction, women are always fainting. I'd never found that particularly believable, never having seen one actually do it. So I was unprepared when Chloe's legs collapsed under her. I managed to catch her before she hit the deck.

"Khorat!" I yelled as I picked her up and carried her into her cabin. I'd barely laid her on the bed when Khorat arrived with an Ekhemasu who I assumed was a medic. The latter proceeded to gingerly examine a member of an unfamiliar species.

"It is unfortunate that Nafayum is no longer available for consultation," Khorat remarked as we sat in his tiny— on Ekhemasu standards—office. "But given the unaccustomed strains and stimuli to which her body has been subjected, some chemical imbalances are hardly surprising."

"Yeah, that's probably it," I said, taking a fortifying swallow of the sort-of-gin. "I was feeling pretty woozy myself." But neither that line of reasoning nor the booze could make me forget the stricken look I'd seen on Chloe's new face.

The hatch beeped for admission, and the obviously relieved medic entered. "She is conscious," he reported, "and apparently suffering from no ill effects. I have told her to rest for a time."

"Thanks, Doc. Can I see her?" I glanced sideways at Khorat. "Alone?"

"Yes, although she should not be fatigued."

I hastened to the sick bay, where human-sized bedding had been improvised. Chloe was lying on her back with her eyes closed, but she didn't look asleep. Instead, she looked like she was thinking with a veritable fury of concentration.

"Hi," I said tentatively. "How are you feeling?"

Chloe's eyes snapped open, and for an instant the stunned look reappeared. But only for an instant, for she clamped a neutral expression down like a steel shutter.

"Oh, hi, Bob," she said in a voice as controlled as her features. "I'm fine, just tired."

I took Chloe's hands. To my relief, she didn't jerk them away. "Chloe, please tell me what's the matter."

She took a deep breath, and a smile trembled to life on lips that weren't quite as full as they had been. "Nothing's wrong, Bob. Nothing. I'm just not feeling myself yet, and it was disorienting, and . . . Bob, could you let me rest for a while?"

"Oh sure. Sure. Best thing for you." I hastened to leave her alone.

A few hours later, she emerged from the sick bay, to all appearances calm and cheerful. And so she remained for the next couple of Earth days, as the Ekhemasu completed their preparations for departure.

But it wasn't the same. From time to time, I caught her staring at me in a way she never had before. I told myself she was just intrigued by my new face. But I knew there was more to it than that, although I couldn't imagine what. And despite the bewildered hurt I felt, I didn't dare force the issue by demanding answers.

There was only one thing of which I was reasonably certain: behind her consciously maintained barrier of superficial normalcy, she was still thinking very, very hard.

CHAPTER SIXTEEN

The dry-planet-dwelling Ekhemasu had no nautical tradition of giving ships names. Not being a swabby, I was untroubled by any superstitions about bad luck arising from the lack.

A fat lot I knew.

At any rate, our unnamed ship naturally followed the day/night cycle of Khemava. So once again Chloe and I had to establish our own schedule, which had nothing to do with that of our hosts. At least we could set the lights in our cabins so as to simulate the twenty-four-hour period for which we had evolved. This was easier on our metabolisms, but didn't always facilitate interaction with Khorat.

For example, we woke up one morning (as defined by us) to discover that we had slept through the ship's departure from the Khemava system.

"We saw no point in awakening you," Khorat explained when we sought him out in the observation lounge. The semicircular screen was set for view-aft, and the stars were streaming past us and receding at the impossible rate we remembered from our voyage to Antyova. For all the rock-steady artificial gravity, I had to fight a momentary impulse to grab on to something.

"But why the rush?" Chloe asked. "I didn't think we were scheduled for departure for another twenty-four hours at least. What happened?"

Khorat turned to face us, and his aspect quieted us. He seemed shaken to the core. "Circumstances have altered. A ship arrived at Khemava bearing new information from our Tonkuztra sources in the Osak *gevroth*, who in turn had obtained it through their infiltration of their Tosava rivals." The old Ekhemar trailed to a halt, and I realized it wasn't just a pause for dramatic effect. He was, quite simply preoccupied . . . and, I began to suspect, even more shaken than I'd thought.

"And . . . ?" I prompted.

Khorat pulled himself together. "It seems we badly underestimated Novak and her confederates. We thought they would still be in the organizational stage. In fact, their time ship is approaching readiness, sooner than we ever dreamed possible. They must have begun preparing the ship itself, in all respects other than the actual time-displacement apparatus, in anticipation of success in obtaining that apparatus. It is the kind of total commitment possible only to the true fanatic."

"So," I demanded, "where does this leave us?"

"Our strategy of infiltration, using the two of you, is almost certainly no longer viable. Novak must already have her personnel in place. So, however much it runs counter to our natural instincts, we will probably have to resort to brute force methods and disable Novak's ship before it commences its temporal displacement."

Chloe's newly gray-green eyes were round. "Are you saying that this ship is *armed*?" I didn't feel as shocked as she sounded—blame it on my background—but even I could guess at the magnitude of the illegality involved.

"Not heavily armed," Khorat said hastily. "That would be quite impossible for a ship this size. The weapons of space warfare are, of necessity, massive—or so I'm told. It isn't exactly my subject."

"Yeah," I nodded. The Project had learned something about the way war was waged among the stars. "That's why capital ships are generally designed as close as they can get to the fifty-thousand-ton upper limit imposed by the interstellar drive. Laser weapons, no matter how advanced, can't get away from one hard fact: all other things being equal, the greater the diameter of the focusing optics, the greater the effective range. And as for missiles, field drives—even ones designed to burn themselves out in a single suicide run—can be miniaturized by only so much. So missiles that can catch faster-than-light ships have to be big, which means a ship has to be *damned* big to carry a useful number of them."

"You put me to shame with your knowledge of these matters," said Khorat graciously. "You will understand, then, why we were only able to equip this ship with a single small laser weapon—not intended for an antishipping role at all, but rather for short-range defense. Nevertheless, within its limited range it should be capable of inflicting disabling damage on a space vessel."

"Unless that vessel blows us into dust bunnies first," I commented gloomily.

"Remember, Novak will not have a purpose-built warship either. In fact, our assessment is that it won't be armed at all. Why should it be? Its destination is a time and place where no other space vehicles exist. Ship-to-ship weapons would have no targets!"

I considered this. It seemed to hold up . . . except for one little problem Khorat had overlooked. The peewee laser cannon the Medjavar had welded onto their ship would be manned—well, you know what I mean—by beings evolution had neglected to equip with a killer instinct. That hadn't occurred to Khorat for the simple reason that he himself was one of those beings.

"So, Khorat," asked Chloe, "if the original plan—the one involving us—has gone by the boards, then what are we doing here?"

"Complete with our new bodies," I added.

Khorat showed the signs I'd learned to read as reflecting discomfort. "It is true that Nafayum's work has probably gone for naught. But, as I have indicated, this news forced an urgent revision of our plans, leaving no time to send the two of you back to Khemava. Besides . . . are you sure you would have *wanted* to be left behind, to wonder whether we had succeeded?"

"Now that you mention it, no," I admitted.

"One other question." Chloe spoke with an intensity which, like so much about her these days, I didn't understand. "You're noted for your contingency plans, Khorat. What's the fallback position if we're *not* in time to catch Novak's ship 'before it commences its temporal displacement,' as I believe you put it?"

"In that event," said the old Ekhemar slowly, "we will have no alternative but to set out in pursuit."

For a heartbeat or two, I genuinely didn't get it. Maybe it was because I was staring at Chloe, who had closed her eyes and was nodding repeatedly as though at the unsurprising confirmation of a suspicion. But then, for some reason, I remembered Khorat's slip of the tongue when we'd first come aboard: something about the modifications to this ship, and the fact that some of them might not be illegal, strictly speaking. . . .

"Khorat," my mouth said for me before my mind had really come to grips with the notion, "are you, by any chance, implying that this is a *time ship*?"

"We truly believed that the capability would not be necessary. We still hope that it will not. But we had to face the possibility. We began fitting this ship with it at the same time we began installing the laser weapon."

"But Novak stole the data! And you told me the Medjavar don't believe in making copies."

"In this case, we made an exception. The potential consequences of a theft of this knowledge—not that we ever really believed in the possibility—were such that we had to reserve to ourselves the capability of countering it. Indeed, we extended Imhaermekh's theoretical work. We discovered . . . Well, remember the analogy I drew between time travel and falling? And my remark that there are dimensions in which one can 'fall' faster than in others?" Khorat paused, and I sensed his irritated frustration with the need to express these concepts in baby talk lest the translator simply shut down. English was as about as well-suited to this discussion as Mycenaean Greek would have been to teaching a class in TV repair.

"At any rate, we have knowledge that Novak did *not* steal. Using that knowledge, we have equipped this ship to access those 'faster' dimensions."

"So," I asked, "you think you can catch her if she doesn't get too much of a head start?"

Khorat gave the small backward jerk of the head that was his race's equivalent of a human's wince, and I tried to imagine how my question came across in translation. "That is, I suppose, one way to put it. But, to repeat, we have every hope of arriving before it becomes necessary to use this capability. So with any luck the whole matter will prove academic."

"Luck is like government," I philosophized. "Everybody needs a little of it, but only a fool relies on it."

The voyage to the Solar System took about as long as our previous journey to the Antyova system had. It just didn't seem as long.

I spent the time getting checked out on the laser weapon. I'd never had a chance to observe galactic-level shipboard weaponry. The Project had produced a few such weapons, at staggering expense. But they were just for show, as part of the deception. Otherwise, there was no point. We didn't have a prayer in hell of actually going toe-to-toe with any of the starfaring powers.

What I saw confirmed what I'd read. In theory, greater ranges could have been obtained by designing focusing optics that unfolded repeatedly to vast diameters until the ship itself was like a small spider in the center of a large web. But in practice, such an array would have been hopelessly vulnerable—not just to enemy action and space junk, but also to Murphy's Law. As always with military hardware, rugged reliability counted for more than any number of fancy-pants refinements. This weapon, like all of its kind, was almost entirely contained in the ship's hull, into which it was normally faired. Only when it was time for action did it exude a small focusing array resembling your idea of a radar dish. It was not a serious weapon for space warfare as the great Delkasu empires waged it. In human naval terms, it was like the popgun carried by a Coast Guard cutter. But for what Khorat had in mind, it ought to serve, just as a Coast Guard cutter could stop a smuggler's cabin cruiser.

The fundamental principle wasn't unfamiliar to me, inasmuch as the Project had arranged for the laser to be "invented" in 1959. Of course, the superconductor-loop "capacitors" stored energy at a density Earth's mainstream science denied was even theoretically possible, and there were a lot of other engineering details that smacked of Clarke's Law. But I could handle the basic concepts, rather like a Renaissance person looking at an automobile; the electrical systems would have been a mystery, and the internal combustion engine would have seemed fantastic (although I'll bet Leonardo would have picked up on it in no time), but the wheels and gears would have presented no problem.

The time machine was another matter.

I persisted in thinking of it as that, since the translator's "temporal displacement field generator" had too many syllables. It was a small thing, and as Khorat had explained it didn't draw much power. And yet, staring at it, I was like my imaginary Renaissance man studying an X-ray machine. I soon gave up.

Instead, I occupied myself with dry runs on the laser cannon. The controls took some getting used to. This was even more true of the handheld weapons in a locker that the Ekhemasu mostly avoided with visible distaste. I pestered Thramoz, who was the equivalent of a human ship's master-at-arms, until he let me try the things out. They, too, were based on the laser principle; galactic-level energy storage technology made this practical for a weapon I could lift with no more difficulty than, say, a BAR. Designed by and for Ekhemasu, it was awkward as hell for a human to hold and fire, but the total lack of recoil would help make up for that.

I anticipated an argument when I suggested to Chloe that she also familiarize herself with the weaponry. She surprised me by falling in with the idea at once. The bulk and weight of the portables were more of a problem for her than for me, but she actually adapted better to handling the Ekhemasu-style grips and firing mechanisms, not having my burden of drilled-in habits to unlearn.

As we went through these sessions, I continued to observe her, trying to understand the change in her. She was still quite obviously concealing something behind shutters of superficial normalcy. But there was a subtle change in what that something was. Before, it had been appalled fear and uncertainty, whose origin was a mystery to me. Now, I sensed, all that had been replaced by a deep certainty, and an irrevocable decision based on that certainty—a certainty, and a decision, which I could not be allowed to share. And that still hurt.

So matters stood as we approached the Solar System.

It came as no surprise that our ship had a state-of-the-art stealth suite, and was not announcing its presence through regular channels to the Project's *faux* governmental authorities. Nevertheless, it came to a halt somewhere outside the Oort Cloud, where the Sun was still just another zero-magnitude star.

Chloe and I had no idea what was going on, for Khorat was inaccessible, deliberately or otherwise. So, with nothing better to do, we took ourselves to the observation lounge. We arrived just in time to see a small vessel enter the viewscreen's pickup as it rendezvoused with us. From the size of it and other indications, the stranger was a ship designed by and for Delkasu.

There was no physical contact between the two ships. The new arrival merely held position off our starboard side for a time, during which we assumed radio communications were being exchanged. After a while, the other ship swung away and disappeared. Almost immediately, the alarm sounded and our ship went back into field drive—but rather slowly, judging from the apparent motion of the stars.

Shortly thereafter, Khorat entered—he must have had a pretty good idea where we'd be. By this time, we'd been among the Ekhemasu long enough to recognize a bearer of bad tidings.

"That ship belonged to the Osak *gevroth*," he began, earning my gratitude by not going through the motions of pretending he didn't know we had been watching. "Their sources of information indicate that Novak is even closer to departure than we thought."

"Then why are we dawdling?" I demanded, waving my arm at the viewscreen.

"Security reasons," said Khorat succinctly.

"Security? You mean you're afraid Novak will find out we're coming? And what has that got to do with our speed?"

"Not her. We don't know what galactic ships are currently in this system. If there are any, and they have the proper sensors, a field drive operating at transluminal velocities is easy to detect—indeed, difficult to miss. Remember, the Medjavar's possession of this ship is not generally known. We could be badly compromised."

My mouth was half-open to inquire just exactly what difference that would make, given what he himself had told us about the consequences of Novak getting away into the past. But then I thought better of it. What was the use? I knew from experience how security procedures could take on a life of their own, like religious rituals that had lost their meaning. And what about a habit of concealment that dated back thousands of years?

"All right." I sighed. "So we're proceeding at less than lightspeed, despite the news you've just gotten. Does this mean we're going to have to travel into the past after all?"

"It appears increasingly likely," Khorat admitted, "that we will indeed have to pursue Novak and destroy her ship while in temporal transit."

"Well," I said . . . and found myself at a loss for anything further to say.

Chloe spoke up hesitantly. "Khorat, don't get me wrong: I don't in any way condone what Renata has done. But you talk like destroying her ship is the only option. Couldn't we at least try to . . . well, apprehend her and bring her back to the present day?"

Khorat turned his huge, somehow melancholy eyes on her, and spoke after a long pause. The voice in my earpiece was so expressionless it was barely recognizable as Khorat's.

"Oh, no. That's quite out of the question. Traveling

forward in time is a theoretical possibility—indeed, Imhaermekh succeeded in sending subatomic particles a few microseconds into the future—but as a practical matter the energy curve involved rises swiftly to infinity."

For a moment, we sat in a silence of bewilderment . . . or, perhaps, of unwillingness or inability to credit what we'd just heard. Chloe finally broke it. "Khorat, I'm not talking about traveling into the future. I'm talking about returning to the time you set out from in the first place."

"That's not the way it works." Had a hint of compassion crept into the artificial voice? "There is no such thing as *the* future or *the* past. There is only time on one side or the other of the constantly advancing wave front we call the present. It is analogous to the relativity theories your civilization has already evolved: a time traveler's 'native' point in time has no 'privileged position.' Or, to put it another way, once one goes backwards in time, one's original point of departure becomes part of 'the future.' The *unattainable* future."

"But . . ." I shook my head and tried again. "But in that case how do you get back to where . . . I mean *when* you came from?"

"You don't." Khorat's bluntness was merciless. "It is strictly a one-way trip."

It is possible for anger to reach such a level that it defeats itself, leaving you strangely calm. Staring at Khorat, I found I had entered into that state of emotional overload.

On the fringes of my consciousness, I heard Chloe's quiet voice. "Does Novak know this?"

"She must. She has all the relevant data at her disposal." Khorat turned brisk. "And now I must consult with

my colleagues, as we will be nearing your sun shortly."
He departed hastily.

For a moment, I stared at the hatch through which he
had disappeared. I discovered that the eerie calmness I'd
felt was like the eye of the hurricane: a deceptive pause
in the storm. Without a word I strode out of the lounge
and toward my cabin. I could hear Chloe following me.

As soon as the hatch closed behind us, I smashed my
fist hammer-style into a bulkhead. The pain broke my
inhibitions. "That lying cocksucker!" I roared, indifferent
to whether or not the cabin was bugged. "That
motherfucking son of a bitch! He never told us!"

You have to understand: I was born in 1936, to middle-
class American parents. In the world I came from, men
were about as foul-mouthed among themselves as they
would be in later times—this always seems to come as a
shocking surprise to my juniors—but you simply didn't
use obscenities in the presence of a lady . . . unless, that
is, you were so enraged as to be past caring about such
things. And I had never been so furious in my life. I raved
on until I ran out of breath.

"Well," Chloe ventured, "he never actually claimed it
was possible to return from a temporal displacement into
the past."

"No, he just kept quiet and let us take it for granted!"
I grasped her by the shoulders. "Chloe, if we arrive in
Earth orbit and find that Novak's ship is no longer there,
you and I are going to have to stop Khorat."

"Stop him? How?"

"Take over the ship!"

"Take over the ship?" she echoed. "The two of us? But
there are . . . how many Ekhemasu aboard?"

"It doesn't matter. We know where that small-arms locker is—and I can get into it."

"But . . . what if some of the crew have already drawn hand weapons by then? I'll bet Thramoz, at least, will have."

"So what? Chloe, the Ekhemasu are descended from a million generations of herbivorous herd animals. I've seen it, even in Thramoz: put them in a combat situation, and their chromosomes will tell them to run—or, if there's no place to run, freeze up in the hope that if they hold still the predators won't notice them."

"You're serious, aren't you?" she asked quietly.

"Damned right I'm serious! Khorat has gone 'round the bend. He's ready to charge off into interdimensional chaos even though he knows he can't get back. It's up to us! Are you with me?"

Chloe stared at me, and at first I saw the same thing I'd seen in her since the day we'd met in the passageway and seen each other's new faces: a drawing of shutters, behind which her thoughts seemed to be racing furiously. But then, abruptly, all that was gone and, despite everything Nafayum had done, the old Chloe was back. All my fire and fury drowned in her smile.

"Yes, Bob. Yes. I'm with you. But first . . ." Her arms went around my waist and drew me close, with more strength than I'd known she possessed. "Bob, I can't wait any longer. I need you, Bob, and we may not have another chance. Please take me!"

To say I was stunned would be an understatement. "Chloe," I said weakly, "we've talked about this for God knows how long . . . and the same arguments still apply—"

"I know, my love. And I don't care anymore!" Before I

knew what was happening, her left arm snaked around my neck and drew my head down, and she kissed me with a fierce hunger.

There is, I truly believe, nothing so overwhelming as instant, unanticipated eroticism. Everything else was forgotten as I responded to her kiss.

We finally broke apart to catch our breath. She backed off a step, smiled roguishly, and drew me by the hands. "Come."

I let her lead me to her cabin through the empty passageway—the Ekhemasu were otherwise occupied. As soon as we were inside, she poured us drinks of the Ekhemasu attempt at gin.

I didn't need alcohol at that point. But I was willing to abide by whatever rituals she wanted to impose. I tossed off the drink, then took her in my arms.

I had never known what lovemaking could be, before experiencing her.

I awoke with a horrible combination of headache and nausea, not unlike a migraine. But it wasn't a migraine, because it began to recede as soon as I managed to swing my legs out of the bed and get shakily to my feet.

Chloe was gone. The cabin was empty.

I got back into my clothes, stumbled to the hatch and, with gradually increasing steadiness, made my way aft to the observation lounge. It, too, was empty. So I started forward, toward a hatch I had never entered, nor been invited to enter.

I'd seen the Ekhemasu open it by placing one of their three-digited hands on a pad on the bulkhead beside it. I assumed it was coded for those alone—and, even among them, probably for authorized personnel only. But, for lack of anything else to try, I pressed the pad. To my surprise, the hatch slid silently open. I stepped through into the control room.

It was dimly lit by the glow of instrument panels, and by the stars and the cloud-swirled blue globe that shone in the hemispherical viewscreen that enclosed the forward end. Two figures were silhouetted against that cosmic panorama. One was an Ekhemar who, as I approached closer, I recognized as Khorat. The other was easier to identify—effortless, in fact, as there was only one other human aboard.

"So we're already entering Earth orbit," I said, for I knew that blue globe.

Khorat turned to face me. "Ah, you are awake. Yes, we have arrived. And Novak has departed—barely ahead of us. We are positioning ourselves to proceed on the same temporal . . . vector."

I wasn't really listening to him, for Chloe had also turned, and our eyes met. We stared at each other wordlessly, and her face reflected more conflicting emotions than I'd thought a human soul could contain.

There were so many things I could have said . . . but I said nothing. For among all the storm of thoughts in my head, one rose like a whitecap above a raging sea: the Mickey she'd put in my drink must have been prepared *beforehand*. It was easy, looking back clear-eyed, to see how she'd slipped it in—her back had been to me as she'd poured—but it had to have been already there.

"Prepare for temporal displacement," Khorat said quietly.

Something happened to the universe in the viewscreen.

It was difficult for the mind to grasp just what that some-thing was. But then it was over, and the stars went out. But in an indescribable way it was as though they had never been, or were anticipated in the future, for we had entered a realm in which time had a different meaning.

We were committed.

CHAPTER SEVENTEEN

The characteristics of the space we were in didn't grow less weird with familiarity. The strange, subliminal sense that things had happened, or been said, before did not go away. Sound had a hollow, wavering quality, and motion took place as though in a series of rapid photographic frames. And the viewscreen was difficult to look at. It wasn't even blackness; it was just *nothing*.

But to tell the truth, I hardly noticed the eeriness, for my thoughts were in a whirl. My bewildered anger and hurt over Chloe's betrayal—*Why?* I longed to cry out to her, but of course I couldn't in the control room—was almost canceled out by despair at the knowledge that it was too late to stop Khorat in his crazy quest, for we had been plunged irrevocably into the past. I felt adrift, cut off from both my time and my love.

It was too much. There seemed nothing adequate to say. So I settled for, "How fast are we going backwards in time?"

"I beg your pardon?"

"Damn it, Khorat, you know what I mean! At what rate are we going into the past? What's the time right now in our universe?"

"The question cannot be answered with precision, as we have no referents." Khorat indicated the nothingness in the viewscreen. "As I mentioned previously, there are innumerable dimensions—as I must refer to them—in which temporal displacement can take place. While one can theoretically drop into any one of them that is attainable at all, it is safest to progress through them one at a time. We have, I believe, completed those translations." Khorat glanced at an Ekhemar seated at a nearby computer station, and received a gesture of confirmation. "If our theoretical projections of the ratio of displacement are correct, then for each unit of subjective time that passes within the field encompassing this ship, we are receding into the past by slightly in excess of seventeen thousand of those units."

I did some quick mental arithmetic: a little less than two years per hour. . . .

Chloe had clearly done the same calculation, and gone an additional step beyond it. "So Renata is looking at a trip of about three and a half days, to reach the period she's after."

"Actually, over four of your days, or one of ours. Remember, her temporal displacement is proceeding at a significantly lesser rate than ours. This gives us ample time to . . . overtake her."

"How long?" I demanded.

"Once again, I cannot give you a precise answer, as we do not know the exact rate of her displacement . . . or of our own, come to that. But theory predicts that this ship and hers should become mutually contemporaneous between not less than seven nor more than nine subjective hours from now."

"But," I protested, "how can we tell when it's happened? I mean, her ship is in another dimension, right? So how will we be able to detect it?"

"By its gravitational potential. You see, we have sensors based on the gravity waves which, I believe, your world's mainstream science still regards as hypothetical at best."

"Yeah," I said shortly. My patience with being patronized had been wearing thinner and thinner. "We've heard of these devices. I understand they're very bulky."

"True. This ship can only accommodate a very short-ranged sensor suite. But that is all that is required. You see, we commenced our temporal displacement at no great distance from where Novak did—and objects in this state of dimensional phasing conserve their spatial relationships in our own universe. And, for reasons concerning which I'll have to refer you to the specialists, the gravitational 'shadow' which makes the sensors possible is detectable across the dimensional divide."

"But," I persisted, "we won't be able to see her ship until we 'become contemporaneous' with it?"

"Not altogether true. Once we detect it, we will immediately begin to come into phase with it. Once we get 'close' enough to it, dimensionally speaking, it will become visible, albeit indistinctly. Indeed, under these conditions we should be able to appear to physically interpenetrate with it—a somewhat unsettling sensation, I would imagine." Khorat paused reflectively. "Come to think of it, if the two ships came into full dimensional synchronicity, permitting actual physical interaction, while such an interpenetration was taking place, it would end the problem rather definitively."

"It would end *us* rather definitively," I pointed out. "You're not really planning to . . . ?"

"Oh, no. It was only a thought." But Khorat's tone was altogether *too* damned thoughtful for my taste.

"Then what *is* the plan?" Chloe sounded like she wanted to get Khorat's mind off this particular track without delay.

"The impellers, being reactionless in nature, will function under the conditions of temporal displacement, though at a reduced level of efficiency. In other words, we can maneuver, albeit sluggishly. We will establish synchronicity with Novak's ship at the closest range we can safely manage, and . . . use the laser weapon."

"And what then?" Chloe persisted. "Assuming that all goes according to plan, where does that leave us?"

"We will immediately disengage the temporal displacement field generator, and drop back into the normal universe. As I have indicated, we should be only twenty years or less into the past."

"But Khorat," Chloe continued remorselessly, "our history has no mention of an Ekhemasu ship appearing in Earth orbit. And your history doesn't include slightly older versions of you and Thramoz and the rest showing up on Khemava. So won't we be doing the same thing you told us Novak would do by changing the past?"

Khorat tried to look away, but Chloe met those huge dark eyes and held them. There was an urgent intensity in her that could be sensed even from beyond the gulf of alienness. He spoke expressionlessly. "We have anticipated the possibility that this situation might arise ever since we . . . dealt with Imhaermekh. So we took steps. Some time ago the Medjavar prepared a habitat in a hollowed-out asteroid in the trailing-Trojan position of our sun's fourth planet. Then it was left to robotic maintenance, unoccupied and unapproached. Only a few individuals know of its existence. Only a *very* few, of whom I am one, know its location. We will remain cloaked when we appear in Earth orbit. We will then proceed back to the Khemava system, to that habitat. There we Ekhemasu will pass the remainder of our lives, unable to influence history."

By now, I knew the capabilities of the translator software too well to doubt that what I'd just heard was precisely what Khorat had said, and meant. So I tried to cope with it on its own terms. I failed. The philosophy behind it was simply too foreign. Compared to the Medjavar, the monks of Mount Athos were regular guys.

"So," I finally managed, "you and the rest of this ship's crew have been sitting tight inside some asteroid for the last couple of decades, while at the same time you—that is, the *you* I'm talking to right now—have been on Khemava, and on Antyova II meeting me, and . . ." My head was starting to spin.

"We can only hope so." Khorat's bland insouciance was returning. "That would mean that our present mission succeeded."

My head spun faster.

"And what about Bob and me?" I silently applauded

Chloe for not losing sight of that little matter. But her tone was still strange, and her face wore the look of a soldier advancing into a minefield.

"We are not devoid of ethics. Our intention is to return the two of you to your own world as soon as it is safe to do so—that is to say, as soon as we can manufacture identities for you. Among Earth's teeming billions, you should not be able to alter history in any measurable way . . . and I hope what I have told you will persuade you not to try. At a minimum, we will require your solemn promise that you will make no attempt to contact your own younger selves."

"So," I breathed, "was this what you really had in mind all along when you had Nafayum do a makeover on us?"

"By no means. What you were told about our plans was quite truthful . . . at the time. Of course, I cannot deny that some such contingency as this entered our minds."

A contingency you never thought to mention to us, I thought darkly. Chloe remained inscrutable.

Thramoz got up from behind a computer station—the weapon station, I assumed—and spoke matter-of-factly. "We should all get into survival suits, while there is nothing for anyone except watch-standers to do."

"A sensible suggestion," said Khorat, obviously grateful for the interruption.

Suits had been prepared to my and Chloe's measurements. Aside from their size and shape, they were like the Ekhemasu models, which means they bore little resemblance to your visualization of a "space suit." They were flexible, lightweight, form-fitting jumpsuits made of quasi-alive, self-repairing nanoplastic. No bulky air tanks or anything; just a small belt-mounted bottle with enough air to pressurize the suit, after which it could keep you alive for weeks on your own recycled exhalations and wastes. All you had to do was slip on gloves and pull over a flexible transparent hoodlike helmet. As everyone got suited up, Chloe and I were never alone. (Was it my imagination, or did she arrange it that way?)

Then we waited. The hours crawled by with an unnatural slowness that had nothing to do with the peculiarities of the space in which we were falling backwards through time.

When it finally came, the alarm seemed deafening.

"Novak's ship has been detected," said Khorat unnecessarily, amid the crackling tension that suddenly pervaded the control room. "We will now begin to close with it, in dimensional terms."

"Why can't we just go directly to the same dimension Novak is in?" I wondered aloud.

"That is theoretically possible. But interdimensional energy differentials make it unacceptably risky. It is safer to transition gradually from one dimension to another, as we are doing now."

Even as he spoke, the disturbing blankness in the viewscreen began to change.

It was barely perceptible at first, as though a mist was trying to solidify into the form of a spacecraft a few thousand yards to port and a little ahead of us. Then it came into focus . . . but a ghostly, transparent kind of focus. Then it began to flicker and go out. The control room crew went silently but unmistakably to a higher pitch of concentration.

"Novak, or her pilot, is doubtless trying to evade us by

shifting dimensionally," Khorat explained. "Of course, she can only shift 'downward,' inasmuch as her ship was already at its highest attainable level of temporal displacement. This simplifies our problem in matching her shifting." And even as we watched, the phantom ship began to firm up again.

Novak tried a new tack, attempting physical evasive action now that the dimensional variety had failed. But I could now see what Khorat had meant about the sluggishness of impeller-driven maneuvering in this strange medium. Our quarry—it looked like a ship made of glass— swung away from us with no more apparent swiftness than a sailing vessel beating into the wind. We followed suit, but such maneuvers were evidently hard to control as well as slow. Before our pilot could compensate, he had overshot Novak's ship . . . and, for a second we occupied the same space it did, in a slightly different dimensional phase.

That interpenetration was utterly indescribable. For an instant, I was only a few yards away from what looked like the ghost of Renata Novak, her mouth open and shouting inaudible commands. Then we were past.

"Stand by for dimensional synchronicity," the pilot called out. Thramoz, at the weapon station from which he could directly control the laser cannon, stiffened into a posture of tense expectancy.

But I was conscious of none of this, for my mind was empty of all save the stunning realization of what I had, at the last split second, glimpsed through the transparent inner complexities of Novak's ship. There could be no mistake, for it was a shape I'd come to know lately.

"Khorat," I blurted, *"she's got a laser cannon!"*

The old Ekhemar stood immobilized by shock. With a

curse, I turned away from him toward the pilot's station.

"Abort!" I yelled.

It was too late. At that moment, the two ships came into full dimensional synchronicity. With shocking abruptness, Novak's ship was there in all its solid reality.

Thramoz shouted something and jabbed at his controls.

With a hideous din of tearing metal, the ship cried out its agony. Concussion threw us to the deck.

Even laser beams using the wavelengths detectable by human eyes are invisible in vacuum. Still more so are the X-ray lasers that are standard shipboard armament.

Otherwise, though, the Hollywood version was surprisingly accurate. Rather than a continuous beam—impractical for a lot of reasons—a weapons-grade laser delivers a short, intense pulse of energy to a small area of its target, which it vaporizes, causing an explosion like the one whose shock waves had sent us sprawling.

But I'd underestimated the Ekhemasu . . . or at least Thramoz, an atypical specimen of the race. He must have fired in the same nanosecond as Novak's human gunner, because—incredibly—the two beams had struck with such simultaneity that both laser weapons were disabled.

"Furthermore," Thramoz reported to Khorat, "we believe the target has lost its ability to shift dimensionally, or to maneuver under impeller drive. Otherwise, it would be doing one or the other now, to evade us."

"But it can still return to the normal universe?" Khorat asked anxiously.

"Presumably. That merely requires disengaging the temporal displacement field generator. But Novak will not want to do so yet, as we are still less than twenty years into the past, far short of the era she is aiming for."

"But she can still do it whenever she chooses." Khorat's body language held more despair than the translator could put into a voice.

"What about us?" I demanded. The ship's air held an acrid smell of electrical fires, and I could hear a distant commotion that smacked of damage control.

"Our life support, navigational and drive systems are in no danger," Thramoz told me. "Only our laser weapon is damaged beyond hope of repair. Presumably, Novak targeted it first, intending to finish us off at her leisure afterwards."

"You prevented that," Chloe told him fiercely. "You nailed them to the wall!"

Thramoz looked about as comfortable with the compliment as a human would have been with praise for virtuosity as a cannibal chef. "Well, computer analysis indicates that our laser cannon was the more powerful, so our one shot caused more damage than theirs."

"So," I summarized for him, "they're sitting out there dead in the water, incapable of firing on us or getting away from us."

"But quite capable of reentering the time stream at whatever point Novak chooses," said Khorat in a voice of gray emptiness. "We can, of course, follow suit. But without a ship-to-ship weapon, we would have no more ability to thwart her than we possess here and now." His eyes strayed to the viewscreen and Novak's ship, visibly damaged and leaking a mist of air.

I knew in the pit of my stomach what he was thinking. He did, in fact, have a weapon left: our ship itself.

Desperation, not necessity, is the mother of invention. I spoke before even thinking the idea through. "Wait a minute, Khorat. We can *board* that ship!"

"Board?" Khorat repeated blankly.

"Sure. We've got an access tube, don't we?" The question was rhetorical; spacecraft air locks incorporated the device as standard equipment. Normally, it would extend itself to another vessel's air lock, forming a passageway through which one could stroll in shirtsleeve comfort. Well, not so much stroll as float, being outside either ship's artificial gravity field. This time, though . . . "You've told me Novak can't maneuver. We'll draw alongside, use the tube to attach ourselves to the side of the ship like a leech."

"And then?" Khorat queried. "Do you expect Novak to let us inside?"

"No, I expect us to blast our way in! Thramoz, I recall seeing a kind of semiportable laser weapon in your goodies locker."

"Yes! And this will allow us to utilize it. It can penetrate the hull of an ordinary civilian craft like that, allowing us to enter and—"

I shook my head. "Not 'us.' Think about it, Thramoz: that ship is designed for humans. Once inside, you wouldn't be able to squeeze through the passageways and hatches."

"That's right." Chloe moved to my side. "It has to be Bob and me."

"Like hell!" I exploded. "You're staying here."

"But I've checked out on the hand weapons! And besides, do you really think you can take that ship single-handed?" She laughed scornfully. "Blackbeard the pirate!"

"Novak only has a few people, and after the hit their

ship took you can bet some of them are out of action. And
the ones who aren't will be in a state of shock. And I'll
have the initiative. And . . . and . . . and you're not coming,
that's all!"

"Very well," Khorat said heavily. "You may make this
attempt. We can hardly lose anything by it. If you fail, we
can still exercise . . . the other option remaining to us."

Thramoz and I lugged the semiportable laser projector to the ship's service air lock and set it up. Then we
pressurized our survival suits as a precaution—whatever
else could be said of the medium we were in, it was
nothing that could be breathed—and settled in, Thramoz
behind the semiportable and me awkwardly cradling
something the size of a light machine gun. In the port-
hole of the air lock's outer door, Novak's ship hung
suspended in the middle distance.

Thramoz signaled the control room. Artificial gravity
kept the air lock floor steady under our feet as the ship
swung around on an intercept course.

Novak still had maneuvering thrusters, with which she
tried feebly to evade us. That game didn't last long. We
pulled alongside, and the flank of her ship filled our field of
vision. Thramoz touched a control panel, and the access
tube began to telescope outward until it met the other ship's
hull in a magnetic kiss. Thramoz opened the air lock's outer
door, and we looked down a tunnel with a closed end.

I nodded to Thramoz. He touched the firing stud.

Not even galactic technology could scale an X-ray laser
down to the size of our semiportable, and at any rate it
would have been useless in atmosphere, which absorbs
X-rays. So the beam Thramoz unleashed was in the visible-
light wavelengths, and it left a sparkling trail through the

air that had flowed outward from our air lock. But that trail was banished from our sight by the minisun that erupted at the far end of the tunnel, and an instant later a shock wave sent us staggering. These energies were not meant for an enclosed space.

Thramoz and I exchanged a quick look through out helmets. Then I launched myself into the weightlessness of the tunnel.

The transition was sickening, and I might have puked had I not had other things on my mind—notably, fighting the outflow of air from the ruptured hull ahead. That was an annoyance, but also a cause for exultation: we had burned our way through! I floundered forward and grabbed a curling piece of wreckage, pulling myself forward.

Getting through was no problem; there was barely enough intact hull material around the perimeter of the tunnel for the access tube's magnets to adhere to. Weight descended on me as I entered an artificial gravity field. It was full Earth-normal weight, to which I'd grown unaccustomed, but I was expecting it. I landed on my feet in a ruined passageway.

A survival-suited figure loomed ahead of me in the dim emergency lights. There was no one aboard that ship I was concerned with keeping alive; I brought up my laser weapon and used the awkward firing mechanism. The suit's nanoplastic was tough, but not that tough. Superheated body fluids erupted outward in an explosive energy transfer that smashed him (or her) back against a bulkhead as viciously as a large-caliber bullet would have.

I swung my weapon to left and right, alert for fresh targets. There were none in sight. But to the right, the hull was especially damaged, with great rents through which I glimpsed our ship, at the far end of the access tube.

And, out of the corner of my eye, I glimpsed something else.

From a little farther forward along the hull, a long jointed rod was unfolding itself and reaching toward our ship. I had no idea what it was or what it was for. But at its tip was something that held the unmistakable look of jury-rigging, as though it had been hastily attached.

The thought ripped through me in a silent scream: *limpet mine!*

As I watched, helpless, the tip reached our ship's flank and drew away, leaving the improvised object clinging there.

At that instant, as I stood paralyzed by horror, a weight at least equal to my own landed on my back, smashing me down to the deck and twisting my left arm behind me and upward.

Even as I struggled, I had a full view of the shattering explosion that sent our ship reeling away, clearly wrecked beyond hope of repair, leaving the access tube still attached to this ship, flopping obscenely about like a cut umbilical cord. Maybe it was just my imagination, but I thought I could see the survival-suited figure of Thramoz tumbling away from the open air lock into the depths of this lunatic space.

But I hardly noticed, for at that moment my entire soul was one vast, silent shriek of *Chloe!*

Something hard crashed against the flexible nanoplastic of my helmet. The pressurization cushioned the blow, and I didn't lose consciousness. But my head spun, and I lost my grip on the laser weapon I couldn't use anyway at such close quarters. Whoever it was who was grasping me from behind heaved my unsteady form upright.

I stared into the face of Renata Novak, silhouetted against a crescendo of secondary explosions that completed the destruction of the ship that had contained Chloe.

CHAPTER EIGHTEEN

"Do you have any idea why you're still alive?" Novak's question didn't seem to call for a reply, so I kept quiet as she answered herself. "Two reasons: first of all, I want to know just exactly who the hell you are, and what you were doing aboard what was obviously a Medjavar ship."

Realization brought me out of my sinkhole of despairing horror, and stilled my tongue before I could stupidly blurt something out. *She didn't recognize me.* Not having looked in a mirror lately, I'd forgotten that, thanks to Nafayum, I still had one card left to play.

"Don't you also want to know where Chloe Bryant and Robert Devaney are?" I asked, meeting her hate-filled eyes.

"Not particularly. If, as I suspect, they were aboard

that ship, you're not likely to admit it. And even if they are still alive, somewhere and somewhen, there's nothing they can do to stop me now."

"Stop you? Lady, you're already stopped! You may still be able to drop out of temporal displacement whenever you want to, but do you really think you'll be able to land this piece of wreckage you're flying?" I gestured at the ruined passageway around us and the rents in the hull. "If you try to reenter the atmosphere, all you'll do is burn up from friction and give the people on early nineteenth century Earth an extra shooting star to make wishes on. Why don't you just pack it in?"

For the barest instant, Novak blinked with puzzled annoyance, as though there was something vaguely familiar about her mysterious prisoner's voice, something she couldn't quite place. But then the look was gone, expunged by one of vicious gloating.

"You're mistaken. And that brings me to the second reason I haven't let Evan here kill you. I want you to live long enough to know you've failed. Bring him!"

The last two words were addressed to Evan, who jerked my arm even further up behind me, sending pain tearing through the shoulder, and shoved me forward. We followed Novak through passageways into areas that looked like they still had structural integrity, ending up in the control room, where Novak slapped a switch. I heard the rumble of closing airtight hatches behind us. Novak depressurized her survival suit and removed the helmet. Evan did the same for himself and me with his free hand. Then we continued forward into an open air lock whose most conspicuous feature was a round hatch in the middle of the deck.

Novak pointed at the hatch in the deck. "Do you know what's down there?" I did, but saw no reason to deprive her of the pleasure of answering her own question. "The lifeboat. It is undamaged, being recessed into the underside of the ship, as you probably know is standard."

I did, in fact, know that. The so-called lifeboat that all spaceships carried was, in fact, a very small lifting body with rudimentary impellers that could bring it to a landing on a planetary surface—in the ocean, if necessary, for it had flotation capacity though no aquatic propulsion. A human-designed one could hold four people in cramped quarters. It also had a limited cargo capacity. I had a sick feeling that I knew what Novak was going to say next.

"We took all possible precautions. The database containing all the Project's data about galactic technology, and all the necessary interfacing equipment—including media for presenting it in readily understandable format, rather like what the Delkasu use for teaching aids—is in the lifeboat."

It didn't occur to me to doubt it. I knew galactic data-storage capabilities—far beyond what you know, operating on the molecular level—well enough to know the staggering amounts of information that could be crammed into a database of ridiculously small physical size.

"So," Novak went on, "we don't need to land this ship. We'll take the lifeboat down and let the ship continue on course, burning up in atmosphere as you've correctly said it will. So you see, you and friends—your *late* friends— have accomplished nothing. *Nothing!* Do you hear me?" She got her breathing under control, and gestured to Evan. We returned to the control room.

Evan released me and gave me a shove that sent me

sprawling. I looked up at Novak, aiming a small hand weapon at me. I recognized it as a needler, shooting tiny fléchettes by electromagnetic pulse. It wasn't a serious combat weapon, being useless against the body armor that galactic technology could produce, but in the present circumstances it got the point across. Evan, clearly a traditionalist, was fondling a knife. I recognized him from the raid on the Sanctuary.

There was no one else around. I decided that Novak and Evan were the only survivors. A small ship like this couldn't have held many, especially with a laser cannon crammed into it. And Novak's reference to *the* lifeboat seemed to confirm it.

"And now," said Novak, "we can get back to my first reason for keeping you alive. There's something about you that makes me feel I ought to recognize you—I assume you're from the Project—but I can't put my finger on it. What's your name?"

Like a nerve pain of the soul came the memory of my last moments with Chloe. "Blackbeard the Pirate," I said dully.

Novak thrust her face down toward mine—I was still crouching—with a glare. "Don't be a smart-ass! For your information, I'm all that's standing between you and Evan. He'd love to use that knife on you. He and Victor—the man you killed back there—were very good friends."

"Yeah," I said, eying Evan. "I'll just bet they were."

I didn't quite succeed in covering my rib cage before Evan's foot crashed into it. I rolled over on my back, gasping with pain, and looked up into Novak's face.

"Since you choose not to be cooperative, I think I'll let Evan punish you for that remark in, shall we say, appropriate fashion." She nodded at Evan, who flourished his knife, smiled, and advanced toward me.

Something Hollywood has never gotten right about weapons-grade lasers is the sound they make in atmosphere: a sharp *snap!* as the air rushes back in to fill the narrow cylinder of vacuum that has been drilled through it. It isn't nearly as loud as a gunshot, but it's damned startling if you're not prepared for it . . . as I wasn't prepared for the sparkling lance of ionized air that speared Evan's chest. He reeled back in a pale pink spray of vaporized blood and water.

My eyes went to the hatch that opened into the control room, and the figure that stood there holding the Ekhemasu weapon I'd lost on capture. I would never have thought Chloe could have lifted the thing under this ship's Earthlike gravity field.

Novak saw her too. With a wordless snarl, she swung toward the new arrival—as unfamiliar-looking to her as I was—and brought up her needler.

My body still felt pain, but at that instant my mind wasn't processing it. I sprang to my feet and crashed into Novak, grasping the wrist of her gun hand and forcing it upward. I heard a sinister metallic tinkling as fléchettes sprayed the overhead. I tightened my grip and wrenched, and Novak dropped the needler. She continued to struggle like a wildcat.

Chloe heaved the laser gun aloft and brought its stock down against the side of Novak's head with an alarming sound. Novak went limp. I let her fall to the deck and stared at Chloe, who had dropped the laser gun and was catching her breath.

"How . . . ?" I began.

"I followed you into the access tube," she gasped. "Thramoz tried to stop me, but I wiggled past him. "Then that explosive charge went off. The tube's connection to our ship was ripped away. But it was still connected at this end, and I had my suit pressurized. I held on inside the tube, and pulled my way forward into this ship, through the hole that had been blasted through its hull. By that time, you'd been captured; I got inside just in time to see you get led away. I picked up your weapon and followed. Fortunately, I was inside the airtight hatches before Novak closed them."

I could only stare at her. I still didn't understand her actions toward me, back aboard that other ship, but it no longer mattered. There were so many things I needed to say to her . . . but first things first.

"The data Novak was taking is in the lifeboat," I explained, gesturing at the forward air lock and, as a matter of ingrained habit, scooping up the needler. "We can get away in it, and just let this ship burn up on reentry. Let's do it now, before we get any farther into the past. I've lost track of how many hours have passed since we went into temporal displacement, at about minus two years per hour, but it hasn't been many."

"Do you know how to disengage this ship's temporal displacement field?" she asked.

"I'm willing to take a crack at figuring it out. And even if I can't, I've got a theory that after the lifeboat passes beyond the boundaries of that field—which it will do just after being deployed—it will drop back into the normal time stream, leaving this ship to keep going back in time until its power runs out."

"That makes sense," she nodded. "The lifeboat doesn't

have a time machine of its own."

"Right. So one way or another we'll drop back into the time stream, destroy Novak's database, and try to make a go of it wherever . . . I mean *when*ever we end up. And the further that is into the past, the harder a time we'll have adapting. So let's get busy!"

For an instant, Chloe's face wore that strange, shuttered look again. But then it was gone, replaced by a brave smile whose artificiality I was too preoccupied to notice, although I can recall it now. "Yes, of course, Bob. You're right. It's the only way."

It took us no time at all to locate the switch that activated the lifeboat deployment sequence. It was just inside the inner door of the lifeboat air lock, and it was delayed action, giving the occupants just barely enough time to get into that air lock before it closed irrevocably—this was for ultimate emergencies, remember—and strap into the lifeboat before it was flung free of the ship. All very standard.

The time machine was another matter.

"As nearly as I can figure it," I said, after a frustrating computer search and a tentative examination of instrumentation that had obviously been cobbled onto the ship's control board, "this is also delayed action. It takes a couple of minutes after you start the shutdown sequence before the field collapses and you snap back into the normal universe."

"But are you sure you know how to actually commence the shutdown, as opposed to just making these lights flash on and off?"

"Hell no, I'm not sure! But we can activate this—or try to—and then slap the lifeboat switch and get into the lifeboat. If the field shuts down like it's supposed to, all well and good; we land on Earth and this ship burns up. If not, then the lifeboat launches anyway and we go to Plan B."

"All right," Chloe said matter-of-factly. Our eyes met. On a sudden impulse, I kissed her. She responded hungrily . . . almost desperately. I tasted tears on her face. I should have asked myself why. But instead I drew away and commenced field shutdown. Then I entered the lifeboat air lock and opened the hatch in the deck, revealing the lifeboat's tiny passenger compartment below. Chloe followed. On the air lock's threshold, she paused, her hand halfway to the switch.

"What about Renata?" she asked.

"Huh?" I'd forgotten Novak just as completely as I had the equally motionless Evan. I looked back and faced Chloe. "What about her?"

"Shouldn't we—?" She turned around and started back into the control room.

With a scream, a face from hell reared up in her path.

I'd thought Novak was as good as dead, and certainly immobilized by concussion. I'd forgotten the way hysterical strength can power a body beyond what is medically plausible, if the restraining band of sanity snaps. And the blood that caked Novak's hair and streamed down her cheek wasn't what gave that face its horror—it was the absolute lack of humanity. It was a mask of hate from which all reason had fled.

She was like a fury out of the darkest reaches of myth. And she was brandishing Evan's knife, about which I'd totally forgotten.

Like a Cossack swinging a saber, she slashed at Chloe with the knife.

Desperately, I lunged forward and pushed Chloe out of the way of that onsweeping edge, into whose path momentum carried me. Pain exploded as Novak whipped the knife across my face, laying my left cheek open to the bone.

Sickened, blinded, I staggered backwards and fell through the hatch into the lifeboat. As I caught myself and struggled back up into the air lock, I saw Chloe tackle Novak and grasp her knife hand before it could commence another swing. She gave a twist. Novak screamed and dropped the knife. Chloe bore her backwards through the air lock door, into the control room. Just beyond that threshold, they grappled, straining against each other.

The left half of my face was a fireball of agony, and blood was already trickling down my neck into my survival suit. But I staggered upright, just in time to hear a voice that was pure Chloe.

"You really don't know who I am, do you, Renata?"

For a moment, stunned realization wiped Novak's face clean of madness, and she loosened her grip. It gave Chloe a chance to wrench one arm free and bring the elbow sharply up into her opponent's face, bloodying her nose.

I started to reel toward Chloe. Our eyes met for an eternity that could only have lasted a fraction of a second— a flash of frozen time in which her face held more emotions than a lifetime could or should contain. She opened her mouth and said something to me, but Novak screamed again, so I couldn't hear it.

Then, as though in slow motion, Chloe's free hand came up and slapped the lifeboat switch. The airlock door began to slide shut.

"*Chloe!*" I shouted, stretching my sliced facial muscles

and bringing a renewed deluge of blood, and a spasm of pain that almost made me lose consciousness. But even as the universe spun around me, I forced myself forward, toward that inexorably closing air lock door and the two struggling women just beyond it. . . .

It clanged shut just before I reached it. A red light began to flash stroboscopically, and a warning siren began to wail.

I crashed against the air lock door, heedless of my agony, pounding on it with futile fists. I glimpsed Chloe through the transparent bull's-eye for a last instant, before her struggles with Novak took her out of my line of sight. The siren continued to ululate.

"Ten seconds to lifeboat deployment," a robotic voice called out. Ten seconds . . . after which the lifeboat would be gone and the air lock would be open to space. . . .

I was beyond thought. All I could do was react. I got into the lifeboat just before the hatch automatically closed. I had barely strapped into one of the couches when the universe seemed to drop out from under me. I looked through the lifeboat's curving transparency and saw the half-wrecked ship recede rapidly into the weird emptiness of that extradimensional realm.

Then, with mind-shattering suddenness, the real universe was back, and the lifeboat was hurtling down into the tenuous upper atmosphere of the blue planet below.

My theory had been correct: as soon as it had left the ship's temporal displacement field, the lifeboat had reentered the flow of time at whatever point the ship had reached. For a heartbeat, I looked up and scanned the blue-black sky of those altitudes for the fireball that would mark the ship's death. Not seeing it, I felt relief rise in me, only to be smashed flat by the realization that at the moment of my departure the ship had still been in temporal displacement, headed still farther backward in time. So, assuming that my tinkering had succeeded, that fireball *had already happened*, and by now had faded from the sky.

On the other hand, it might not have happened at all. Maybe I'd failed, leaving that ship a Flying Dutchman of the oceans of time.

Was Chloe dead, or in limbo?

The lifeboat began to bump and vibrate—it was too tiny to mount artificial gravity generators—and I could hear a thin scream of cloven air. Looking forward through the transparency, I could see the craft's nose begin to glow a dull furnace-red. But its design took account of the possibility that its occupants might be incapacitated, or include no qualified pilot. Its automatic pilot was capable of analyzing its surroundings in terms of gravity, atmospheric density, and everything else needful to achieve a safe planetary landing.

So I had nothing to do except grit my teeth against the bucking ride that brought renewed pain with every vibration, and force myself not to think about all I had lost. That would come later.

CHAPTER NINETEEN

I lay under the wide blue sky of my birth planet, bathed in its sunlight, rocked by the swells of the Atlantic.

I knew it was the Atlantic because, shortly before touchdown, I had glimpsed what was unmistakably the eastern seaboard of North America. After that, I could only hang on as the lifeboat burned out its paltry power sources performing the one atmospheric reentry it had in it, with no margin for picking and choosing among sites for a safe landing. Safe, but not necessarily comfortable. Even strapped in, the arrival in the ocean was bumpy enough to renew the pain and the blood flow. Only after the lifeboat had settled could I stand up and seek out the first-aid kit. I smeared antiseptic gel on the gash, and used an adhesive strip to keep the lips of the cut together. Then I opened the transparent bubble. The salt air came flooding in, so warm that it had to be summer.

But summer of what year?

It was a difficult question. My watch told me that about seventeen hours of my life had passed since first going into temporal displacement. At the rate Khorat's ship had been maintaining, that would have put me more than thirty years into the past. But we'd spent part of that time in the "slower" dimension Novak had been using, so it was impossible to say for certain. At any rate, I wouldn't be seeing any Spanish galleons or clipper ships on these seas.

The question was whether I'd see anything at all. The lifeboat had an automatic transponder, but there was no one on Earth, or even in the Solar System, with the capability of picking it up. And I wasn't going anywhere; the lifeboat had done what it was designed to do, and burned out its tiny one-shot impeller doing it.

So I took stock. There was a small supply of concentrated rations and drinking water, both of which I used. There was also a flare gun, and I found myself face-to-face with the unwelcome question of whether I *ought* to use that if I sighted a ship or a plane. Whatever year I was in, the discovery of this lifeboat couldn't fail to change history.

It was an awkward ethical problem, and I should have been pondering it deeply. Instead, I found myself thinking about Chloe, and trying to understand.

Ever since she'd regained consciousness after fainting at the sight of my new guise, I'd been taken in by her pose of normalcy because I'd wanted to be taken in by it. I could see that now. Then had come her seduction of me—there was no other word—in a blaze of passion she couldn't possibly have faked . . . but *must* have faked, given what she'd been doing at the same time. But after that crushing piece of treachery, she had followed me unhesitatingly into hell . . . and then, at the very end, sundered us permanently, with calm determination.

And what was it she had said to me, at that last instant? I had seen her lips moving, and I thought they had formed the words *I love you*. But maybe that was just what I wanted to think. I couldn't be sure.

Now I would never be sure of anything.

Try I as might, I could understand none of it. So I let a kind of numb fatalism take me as the sun climbed to the zenith and began to sink in the west, occasionally going behind scattered clouds and giving some relief from the heat. I finally dozed off.

When I awoke, it looked like late afternoon . . . and I saw that the decision as to using or not using the flare gun had been taken out of my hands. A ship was approaching from out of the westering sun, by whose reflected light it had probably spotted the lifeboat. And even if I'd been feeling heroic—which I wasn't—I had no way of scuttling the lifeboat. It was built to float, not to sink.

The ship drew closer, a lean greyhound shape flying a forty-eight-star US flag. I recognized a World War II-era destroyer—no missile launchers, just five-inch guns in boxy turrets and 40 mm AAA in gun tubs. There was also no helicopter on a stern platform. Instead, a launch was lowered.

"Ahoy, there!" called the young lieutenant (j.g.) in charge, as the launch drew alongside. He was wearing officer's short-sleeved khakis, confirming that this was no earlier than the 1940s. "Do you speak English?"

"Yeah," I replied listlessly. The kid's open face reflected

a mixture of relief and bewilderment at hearing Americanese from the oddly dressed occupant of this even odder life craft. I got the impression that the sweat on his brow wasn't entirely due to the weather.

"Here," he called, tossing me a line. "Secure that, and we'll tow you to the ship . . . and get you to sick bay."

They towed my lifeboat around to the fantail, where depth charges were racked. As the destroyer's stern came into view, I read her name: USS *Elijah Ashford*.

Now why, I asked myself, did I feel there was something familiar about that name—something I ought to remember? And why did I feel a shiver running up my spine, as though rising from realms below that of conscious thought?

I continued thinking about it as they hoisted me aboard and took me to the small sick bay. The medical lieutenant's expression was eloquent as he examined my left cheek.

"Hey, you should see the *other* guy," I quipped feebly.

The doctor gave me a brief professional smile, and got busy stitching up my cheek. Even with the painkiller he injected into my face, it was almost unpleasant enough to take my mind off things. Almost . . . but not quite.

"There," the doctor finally said. "You'll be okay. But I'm afraid you're probably going to have one hell of a permanent scar."

"The least of my worries," I mumbled, using the non-numbed right side of my mouth. "Thanks, Doc. Oh, by the way, about my life craft—"

"Don't worry about that. They're winching it aboard now. It's a very unusual craft." He gave me a curious look, but was too polite to say that the lifeboat wasn't the only thing that was unusual. "The skipper is anxious to talk to you when you're able."

"I'm sure he is," I sighed.

"In fact, that's probably a messenger from him right now." The doctor turned to a sailor in the hatchway. The sailor said something I couldn't quite make out. The doctor shook his head firmly.

"No, not yet. He's suffering from exposure and mild shock, in addition to having lost a fair amount of blood. Tell Commander Bryant that I'll send word as soon as—"

I heard no more. At the sound of that name, a tidal wave of realization crashed over me and swept me under, and my consciousness drowned in the swirling depths.

When I awoke, there was a blessed moment of forgetfulness—the last I was ever to experience. Then it all came back to me. My eyelids, which had begun to flutter open, squeezed shut again, and I thought furiously in darkness.

Chloe Bryant had known. She had known just after seeing the face Nafayum had given me. Her few seconds of puzzled nonrecognition had been due to my lack—then—of a facial scar. But after that, she had known . . . and understood.

As I understood now.

Khorat had been wrong. There was no possibility of obliterating subsequent history by temporal meddling; it was simply a matter of things coming to pass that already had. Yes, Chloe had understood. With that clear, fine, tough-minded intelligence of hers, she had realized what was going to happen, and why it *must* happen.

But we couldn't be *absolutely* certain that Khorat was wrong. Chloe had seen that too. There was always the chance that reality helps those who help themselves. That was why Chloe had scuppered my wild idea of taking over the ship and stopping Khorat. But, in the usual mixed-up way we humans do things, she had also seen that our reasons for denying ourselves the final consummation of our love no longer applied. So the calculation had been there, but the passion—the long-denied passion—had been real.

And just as real had been her sheer, cold courage at the very end, when my slashed cheek had removed the last possible doubt in her mind, and she had unhesitatingly consigned herself to death or worse because it was the only way to *force* me to fulfill the destiny on which everything depended. A destiny in which she had no part.

And I couldn't take chances either. Khorat had been right about one thing, as I knew because my own knowledge of my own race confirmed it: if humans knew time travel was possible, they would never rest until they had attained it . . . and set in motion the unraveling of the universe.

So I knew what I must do, lest Chloe's sacrifice be meaningless.

I finally opened my eyes. I wasn't in the sick bay. They had moved me to a two-man officers' bunkroom, and laid me on the lower bunk. The tiny compartment held the usual fold-down writing desks, and chairs. Sitting on one of those chairs was a stocky man in khakis with lieutenant commander's gold oak leaves.

"I'm glad you're finally awake," he remarked affably.

"Have you been waiting for me long, Skipper?"

"Not very. But I wanted to talk to you in private. I'm hoping you can satisfy my curiosity about certain things."

I looked at the strong, unforgettably ugly face I'd seen on a slide, once upon a time, at a secret facility in the Alaska panhandle—yes, the bulbous nose with the cleft tip was there in all its glory—and smiled as widely as I could without intolerable pain.

"I hope I can, too. It's the least I can do to repay you for rescuing me."

"Yes, well, there are quite a few questions in connection with your . . . presence here. Let's start with the most obvious one: what name do you go by?"

I met his eyes—blue eyes, his only point of resemblance to his daughter—and gave the answer that history required of me.

The homely features hardened. "Okay, mister. If you want to play games, I'm willing to play along . . . up to a point. But in the end I'm going to need straight answers. That getup you were wearing, for example: at first I thought it was some kind of flight suit, but it doesn't really look like one, and nobody can figure out what that stuff is that it's made of. And as for your life craft . . . I've been going over it, and it's not clear what most of the gizmos in it even *do*. For one thing, what propels it in the water?"

"Nothing does, Skipper."

"Oh? I hope you're not going to tell me it just fell out of the sky. It can't be an aircraft; it has no propulsion for that either, and it hasn't even got wings. And—ha-ha!—I don't think it's one of those 'foo fighters' that nervous flyboys were reporting over Germany toward the end of the war. You're obviously an American, of some national origin or other."

"To take those points in order: actually, it *did* fall out of the sky. And . . ." I recalled the story as I'd heard it when I was learning of the Project's origins. "I speak American English because my brain was provided with that language—plus detailed background information—electronically, by means of direct neural induction." I held up a forestalling hand. "I've got a pretty good idea of what you're thinking. But if I gave you the straight answers you want—and I'm more than willing to do so—you'd be even more convinced I'm crazy than you already are. All I ask is that you give me a chance to demonstrate that what I say is true, however fantastic it may sound. For that, I need access to my life craft. You've got it aboard this ship, don't you?"

"Yes. I've got it covered with a tarp and under guard. There's been a lot of loose talk about it among the men."

"Very sensible. When you've seen what I have to show you, and hear what I have to say, you'll realize the over-riding need for secrecy. Your crew will have to have that impressed on them in the strongest possible terms—maybe with some vague hints about 'atom bomb stuff'—so they'll keep their mouths shut about what they've seen."

"You don't know sailors," said Commander Bryant dryly.

"Oh, maybe some of them will get drunk and blab. But it probably won't be taken any more seriously than any other sea stories." In fact, I *knew* it wouldn't. "But we'll worry about that later. How about it, Skipper? Will you let me demonstrate to you—in private—why you should take me seriously? You've got absolutely nothing to lose. If it turns out I'm not as good as my word, you can heave me into the brig and deny me access to sharp instruments."

"I probably ought to go ahead and do that right now. Only . . . damn it, you don't act like a crazy man! And that craft of yours is real enough." He reached a decision. "All right, I'll give you your chance. You say you can show me whatever it is you want to show me in the life craft? I recall seeing something in it that had a kind of . . . screen. Sort of like these television sets I've read about in magazines."

"Yeah, something like that." Television, I recalled, had been invented in 1929, but hadn't amounted to anything until after World War II, when regularly scheduled broadcasts had begun. Of course, that flat screen was just for the elementary stuff. Commander Bryant was going to find holographically projected 3-D images in the middle of the air a lot less familiar. "And yes," I continued, "we can do it in the life craft, on its own power supplies." For now, the computer could run on its own emergency reserve of stored power. Later, local sources could be adapted; it no doubt had instructions for doing just that, starting with the kind of electrical generation that could be rigged up in early nineteenth century England. "By the way, could I trouble you for something to wear so I'll be a little less conspicuous?"

"I think that would be wise. One of my officers is a tall guy like you; I'll borrow a set of khakis."

"Thanks."

"Don't mention it. And afterwards, you can show me all the miracles you've got stored up in that craft." The words were scornful; the tone tried to be . . . and didn't quite succeed.

"No miracles, Skipper. Just a lot of new data . . . and a warning that I'm here to deliver."

Ashford nosed her way into Hampton Roads, past Sewell's Point in Norfolk and then up the Elizabeth River to the destroyer piers at what was, with typical swabby eccentricity, called the Norfolk Naval Shipyard even though it was in Portsmouth.

What awaited us was the typical scene that greeted a returning warship: families lined up to greet husbands and fathers, after which the unmarried sailors would disembark and set about doing that which unmarried sailors do in places like Hampton Roads.

I had persuaded Commander Bryant that it would be a mistake to call for a massive security cordon that would only set the rumor mill grinding away. Let our arrival be as normal as possible; nobody would notice the tarpaulin-covered object aft. Later, at night, it could be off-loaded and turned over to the people who were eagerly awaiting it in response to the radio message he'd sent ahead, in a code that was hardly ever used.

"They're waiting for you, too," said Commander Bryant, grim-faced. Actually, that was the only kind of face he'd worn lately. "After I turn you over to them, they're going to fly you to Washington, by direct order of President Truman. He's agreed to meet with you as you requested."

"I thought he might," I replied absently. We stood on the bridge, watching the joyful scene on the pier. As per tradition, the captain would be the last to disembark.

At last the time came when we could leave the ship, amid the traditions that accompanied the captain's departure. We descended the gangway and stepped onto the pier. . . .

"Daddy! Daddy!"

I swung toward the source of the cry, just in time to see a smiling woman in 1940s dress lower a camera of the same vintage. But I barely noticed her. My universe had narrowed to the five-year-old girl who broke away from the woman with the camera and ran, light brown braids flying in the sea breeze, to embrace Commander Bryant's legs and gaze up into what was, for her, the handsomest face in the world.

"Chloe!" Commander Bryant lifted her up into a hug, then set her down. He turned to me with a sheepish grin. "Uh . . . my daughter," he explained unnecessarily.

In the back of my mind, I'd known this moment was coming. But I'd kept the knowledge there, back among all the clutter of things we hope will go away if we don't think about them. But it hadn't gone away, as such things generally don't, and now the moment was here, bringing with it the recollection of one of the more unwelcome conclusions I'd reached in that time of dark, silent thought in the bunk.

Renata Novak's work would outlive her. The poisonous seed she had planted with her faked evidence would sprout, and flourish . . . and I would have to let it. If the truth about Novak came out, it would result in further inquiries, which might well lead the investigators to the secret of time travel, which must never be revealed. So the time would come when I must stand helplessly by and let the name of Chloe Bryant take its place alongside those of Benedict Arnold and Judas Iscariot.

All this ran through my mind in less time than it took the little girl to raise her huge blue eyes—huger than I remembered, in that small child's face—and look timidly up at the strange man with the hideous scar. Then she smiled.

Somehow, I managed to smile back.

I know I did, because—not least among all the gifts she had given me—she had told me that I would, never dreaming who was sitting in her audience in that auditorium in Alaska. *"I've never forgotten that smile he gave me—nor have I ever been able to interpret it, except that I could have sworn it held a deep sadness. For a second, I thought he was actually going to cry. But I also sensed a great love."*

For a moment, the fate of the universe was forgotten, and all I wanted to do was fall to my knees and sweep that lovely little girl into an embrace, and cry: *"It's me, Chloe! Don't you know me, in a way that defeats time itself? No, of course you don't. But please forgive me for what I must do. I hope you can, because I will never be able to forgive myself."*

The moment passed. I walked away, not looking back. I knew I would never see that little girl, or the young woman she would become, again. I would take great pains to make certain that I would not.

I also knew I would not seek out a certain brat of a ten-year-old boy, even though I knew exactly where he was living in this year of grace 1946. But I wouldn't forget about him, because in 1963 I would make certain he was taken into the Project, as he *must* be. Afterwards, when he glimpsed me outside a Quonset hut, I wondered if I would glimpse him as well. I rather hoped not. But then I remembered there had been a very brief moment of eye contact. So I was to be denied even that.

I put it out of my mind as I walked on toward the Secret Service men who awaited me at the foot of the pier.

EPILOGUE

"So that's it," the President finished. He was bone-tired, and hoarse from talking. "Now you know what your predecessors have known. And, like them, you know why it must never be revealed."

There was a moment of dead silence in the Oval Office.

"No," said President-Elect Harvey Langston.

The President's head jerked up from its incipient slump. "What did you say?"

"No!" Langston stood up. There was a wild look in his eyes, and his voice began to hold the shrillness from which his handlers were always careful to rein him in. "I've heard enough! This is all . . . it's unconstitutional! It's a violation of the public's right to know! The multinational corporations must be behind it! Or the Jewish bankers! Or the

Trilateral Commission! Or the Illuminati! Or . . . the *Vast Right Wing Conspiracy*!"

"For God's sake!" the President exploded. "Can't you, for once in your life, stop thinking in slogans?"

"I'm going to expose it all!" Langston showed no sign of having heard. "I'm going to blow this wide open! I'll tell the world! Yes, I'll use my inauguration speech to do it!" He turned and strode to the door, then paused. "Don't try to stop me!" he declared theatrically. The President didn't move. Visibly miffed at the anticlimax, Langston stomped out, slamming the door behind him.

The President sat in silence, head lowered, for a few moments. Then the faint click of an opening side door reminded him that he hadn't been entirely truthful when he'd told Langston they had been alone.

A tall, gaunt man entered. As always, the President felt a chill slide up and down his spine as he looked at the messenger from the stars.

How old was Mr. Inconnu? The President had often wondered. By all accounts, he had seemed in his early thirties when he had arrived on Earth in 1946. If so, that would make him at least a hundred now. In some ways—the deep lines in his face, the whiteness of his thick hair—he looked it. But his mental and physical health seemed unimpaired. His explanation—that the colony of human exiles he'd escaped from, somewhere in the remote reaches of the galaxy, had had access to the life-extending biotechnology of their alien masters—must be true.

"You heard," the President said. It was a statement, not a question.

"Yes, Mr. President."

"He means well." For some perverse reason, the President felt driven to defend the man he despised. "He's genuinely sincere in his beliefs. He just can't grasp the distinction between the slogans he grew up on and reality. He thinks they *are* reality, and not just noises for morons to chant as a substitute for thought."

"That's precisely the problem. Mr. President. Our worst nightmare has always been the election of an ideologue to the presidency, but the political realities have always spared us that. Now, after this freakish election, it's finally happened, and it's even worse than we've feared; he's a *stupid* ideologue."

The President swung his chair around toward the French windows and stared into the darkness. "You know, I really believe in . . . this." He gave a gesture that encompassed the room, the White House, the city beyond it, and the Constitution of which they were the visible manifestation. "All right, all right; I know there are a thousand politicians who say that and don't mean it any more than they mean anything else. But by God, I mean it! And that man—" (he waved in the direction of the door through which Langston had departed) "—is the President-Elect of the United States, under the constitutional system we claim to live by. Do we only live by it when it suits us?"

Mr. Inconnu said nothing.

The President's head dropped.

"All right," he said, just above the threshold of audibility. "Go ahead. Do what has to be done."

"Yes, Mr. President. Everything will be taken care of. I'll see to it that you never have to know the details."

"No!" The President's head came up, and more than two centuries of history settled around him like an invisible mantle of authority. "To hell with that. I want to know everything."

Their eyes met, in a shared realization of the need for a form of penance.

"Very well, Mr. President. I understand. You'll receive a full report." Mr. Inconnu's voice held nothing but deep respect. He turned to go. Then he paused, and spoke with a strange kind of hesitant impulsiveness. "Oh, by the way, Mr. President . . . a while back, when you were speculating aloud about the traitor's motivations . . . you were wrong."

"What?" The President blinked, startled. This was the first time Mr. Inconnu had ever revealed any special knowledge of that matter, four decades or so earlier. He had simply let Section Two's report stand. "Are you saying you know something beyond what the investigation turned up after Chloe Bryant's disappearance?"

Mr. Inconnu's features clenched as though in pain, twisting the scar that disfigured his left cheek. (He had never had it removed, as the Project's medical techniques were quite capable of doing. The President had often wondered why.) Then, before the President had time to feel alarmed, his face cleared.

"No," he said quietly. "I have nothing to add to Section Two's findings in the case of Chloe Bryant's betrayal of the Project. Please forget I said anything." He straightened up and spoke briskly, as though his uncharacteristic lapse had never happened. "I'll make all the necessary arrangements, Mr. President." And then he was gone into the night.

The President stared after him for a few seconds, wondering what he'd almost glimpsed. Then he sighed, and turned to his desk's communication suite. His chief of staff had gone for the night, but he'd leave a recorded message to be received first thing in the morning.

"Larry, I want you to contact Senator Goldman's staff, quietly and informally, just to establish a line of communication. At some point in the very near future, it's going to be necessary to set up a private meeting between him and me, with very little notice. Yes, I know it all sounds a little irregular. Do it anyway."

The President broke the connection and sat back with a sigh.

Thank God, he thought, the *Vice* President-Elect, at least, could be reasoned with.

The following is an excerpt from:

Exodus

BY

STEVE WHITE
&
SHIRLEY MEIER

Available from Baen Books
January 2007
hardcover

BOOK ONE

Prologue

There could be no true night with Sekahmant in the sky.

The sun had set, turning the Auriel Ocean molten in shades of red and orange and *murn*, leaving the giant star unchallenged. Of course, it was only a point source of actinic bluish-*vrel* light—no imaginable object could show a visible disk across even a minor interstellar distance—but that light was of an intensity to banish every other star and trigger the color sensitivity of one's central eye. So Harrok, standing on the terrace of his mountainside villa high above the west coast of Kormat, could clearly see the town below, the coast curving northward in a succession of coves separated by wave-lapped mountains, the mercury-like ocean to the west, and the peaks rising in range upon range snowcapped range into the eastern distance.

He could also see this same coast from the tarry deck

of a sailing vessel of the Asthians who would, in later centuries, build the town below his villa, for he was *shaxzhu*, and his memories of all his lives was good. But that was a different kind of seeing.

The view had never failed to move him. What a thought in the Mind of Illudor! So much beauty, to be obliterated by that which now only illuminated it! Harrok was no astrophysicist, but he never doubted the truth of the horror that they had revealed with their orbital instruments. After all, educated people had known for generations that the ethereal loveliness of Sekahmant must someday turn destroyer. But so soon?

A rustling sound distracted him as his daughter stepped from the doorway into the Sekahmant-light. Ankaht was the image of her now discarnate mother, tiny and dark, in contrast to Harrok, whose skin was translucent gold—though dulling with age, now—and whose long, thick neck lifted his head to an above-average height. But these were superficial differences. In what really mattered, they were alike, for she, too, was *shaxzhu*. For both parent and child to possess the gift was rare but not unheard of. It lent the father-daughter relationship a sometimes disturbing closeness.

"The decision has been made," she announced without preamble. She had been linked into the global datanet, which Harrok found himself less and less inclined to do these days, when almost all the news was bad. "The nations have granted the new government all the emergency powers it asked for—in effect, dissolved their own existence. (Excitement, tempered by mourning for the old ways.) And the proponents of extended research and development have been overruled. Construction of the first ships will begin with the technology we have now, although further discoveries will be incorporated into later ships if possible. (Deep reservations.)"

Harrok and Ankaht never misinterpreted one another's emotions. The empathetic sense of *selnarm* was extraordinarily strong among all *shaxzhu*, and especially so among those who were also close blood relations.

"Well," he said, "they had little choice. (Resignation.) The last I heard, estimates of the supernova's date had been moved up to two hundred years from now." *No more than three or four incarnations for me,* he thought bleakly, even assuming minimal time spent discarnate.

Not that any such assumption was likely to be justified, given the draconic population control measures that were being proposed. But, again, what choice was there? There was not enough metal in the crust of Ardu to build a fleet of ships that would carry a significant fraction of the present population, or even keep up with its increase. *More time in the dreary less-than-existence of discarnate status for all of us,* he thought.

But it never occurred to him to doubt that the project would succeed, at least in the sense of saving *some* of the Race, nor was his confidence based on the power-urge of politics or the proofs of science or economics. His certitude was a simple philosophical imperative. After all, supernovae also had their existence in the Mind of Illudor. Could Illudor will His own obliteration? It seemed unlikely. It was also too disturbing a thought to dwell upon—that a Deity might commit suicide—though far less disturbing than the heretical whisper heard more and more of late: that the universe was Illudor's *dream* . . . and that the dream had now turned to nightmare.

He shook off his philosophical musings to listen as Ankaht spoke again.

"I've been asked to join the group that will be planning for the social organization of the ships . . . especially the problem of maintaining cultural continuity for hundreds of years in an environment like that. (Disgust.) We *shaxzhu* will be specially important in maintaining a link with the world we've known. How else will the others even understand there *is* a universe outside those steel walls?" She shuddered. "They want your help, too Father. You probably won't be incarnate when the first ships depart, but your wisdom will be invaluable in the planning stages."

"Of course I'll help in any way I can," Harrok replied. Strong *shaxzhutok* carried obligations as well as privileges and, to be honest, the problems were not without interest. He turned to lead Ankaht inside, then suddenly stopped and loudly clicked the strong, curved claws that tipped his left hand's two primary tentacles. "Oh, yes! I forgot to mention when you arrived this morning; your sister was in a skimmer accident. She's all right, but her new son was killed."

"Oh. (Mild regret.) He was less than half a year old, wasn't he? You don't happen to know who . . .?"

"No. I wasn't there for the birth, and afterwards I couldn't get any sense of who'd picked him. Couldn't have been anyone close."

"I suppose not. Still, it's too bad for whoever he was. I can dimly remember going discarnate in infancy once. What an annoyance! Nothing more frustrating. Anyway, tell Kathmeer I'm glad she's all right. I haven't kept in touch as I should have, but I happen to know that disincarnation would be very inconvenient for her just now. (Grimness.) Inconvenient for everyone, with the birth restrictions we all know are coming."

The reminder of his own earlier thoughts saddened Harrok—sadness which, of course, communicated itself to Ankaht. Silently, father and daughter stepped inside and closed the sliding glass door behind them.

Outside, in an evening filled with wild flixit song and the buzz of second-light insects, Sekahmant continued to glow as if it were an enduring star.

Chapter One

Rebirth

Prescott City had changed.

No, she reminded herself, for the thousandth time but with undiminished irritation. *Not "Prescott City." Just "Prescott."*

She couldn't remember precisely when, during the past couple of generations, the "City" part had been dropped from popular parlance. But by now the shortened name stood triumphant even in official paperwork and maps. To say "Prescott City" was to declare oneself an incorrigible old fogy. And the Honorable Miriam Ortega—onetime chairperson of the Rim Federation's constitutional convention, subsequently its prime minister for five nonconsecutive terms totaling over forty years, and currently chief justice of its Supreme Judicial Court—was not ready to do that. Even though her one hundred and eleven Standard years arguably gave her every right to.

She shook off the thought. The antigerone treatments to which she was entitled from at least two standpoints—her inarguable contributions to the community, and her residence on a planet the least of whose worries was population pressure—rendered her apparent physiological age a very well-preserved late sixties, and therefore deprived her of whatever excuse senile decay might have provided.

Besides, she told herself, *why shouldn't the name have changed? Everything else has.*

Nowhere was the change more clearly on view than here, at the window of the chief justice's private office on the top floor of Government House.

A hundred and fifty-five years ago—the Standard years that everyone still used, the time it took Old Terra to revolve around Sol—Government House had been built to house the provisional government of this planet of Xanadu, then little more than a raw new military outpost whose civilian workforce had mushroomed to the point of needing such a government . . . but not to the point of needing (or being able to afford) an edifice which would have done credit to some long-established colony world. But Government House had been less a building than a grand gesture—a madly extravagant exercise in what Miriam's mother would have called outrageous *chutzpah*.

Xanadu had been colonized halfway through the Fourth Interstellar War, when humanity and its allies had faced the very real likelihood of something far worse than extermination at the hands of the Bugs: survival not even as slaves, but as meat animals who *knew*. It had been colonized because this system, named Zephrain by its discoverers from the Khanate of Orion, had been only one warp jump away from a teeming Bug "Home Hive" system. Those colonists had known full well that they were living on the front lines of a war whose only outcome could be genocide in one direction or the other. By shaping the planet's native stone into neoclassical monumentality, looming above their prefab "cities," those people (Miriam had often wished she could have known them) had made an eloquent declaration of uncompromising commitment: "This world is ours. We can be killed, but we cannot be moved." In the end they had been neither . . . thanks to the man after whom they had named this city, and whose statue they had raised on a column.

Thus it was that, after the war, Government House had been maintained but never modified. And when a young lawyer named Miriam Ortega had moved here after her mother's death, to be near her father, Sergei Ortega, the local Terran Federation Navy commander, it had still loomed over all it surveyed, crowning its hilltop in a bend of the Alph River, even though the city had grown enough to finally deserve the name.

Now, though, the waves of galactic cosmopolitanism had finally washed over the Rim. Government House lay in the shadows of kilometer-high towers of plasteel and synthetic diamond. Abu'said Field, which had once provided it with an impressive backdrop, had long since yielded to the economics of efficient land use, and a new spaceport served Prescott from what were now the city's outskirts. But the extensive grounds of Government House remained sacrosanct, despite being almost beyond price as real estate, and one could almost imagine that Commodore Prescott looked down with bronze eyes over an unchanged scene from atop his column. . . .

Except that now there was a second column beside it. Miriam's eyes strayed to the statue that crowned that one, and she could no longer put off her reason for being here—this meeting that had nothing to do with the Supreme Judicial Court at all.

Unconsciously, she took out a cigarette and lit it. Cancer, of the lungs and otherwise, had long since been banished into the mists of history for everyone with access to up-to-date biotechnology. But her first inhalation of smoke awakened a scowl on a face that had never been conventionally pretty even in her youth. (Although, the more you looked at it . . .) She angrily stubbed the cigarette out and turned to the two men who had been sitting patiently at the conference table.

"Stupid damned habit," she muttered. "I'm going to quit this summer."

The two men kept straight faces. They'd had a lot of practice at it. They had heard those last six words from Miriam Ortega before each of the last 105 of Xanadu's summers, as it swung around its G5v primary in 0.73 standard year.

As usual, the small dapper man in academic-style civvies did a better job of concealing his amusement. Admiral Genji Yoshinaka, RFN (ret.), had the pure white hair his one hundred and twenty-eight Standard years warranted, but his skin held the finely wrinkled firmness of one who had started on the antigerone treatments relatively late. His features were of the cast of Old Terra's east Asia, and in fact he was that rarest of birds in the Rim Federation: a native of the mother planet. He had always been a master at keeping those features unreadable, and age had not diminished his subtlety.

The other man could hardly have presented a more striking contrast. Fleet Admiral Sean F. X. Remko, TFN, was still on the active list—although, at one hundred and forty Standard years—he was beginning to think the unthinkable about retirement), and his bear-like frame was clothed in the Rim Federation uniform. That uniform was essentially the black-and-silver of the Terran Federation Navy . . . but the TFN of seven and a half Standard decades ago, forgoing the changes in style that had since overtaken the parent service—a sartorial eccentricity fraught with political meaning. Similarly, the beard that had been fashionable among male TFN officers then still adorned a face that reflected more ethnic strains than just the ones his name suggested, for Remko was a product of the melting-pot slums of New Detroit, and his bass voice still held harsh residues of an accent that conferred no great prestige.

"All right," Miriam said with the breezy informality that came naturally to her, and which she could permit herself in this company. She sat down at the head of the table. "I declare the trustees of the person and estate of Fleet Admiral Ian Trevayne in session. Thank you both for coming. If there's no objection, I'd like to dispense with the usual financial report. Instead, I've called this special meeting to discuss the latest medical evaluation I've received from Dr. Mendez and his team."

Instantly, the two men took on a look of focused alertness.

"We haven't seen this evaluation, Miriam," said Yoshinaka carefully. Remko emitted a confirmatory rumble.

"I know, and I'm sorry I haven't had time to make it available to you in advance. But I felt we should meet without delay." She paused with the unconsciously dramatic instinct of a veteran politician. "You see, it appears that we may be able to discharge the trust's primary purpose in five Standard years."

They stared at her with the incredulity of long-deferred and often-disappointed hope.

"Let me review the basic problem," she hurried on, while they were still speechless. "Essentially, it is as Dr. Yuan explained to us before his death fifteen years ago, except that since then, advances in medical technology— about which you can read the details later—have now raised the chances of him surviving the thawing process to about eighty-five percent."

Yoshinaka cleared his throat. "Well, Miriam, this is certainly encouraging news. Thawing him out, as you put it, from the cryogenic bath Dr. Yuan used—without the usual elaborate workup—to preserve his life during the Battle of Zapata has always been half of the problem. But *only* half."

"Right," Remko nodded. "Even if the thawing does succeed, it just brings us back to the reason Dr. Yuan froze him solid in the first place: the battle damage that he took at Zapata!"

"Yes." Yoshinaka nodded, and began to itemize. "Extensive radiation damage, especially to the lower body. Spine severed just below the fifth vertebra. Not to mention the effects of extreme anoxia, concussion . . ." Yoshinaka trailed off miserably as he saw the look on Remko's face, and belatedly remembered what the man under discussion had meant to the burly admiral.

But Remko surprised him. He brought his expression under control and spoke steadily. "That's right. And to all that, you have to add the damage done by the quick-freeze itself. Not that I'm criticizing Dr. Yuan, mind you. It was all he could do. But . . ." He made a baffled gesture.

"Yes," Miriam acknowledged. "Dr. Mendez admits that even today the procedure would be risky in the extreme. Even if he survived it, the chances are that he would suffer permanent impairment—especially in light of the radiation damage, which the freezing did nothing for."

"Well, then, we're back where we started," declared Remko.

"Not altogether. What Dr. Mendez is proposing is that we avoid the risks by not even attempting to salvage this body."

Yoshinaka was the first to grasp it. "Cloning?" he breathed.

"The crucial point," Miriam replied obliquely, "is that Dr. Yuan didn't *entirely* forgo the workup to cryogenic freezing. He couldn't omit it for the brain tissue, given the potential for really irreparable damage. So he did a crash job. And Dr. Mendez has been able to confirm that the brain itself is essentially undamaged."

"Just a moment, Miriam," Yoshinaka interrupted. "I think I see where this is heading. And while I'm certainly no expert, I am aware that selective cloning and force-growing of organs and tissue is almost routine by now. I also have no doubt of the ability of Dr. Mendez's people to graft a 'bridge' into a severed spinal cord, and to make the necessary neural connections. But we're talking about a *lot* of replacements, each one carrying a potential for rejection or other failure. So we're still faced with the mathematics of cumulative risk."

"Actually, Genji, you don't quite see it. We're not talking about a bunch of transplants, but only one: the brain itself. Granted, it's a highly—indeed, uniquely—complex transplant. But Dr. Mendez is confident he and his people can do it."

The two men stared at her. For once, it was Remko who spoke first.

"A . . . a full-body clone?" His voice held a succession of emotions: incredulity rising to horrified realization and then to revulsion.

"Miriam," Yoshinaka said sternly, "we all want this. But you, of all people, should know the law on the subject of human clones: they are legal persons, with all the rights pertaining thereto. In fact, this very legal principle provided the incentive to develop the technology of selective body-part cloning. To use a clone of oneself as a . . . a source of spare parts is as illegal—and, I might add, as morally leprous—as using one's child for such a purpose. And if this is true of chopping organs out of such a clone one by one, it must apply equally to taking the brain out of it and putting another one in!"

"I don't know anything about legalities," Remko growled. "But I do know the admiral wouldn't want to have anything to do with this!" Whenever Remko said *the admiral* in that particular tone of voice, there was no doubt in anyone's mind which admiral he meant. "It's ghoulish! He'd rather be . . . the way he is now." He gestured vaguely toward the city, in the direction of the medical center whose subbasement held an obscenely coffinlike tank, perennially filmed with frost.

"Of course I'm aware of the legal precedents," Miriam said evenly. "With all due modesty, I must claim a better knowledge of them than either of you. And I also know how he would react to what you think I'm suggesting. Actually, I think I can claim a better knowledge of *that* as well."

That silenced them. They had only been Ian Trevayne's friends and comrades in arms. Miriam Ortega had been his lover.

"In fact," she continued, "when Dr. Mendez broached the idea, I raised all the objections you've thought of—and also a few you haven't—in the strongest possible language." Both her listeners knew what *that* could mean in Miriam Ortega's case. "He hastened to assure me that what he was offering was a way around these very difficulties. He believes that by a special application of the techniques used to produce individual organs—a kind of 'reverse engineering'—his team can produce a full body clone *minus* one organ: in this case, the brain.

"The clone would be effectively anencephalic—incapable of any higher brain functions. In effect, it would be born 'brain dead.' Now, for a very long time—I'd have to look it up to tell you just exactly how long, but certainly reaching back to the dawn of the Space Age, before the discovery of warp points—the definition of 'death' has been legally settled. In those days, you see, it had become possible to artificially keep a human body 'alive' by the traditional definition—a heartbeat and a pulse—after the brain function had irrevocably ceased. So the definitions had to change. A brainless clone will be legally dead, and therefore will have no rights. It will be kept in that state while it is brought to maturation—a process which can be accelerated by a factor of four, which is why I mentioned the figure of five years. That's how long it will take to grow the clone to the physiological age of eighteen to twenty, while keeping it exercised with the same techniques used for other forms of long-term life support, to prevent muscular deterioration. At that point, we transplant the brain."

"So," said Yoshinaka slowly, "his fiftyish mind will wake up inside a twenty-year-old body."

"His *own* twenty-year-old body," Miriam said firmly. "That's what makes Dr. Mendez so confident of his ability to perform the transplant."

"But . . . Well, as I said before, I'm no expert. But I seem to recall reading somewhere that if a clone is produced from postembryonic cells—cells taken from an adult, that is—then the clone's cells may 'wear out' faster, resulting in premature aging."

"Oh, yes; that problem has been recognized since the early days of cloning, more than five centuries ago. But today we have the antigerone treatments to counteract it."

"All right. You and Dr. Mendez have obviously thought this through. And just as obviously, you *believe* you have thought through the legal repercussions." Yoshinaka held up a hand as the chief justice started to speak. "Yes, I know. It's your field. But hear me out. I don't doubt you're right in principle. But are you sure your desire for this to happen isn't clouding your judgment about whether this will really stand up to a legal challenge? There may be a revulsion from it on ethical grounds, whatever the law may say. As Sean said earlier, there's something about the whole idea that seems—"

"Ghoulish," Remko repeated, but with less vehemence than before.

"Yes. And you should know, Miriam, that when people want badly enough for the law to produce a certain result, they can usually find a way to make it do so."

"Of course. I know all about the 'court of public

opinion.' And I'm *counting* on it!" For the first time, she flashed the expressive smile that had never lost its power to transfigure her face. "Have you forgotten who it is we're talking about? And what he means to the people of the Rim Federation? If you need a reminder, just go to that window over there and look down at the second column out front, beside Prescott's."

This silenced them. Of course they hadn't forgotten. How could they?

Eight decades before, in the darkest days of the Terran Federation's terminal civil war, Yoshinaka had been Vice Admiral Ian Trevayne's chief of staff and Remko his flag captain. They had helped him lead his task force through the rebelling Fringe World systems to Zephrain, gateway to the still-loyal Rim systems. There, he had forged a legend as well as a military dynamo that had taken the last resources of the Fringe Worlds' new "Terran Republic" to finally batter to a halt in the bloodbath of Zapata— blood that had included Trevayne's own. But his sacrifice had saved the Rim for the Terran Federation.

The Federation to which it still stoutly insists it belongs, Miriam reflected. *Even while calling itself the "Rim Federation." And while* not *belonging to the Pan-Sentient Union into which the Terran Federation has now amalgamated.*

Go figure, as Mother would have said.

—end excerpt—

from *Exodus*
available in hardcover,
January 2007, from Baen Books

Flag in Exile 0-7434-3575-3 • $7.99
"Packs enough punch to smash a starship to
smithereens."—*Publishers Weekly*

Honor Among Enemies 0-671-87723-2 • $21.00
0-671-87783-6 • $7.99
"Star Wars as it might have been written by C.S.
Forester...fast-paced entertainment."—*Booklist*

In Enemy Hands 0-671-87793-3 • $22.00
0-671-57770-0 • $7.99
After being ambushed, Honor finds herself aboard an
enemy cruiser, bound for her scheduled execution. But
one lesson Honor has never learned is how to give up!

Echoes of Honor 0-671-87892-1 • $24.00
0-671-57833-2 • $7.99
"Brilliant! Brilliant! Brilliant!"—Anne McCaffrey

Ashes of Victory 0-671-57854-5 • $25.00
0-671-31977-9 • $7.99
Honor has escaped from the prison planet called Hell and
returned to the Manticoran Alliance, to the heart of a fur-
nace of new weapons, new strategies, new tactics, spies,
diplomacy, and assassination.

War of Honor 0-7434-3545-1 • $26.00
0-7434-7167-9 • $7.99
No one wanted another war. Neither the Republic of
Haven, nor Manticore—and certainly not Honor
Harrington. Unfortunately, what they wanted didn't matter.

At All Costs 1-4165-0911-9 • $26.00
The war with the Republic of Haven has resumed...disas-
trously for the Star Kingdom of Manticore. The alternative
to victory is total defeat, yet this time the cost of victory
will be agonizingly high.

HONORVERSE VOLUMES:

Crown of Slaves (with Eric Flint)   0-7434-9899-2 • $7.99
Sent on a mission to keep Erewhon from breaking with
Manticore, the Star Kingdom's most able agent and the
Queen's niece may not even be able to escape with their
lives....

The Shadow of Saganami   0-7434-8852-0 • $26.00
                             1-4165-0929-1 • $7.99
A new generation of officers, trained by Honor Harrington,
are ready to hit the front lines as war erupts again.

ANTHOLOGIES EDITED BY DAVID WEBER:

More Than Honor   0-671-87857-3 • $6.99

Worlds of Honor   0-671-57855-3 • $6.99

Changer of Worlds   0-7434-3520-6 • $7.99

The Service of the Sword   0-7434-8836-9 • $7.99

THE DAHAK SERIES:

Mutineers' Moon   0-671-72085-6 • $7.99

The Armageddon Inheritance   0-671-72197-6 • $6.99

Heirs of Empire   0-671-87707-0 • $7.99

Empire from the Ashes   trade pb • 1-4165-0993-X • $15.00
Contains *Mutineers' Moon*, *The Armageddon Inheritance*
and *Heirs of Empire* in one volume.

1633 with Eric Flint   hc • 0-7434-3542-7 • $26.00
                                     pb • 0-7434-7155-5 • $7.99

American freedom and justice versus the tyrannies of the 17th century. A novel set in Flint's *1632* universe.

THE STARFIRE SERIES
WITH STEVE WHITE:

The Stars at War I   0-7434-8841-5 • $25.00
Rewritten *Insurrection* and *In Death Ground* in one massive volume.

The Stars at War II   0-7434-9912-3 • $27.00
The Shiva Option and *Crusade* in one massive volume.

PRINCE ROGER NOVELS
WITH JOHN RINGO:

March Upcountry   0-7434-3538-9 • $7.99

March to the Sea   0-7434-3580-X • $7.99

March to the Stars   0-7434-8818-0 • $7.99

We Few   0-7434-9881-X • $26.00
"This is as good as military sf gets." —*Booklist*